Dear Reader,

One of the things that I've learnt from your letters (and do *please* keep them coming in – I'm always delighted to hear from you all!) is how much you enjoy the variety of *Scarlet* characters and storylines. That's why choosing the month's books is always such an exciting challenge for me. Will readers prefer the ups and downs of married life to a story about a single woman finding happiness? What about books featuring children?

This month all of these themes appear. The heroines of Clare Benedict's *A Bitter Inheritance* and Margaret Callaghan's *Wilde Affair* are both, in their very different ways, prepared to make sacrifices for the sake of a child's happiness. *The Second Wife*, by Angela Arney, highlights the problems involved when two single parents fall in love and decide to combine family forces. In *Harte's Gold*, by Jane Toombs, the no-nonsense single heroine faces a different sort of family problem: how to protect her susceptible grandmother from being conned when a film company rents their ranch and she has her doubts about the attractive leading man.

Whatever your taste in romantic reading I hope that you enjoy this month's *Scarlet* selections.

Till next month,

Sally Cooper

SALLY COOPER,
Editor-in-Chief – *Scarlet*

About the Author

Clare Benedict was a lonely, half-orphaned, only child when she started her lifelong habit of reading – almost anything – and trying to write. She qualified as a teacher of speech and drama, but gave up her career to bring up her four children. Clare has written short stories, feature articles and literally hundreds of picture and photo story strips for girls' magazines and Christmas Annuals, and was involved with her photographer husband in the shooting of these – casting, costume, locations and props. In addition, Clare has written four romance novels, so her experience was invaluable when she came to write *A Dark Legacy*, her first *Scarlet* romance.

In her spare time, Clare is a passionate film fan, particularly of old black and white movies. Clare says, 'I'm also passionate about my husband, my four grown, handsome, clever children and adorable grandchildren – oh, and the cat!'

Other *Scarlet* titles available this month:

THE SECOND WIFE – Angela Arney
WILDE AFFAIR – Margaret Callaghan
HARTE'S GOLD – Jane Toombs

CLARE BENEDICT

A BITTER INHERITANCE

Enquiries to:
Robinson Publishing Ltd
7 Kensington Church Court
London W8 4SP

First published in the UK by Scarlet, 1997

A copy of the British Library Cataloguing in
Publication data is available from the British Library

ISBN 1-85487-951-0

Printed and bound in the EC

10 9 8 7 6 5 4 3 2 1

PROLOGUE

South West France

When it was time to leave the Villa Des Pines, Juan Sanchez turned from the window that overlooked the courtyard and smiled at Gina.

'Here he comes, *querida*, are you ready?'

'Yes, but – Juan,' she laid a hand on his arm, 'do you think we can get away with it?'

He covered her hand with his own. 'Even if we fail, things couldn't be much worse than they are now, could they? So it's worth a try.'

'You're right.' Gina's determination returned with a rush of adrenalin. 'Let's go.'

It was late afternoon and the housekeeper's son, Gerard Bernat, had just driven his pick-up truck into the integral garage at the rear of the villa.

This was part of his routine; he came every day to take his mother home to the Bernats' small farm and he brought her back every morning.

Gina and Juan had decided that, in order to effect their escape with as much secrecy as possible, this

1

day should follow the same pattern as all the others.

So, after spending no more time at the villa than usual, their accomplice, Gerard, drove away again, operating the security gates with the hand-set he'd been given, just the same as he always did.

His mother turned and waved as she sometimes did if Gina's little stepdaughter, Natalie, was watching from her bedroom window. Except that today Natalie was not at her window nor, indeed, anywhere in the villa.

She was crouching with Gina and Juan in the back of the truck, hidden amongst the sacks and baskets which usually carried farm produce, holding her breath and dying to giggle. It was like a game to her and she was as good as gold.

The pick-up truck climbed the bumpy road to the farm that clung to the lower slopes of the Pyrenees and, when they arrived, Florence Bernat hurried in ahead of them.

She insisted that they should sit at the table in the large kitchen. She served them bowls of her delicious, homemade onion soup, ladled onto thick slices of bread and heaped with grated cheese.

Juan and Natalie did justice to her hospitality but Gina had almost refused. However, she caught Juan's reproving glance and realized that she must not offend the Bernat family. Gerard's young wife, Céline, was already staring at her with a mixture of suspicion and dislike.

A little later, with the shadows lengthening, Gerard drove them to Toulouse. Céline was not pleased.

The round trip would take her husband about three hours and he had to be up early the next morning.

But the girl was in awe of her mother-in-law, so she confined herself to clattering the empty soup bowls onto the bench forcefully, before filling the sink with hot water and the kitchen with steam. She kept her mouth shut but her fit of sulks was unmistakable.

Juan had already phoned ahead to the hire car pick-up point and their car was waiting. It did not take long to transfer their belongings and then, Gina, Natalie and Juan began the long journey through France to the ferryport at Calais . . .

CHAPTER 1

Northumberland

'Keep your eyes on the road!'

'What did you say?' Gina jerked her head up and blinked; her eyes felt as though they were lined with sandpaper.

'You were falling asleep.'

'No I wasn't. And keep your voice down. You'll waken Natalie.'

She glanced in the rear-view mirror. Her step-daughter had toppled sideways in the child seat so that her head rested on Juan's arm. He couldn't move without disturbing her, but he was staring forward intently. He looked hurt.

'I'm sorry, Juan. I shouldn't have snapped at you.'

'That's OK, *querida*. I know you don't mean it.'

Gina swung her eyes back to the road. In the full glare of the headlights it snaked away into the darkness, mile after mile. Had she been losing her concentration? She wouldn't be surprised. The journey north had been long and hard.

And now, the rain, which had started about an hour ago, was getting heavier and the wind was rising. She would need all her wits about her to negotiate these unknown roads in these conditions.

Juan spoke softly from the darkness behind her. 'You know I don't mind driving the rest of the way.'

'No, you've got to start the journey back tomorrow. But we'd better stop and get some strong, hot, coffee – next place we come to. If we can find anywhere open, that is.'

'I doubt that we will. It is late and England, or at least this part of it, seems to have closed for the night.' He sighed.

'Juan, why don't you try to sleep?'

'I can't. I am too worried about you. We must find *somewhere* to get you that coffee and perhaps a sandwich. Even though I have begged you each time we have stopped, you refuse to look after yourself. In fact you have not eaten properly since . . . for days.'

'I'm not hungry.'

'Nevertheless, you will eat – or I shall insist on taking over the driving.'

'Don't try to be masterful, Juan, I'm not in the mood for it.'

'You know you like it.'

He laughed but she could sense the underlying tension. Her own nerves were stretched to breaking point. She wondered if either of them would ever be able to relax again.

'Don't worry, Gina,' he seemed to have read her mind, 'I think we are safe now.'

'I hope so . . . Look! What does that sign say?'

She slowed the car down and they both peered through the rain-streaked windscreen.

'Services, one mile,' Juan read out and he breathed a sigh of relief. 'My prayer has been answered.'

Gina eased over into the left-hand lane and then pulled into the car park behind a brightly lit shop and snack bar, alongside a filling station. She stopped just beyond two big container lorries, undid her seat belt, and turned to smile at Juan.

'We'll follow the same drill as before,' she said quietly. 'I'll go and bring food and drinks back to the car.'

'Let me go.' Juan eased himself away from Natalie and covered her more securely with the car rug.

'No,' Gina said. 'It was OK in France, but we agreed it should be me on this side of the channel. And especially here – with your looks you'd be very noticeable in rural Northumberland.'

Gina buttoned up her jacket and turned up the collar. She pulled a silk square out of her pocket and tied it over her short, dark hair, tugging it forward until her face was partly obscured.

Juan laughed softly. 'You look like an old peasant woman on her way to market.'

'Thanks! But, seriously, it's raining so hard that nobody will think I look strange – just that I'm reluctant to get wet!'

The only other customers inside the long, low

building were the lorry drivers. They were sitting at one of the tables, concentrating on plates piled with sausage, beans and chips and a shared mound of bread and butter. The smell of frying hung in the air.

The two men hardly gave Gina a glance as she walked past them towards the counter. And even if they do look at me, Gina thought, what will they see? Simply a tall, slim female, casually dressed in jacket and trousers of unremarkable grey.

There were still some of the morning's newspapers in a rack beside the till. Because of the way they were folded, not much more than the headlines could be seen. Resolutely, Gina refused to look at them.

Luckily, the woman who served her was tired and barely attentive. If anyone came here straight after I'd gone and asked her to describe her last customer she wouldn't have a clue, Gina thought.

She found herself picturing the scene as if it were in a movie – tough cops questioning the frightened middle-aged waitress in a seedy diner – and she smiled ruefully. For, of course, it wasn't the law she was running from.

'Here, pet, if you're taking that lot back to your car, I'll put it in this box for you.'

Not so inattentive after all then, Gina realized. She nodded nervously. She watched as the woman packed the assortment of sandwiches, biscuits and fruit into the box and then, carefully balanced the two large waxed cups of coffee amongst the food.

'Thank you, that's kind of you. Oh, I'd better have a carton of milk, as well.'

7

Natalie might wake up, Gina thought, better be prepared.

Once back in the car, she draped her scarf over the back of the front passenger seat to dry and loosened her jacket.

As soon as she had passed some of the food over to Juan, she eased the plastic lid from her cup of coffee and sipped it gratefully.

'Mmm, that's good.'

'You think so? Then you are easily pleased, *querida*. Without doubt this is the worst coffee I have ever tasted.'

He sounded so offended that Gina felt laughter welling up inside her. Laughter that was dangerously close to tears.

'Right now, Juan, this is the best coffee in the world,' she said. 'And if you don't agree, you can just thank your lucky stars that you'll be on your way back to the villa tomorrow, where you can brew up your coffee just the way you like it . . .'

. . . Juan takes his coffee as black as hell and as sweet as sin . . .

David's amused tones and his gentle laughter came from nowhere and, then, Gina's tears did spill over as she remembered how they all used to have breakfast together, every morning, on the sun-warmed terrace overlooking the Pyrenees.

'Please don't cry.' Juan leaned forward and touched her cheek gently with the back of his fingers. Gina moved her head away and snatched up a tissue from the box on the seat beside her; she wiped her eyes.

'It's all right, I'm not crying – I'm laughing.'

'Really?' It was obvious that Juan didn't believe her but he didn't challenge her statement any further.

'Look, Juan, if I'm behaving strangely, surely you can understand that it's just a natural reaction to everything that's happened.'

'Of course.'

'Good. Now, let's eat up and drink up so that we can get on our way.'

Thankfully, in spite of this exchange, Natalie did not wake up. The poor child must be utterly exhausted, Gina thought. Let's hope she can go on sleeping until we reach the end of the journey.

Juan insisted that Gina had at least her fair share of the food she had bought and, surprisingly, she found that her appetite had revived a little.

It must be because we're nearly there, she mused, as she studied the map under the car's interior light.

Perhaps, unconsciously, I'm already looking forward to uninterrupted days of peace and quiet . . . Refuge and solitude and a chance to try to come to terms with what has happened . . . begin the healing process . . .

'Gina, take your time with that coffee. Try to relax a little, there's no hurry, now.'

'Yes there is. I want you to have a good night's sleep before you leave in the morning.'

'I could stay with you for one more day, I suppose.

It would set my mind at rest if I could be sure you and Natalie were going to be all right on your own.'

'No, we'd better stick to the original plan otherwise it could all go wrong. I'd hate that to happen after all we've been through.'

Even now, more than twenty-four hours since the beginning of their journey, which had begun more than a thousand miles away, Gina knew they mustn't let their resolution weaken.

Juan sighed. 'You are right. Look, those two lorries are leaving. It will be safe to visit the bathroom now.'

Gina watched as the container trucks pulled out of the car park and took the road leading north. They'll probably be heading for Scotland, she thought.

She and Juan took it in turns to dodge the slanting rain as they visited the separate bathrooms. She was thankful that it wasn't one of those establishments where you had to ask for a key. So far, she was confident that they had travelled up through France and England as anonymously as possible.

Even on the ferry, where they had to get out of the car and go up to the passenger decks, they had been able to find a corner behind a noisy group of French school children. All the other passengers had avoided that area for the entire crossing.

Once they were on their way again, the regular swishing of the windscreen wipers was the only noise in the warm darkness of the car. Soon, judging from the sound of his regular breathing, Gina realized that Juan had fallen asleep.

For a while, she felt safe, enclosed. It was as if, so long as they were travelling, nobody could reach her, nobody could hurt her. But, after a few more miles with no one to talk to, she began to find the silence unnerving. She wished she could turn on the car radio but it might awaken Natalie.

Disturbing memories of the last few weeks nudged at the corners of her mind. The accumulated misery was waiting to pounce – trying to take her mind off the road.

The weather worsened and she gripped the steering wheel determinedly, and peered through the windshield into the driving rain. A side wind buffeted the car and it took all her skill just to keep her speed at a steady forty miles an hour.

Surely there couldn't be much further to go. According to the map, they should be arriving at David's old family home any time now.

She slowed down a little and hunched forward. At a bend in the road the headlights had picked out two stone columns. The name of the house was carved in gothic letters, one word on each column, Northmoor – Hall.

She breathed a sigh of relief. That's it. We're home. The relief didn't last long.

The gates were closed!

Gina almost wept with frustration. With my luck, they're probably locked and chained as well, she thought. She pulled into the verge and brought the car to a halt.

She buttoned up her jacket and tied her silk scarf

over her hair once more. Then she turned and glanced over her shoulder. In the dimness behind her she could make out the sleeping figures of Natalie and Juan. She smiled raggedly. She would let them both sleep just a little longer.

She knew that she only had to ask and Juan would gladly get out and open the gates for her but she didn't have the heart to awaken him. Tomorrow he would face the long drive south, the channel crossing and then on, down through France to the Pyrenees. He deserved some consideration.

'Aah!'

A fierce gust of wind caught the door when she opened it and she wrenched her shoulder painfully as she hung on. For a moment she was frightened that the door would be yanked off altogether but she managed to pull it back and close it behind her before too much rain had blown into the car.

Thankfully, her cry of distress had been carried away on the wind and had not disturbed Juan or Natalie.

To her relief the gates were not locked and they swung open easily. She made sure that each one was secure in its metal retaining latch – she didn't want any accidents now.

She manoeuvred the hired Peugeot estate car into the driveway and, as the wheels began to crunch on gravel, Gina wondered whether she ought to pull up and close the gates behind her. She dismissed the thought quickly. She couldn't face going out in the wind and rain yet again.

After all, it's my house now, she mused as she dabbed her face dry with a wad of paper tissues. I suppose I can leave the gates open if I want to – and, in any case, I'll ask Juan to be sure to close them when he leaves in the morning.

She began to scan the way ahead. The clouds were racing across the sky and the intermittent moonlight revealed that the drive was bordered by tall trees, the branches swaying wildly in the wind.

She had no idea how far the house was from the road. Although her late husband had told her much about his family home, his reminiscences had not included such practical details.

Then the driveway curved round and Gina saw the house in front of her. Her eyes widened. Nothing David had ever told her had prepared her for this moment.

Northmoor Hall was not large as country mansions go, but its elegant lines of grey stone stood out gracefully against a backdrop of wooded hills. Built only about a hundred years ago by one of David's ancestors, the founder of the Shaw industrial empire, the house blended into the grandeur of the northern landscape so perfectly, that it looked as though it had been there for centuries.

No wonder David had loved the place so much. How could he have ever left it, Gina wondered? But, of course, she knew the answer to that. Her husband's work had been even more important to him than his family home – and his work had kept him at his studio and gallery in South West

France, allowing only rare visits to north Northumberland.

In the short time they had been married he had
never found the time to bring her here – but he was
always promising that he would – some day . . .

Gina tried to swallow the aching lump of misery
that had formed at the back of her throat. 'Some day'
had never come for David and her; he had succumbed to a hereditary blood disease that had
haunted the Shaw family for centuries.

While she nursed him he had told her that his
parents had been determined that he should escape
the curse; as a child he had been taken from clinic to
clinic where he had endured all the latest treatments
– some of them experimental – and he seemed to
thrive.

By the time his mother and father had died, when
he was a young man, they must have thought that the
power of their determination, with the help of their
fortune, had beaten it.

How tragic that David had finally succumbed
when he had been at the height of his artistic powers.

Gina still found it hard to accept that he would
never again see the home where he had been born.
Furthermore, the scandal that had followed his death
meant that this was no ordinary homecoming for his
widow and child.

Not even the caretaker of Northmoor Hall knew
that Gina was coming to stay. She knew that Mr
Robson and his wife lived in a cottage in the grounds.
If Gina had written or phoned to warn them of her

arrival, they would have had the house prepared for her, but she couldn't risk any word of her whereabouts getting out.

No, she would see them tomorrow and impress on them that she must have total discretion. Tonight she would simply make Juan, Natalie and herself as comfortable as possible.

She brought the car to a halt as near to the entrance steps as she could and reached down for her handbag. Then she switched on the internal light and examined the bunch of keys. She was grateful that David had always been so methodical; each key was neatly labelled and it was easy for her to select the two she needed.

Gina mounted the stone steps quickly and gained the shelter of the classical portico. Then, standing before the solid front door, she had a moment of total misgiving. Did she have any right to be here?

All the doubts that had assailed her when David had first told her that he was going to make her his sole heir came flooding back. It was the only time that they had ever argued but, eventually, David had overruled her objections and he had made a will leaving everything he owned to Gina.

He could never have imagined what a barrage of criticism she would have to face after he died. Day after day of dealing with the reporters who were eager to brand her a gold digger – and worse – had nearly broken her spirit.

She had barely been allowed to bury David with dignity before the pack descended and began to hound her every move. Even if they thought Gina, and perhaps Juan, fair game, not one of them seemed to care that their intrusive behaviour was ruining the life of an innocent child, David's daughter, Natalie.

Gina had soon realized that they would have to make a break for it – and where better to bring the child than to her father's own childhood home? A home that David had been very protective of.

As his fame as an artist had grown and he had begun to attract attention from the media, he had wisely suspected that he might need a bolt hole one day so he had been very careful not to mention to anyone that he owned a house near the Scottish border.

A house that he had left to Gina along with everything else.

So, why am I hesitating? she wondered. It's too late to change my mind now, and anyway, the house is empty. David was the last of the Shaw family, so unless I believe in ghosts, there's no one here to confront me . . .

Gina looked down at the keys in her hand. One was a simple house key and the other was for the security system. She hoped she'd read the instructions on the label correctly.

The last thing she wanted was to set the alarms going and have the Northumbria police come racing along the moorland roads with sirens blaring. That would really blow her cover.

She stepped forward but, before she could place either of the keys in their separate locks, the door began to open of its own accord. Gina froze. Perhaps there are ghosts here, after all, she thought wildly.

The door swung open to reveal a tall figure, taller than she was, standing there. Gina blinked, surely this was no other-worldly apparition . . . and yet the powerful silhouette seemed hauntingly familiar . . .

Somewhere behind him there was a dull glow as if from a fire burning low in the hearth. But, with the light behind him she couldn't see his face properly, couldn't make out his features. But she knew that he was staring at her.

Seconds seemed to stretch into slow motion as he began to raise one arm towards her. She flinched but, instead of the violence she was half-expecting, his hand merely came up to touch the rain-sodden scarf still covering her hair.

She shivered when his long fingers momentarily brushed against her brow and then her heart thudded painfully against her ribs as her senses told her that they remembered his touch.

He pushed the scarf back until it slithered on to her shoulders and then his hand dropped to his side.

'Ah . . .' he sighed. 'The grieving widow.'

The voice was unmistakably familiar and the muscles of Gina's stomach knotted with disbelief. Was she hallucinating? Could you hallucinate sounds as well as pictures? she wondered hysterically. She was beginning to feel light-headed with fatigue and bewilderment.

But he went on talking. 'When I heard your car approaching, I thought it might be thieves – the hard lads up from Newcastle. This house is isolated and they could have been taking a chance that no one was here.'

Nobody *should* be here, Gina thought, least of all Sam Redmond.

CHAPTER 2

'Why have you come here, Gina?' His tone was hostile, even threatening.

'I beg your pardon . . . ?'

This was all wrong – she should be asking him that question. Suddenly he seemed to melt back into the darkness behind the door. Gina's eyes narrowed as she tried to follow his movements. What was he doing?

'Don't just stand there, come in.'

Great, now he was inviting her in to her own house.

'Close the door after you.'

She started to obey then hesitated. Juan and Natalie were still in the car, should she go and waken them? No, better to get this confusing situation sorted out first – but she left the door ajar.

In that moment's hesitation she lost sight of him, completely. 'What . . .? Where . . .?'

Gina felt a moment of panic as she stared into the darkness, then suddenly the lights snapped on. She blinked and looked around. She saw a large, oak-panelled room dominated by a broad staircase. An old, but probably very valuable, oriental carpet covered most of the floor. Generous sized chairs and sofas, covered in classic chintz, were arranged around a huge stone fireplace. A fire burned low.

But, as she began to focus properly, it was the man her eyes were drawn to. Sam Redmond was standing just a short distance away and he was staring at her. Against all reason she felt as though she were the intruder, not he, and she was miserably aware of her wet and bedraggled appearance.

And Sam? It was three years since she had last seen him; three years since he had left her without a word of explanation. The experience had just about broken her heart.

After the initial misery and the months of wondering what she had done wrong, Gina had vowed to forget him, but seeing him again so unexpectedly, she found herself fighting a surge of longing and desire.

He looked as attractive as ever, damn him. His mane of dark hair looked as if it had been pushed back impatiently from his brow – she remembered the gesture – and his hawk-like features were perhaps even more fine-drawn than before. He was wearing dark jeans and a black polo-necked sweater – casual clothes – but his mood was far from relaxed.

His look was wary, combative; Gina flushed. Sam Redmond had no right, no right at all, to be angry with her.

'Well,' he said at last, 'if you won't tell me why

you're here, I suppose I can hazard a guess. It's not too difficult, is it?'

'What do you mean?'

Instead of answering her, he turned and walked away.

'I . . . where?' For goodness' sake why wouldn't the man stand still? Was he trying deliberately to unnerve her by keeping her on the move?

He paused at a doorway set into the panelling behind the wide sweep of stairs. 'Come in here.'

Sam entered the room with all the confidence of familiarity and Gina followed him into a book-lined study. A large desk dominated the room and on it stood a computer surrounded by reference books, files and manuscript papers. Beyond the desk a fire glowed in the hearth.

A leather armchair stood beside the fire and, beside it, a low table was heaped with newspapers. A tumbler and a half-empty bottle of Johnny Walker Black Label stood on the table next to the papers.

It looked as if Sam had been sitting there until just a short while ago . . .

'You've come here to lie low for a while, am I right?' He was standing with his back to the fire, seemingly at ease, but his expression was guarded.

'Lie low?'

'Come on, Gina, it's Sam you're talking to, do me the courtesy of respecting my intelligence. The way I see it is that things were getting too hot for you and your boyfriend at the villa so you thought you'd better drop out of sight until the hacks let up. Then you'll go back to him. Is that it?'

'Boyfriend?'

'The young Spanish artist – Juan Sanchez.'

'He's not my boyfriend.'

'No?' Sam's gaze dropped to the newspapers on the table beside him.

'No!' Gina hurried towards the table and looked down reluctantly. She knew what she would see.

WIDOW'S GRIEF SOON FORGOTTEN!

The headline shrieked across the double page spread of a series of photographs of Juan, Natalie and herself by the swimming pool of the Villa Des Pines. The photographs had been taken by a free-lance photographer – a paparazzo – shortly after David's funeral.

Gina had swiftly become aware that the paparazzi had homed in on her, but she had never imagined that anyone would hide out in the hills and train a telephoto lens on the villa's high-walled, private grounds.

Not until a flash of reflected light from the direction of the lower slopes of the mountains had alerted her to the fact that they were being watched – and then it was too late.

The low-life jerk who'd snatched these shots had sold them to the highest bidders across Europe – and obviously to the British press too. She sank down weakly to kneel beside the table and pushed the offending newspaper aside. But there was more of the same.

NICE ONE NANNY!

Her late husband's reputation as an artist and teacher had been known world-wide, so his tragic early death was a lead story — especially when it became known that he had left his fortune solely to his child's nanny — who had only recently become his second wife.

GINA GETS THE LOT!

She pushed the paper aside. Not all of the stories were on the front page, but each newspaper had been left folded at the appropriate place. Sam must have been enjoying his fireside reading, she thought savagely.

NOTHING FOR NATALIE!

Gina sighed. So far she had avoided reading the English papers — the French and Spanish press, although a little less vulgar, had been bad enough. And now here they all were waiting for her.

'I can't look at these — they're loathsome!'

With a burst of rage, Gina swept them all on to the floor and then buried her face in her hands. This house was supposed to be her refuge — what cruel twist of fate had ensured that all this evidence of her new-found notoriety would be here waiting for her — along with Sam Redmond?

She became aware that he had crouched down at the other side of the table. She heard the rustle of the papers as he picked them up and then a thump as he put them back where they had been.

'I agree, they're sickening.'

Something about the tone of his voice made her

raise her head and look at him from between her spread fingers.

He was looking down at the paper that was now on top of the pile. She followed his gaze. The page was dominated by a colour photograph taken on the day of David's funeral. It was good, she had to admit – almost like an art print.

In the background, the Pyrenees rose dramatically against the skyline. The small, twelfth-century church in the mid-distance looked as though it had been painted on to the steep mountainside.

In the foreground was the tiny cemetery. Amongst the crowded marble angels, two black-clad people stood beside a new grave. The woman had obviously just placed a wreath of lilies and the man was helping her up – supporting her.

She had seen this picture before – the photographer must have sold it world-wide – but only now did she see how intimate Juan's gesture looked. She looked up and shuddered at the bleakness she saw in Sam's eyes.

'You couldn't wait, could you?' He rose to his feet and stared down at her. 'Your husband barely cold in his grave and you're in the arms of your lover.'

Stung, Gina scrambled to her feet and faced him across the table. 'You've got it wrong!'

'Have I?

'He was comforting me . . .'

'That's one way of putting it.'

'How dare you!'

Gina raised her hand and lashed out at him

24

furiously, but he raised his arm defensively and side-stepped around the table before she could make contact.

She found herself sawing the air and she stumbled. Before she had regained her balance, he reached out and caught hold of both her arms, dragging her forward until their bodies were almost touching.

Gina's head dropped back uncomfortably. The shock of finding herself so close to him took her breath away. She could feel her heart racing as she stared up into his eyes like a mesmerized rabbit caught in the glare of a car's headlights.

In a flash of heightened awareness she knew that he was as shaken by their nearness as she was, but the only sign he gave was a sharp indrawn breath before he spoke.

'Poor David,' he said. 'He didn't deserve to spend his last days on earth with no one but a faithless wife to keep him company.'

'We weren't alone – Juan was with us.'

'Do you suppose that makes it any better?'

'That was the way David wanted it to be. He sent his other students away. Madame Bernat still came every day to look after us but he wanted no one else at the villa except for Natalie, Juan and myself.'

'Are you sure that's the way David wanted it?'

'Of course. What are you suggesting?'

'Perhaps that's the way you wanted it. You and your – you and Juan.'

'That's despicable.'

Gina tried to pull away but Sam held on, dragging

her closer. She could feel his breath on her face. 'Is it?'

'If that's what you believe, then why did *you* stay away? David was once married to your sister – and you were supposed to be his oldest friend – if you really thought he needed protecting then you should have been there.'

Sam's reaction terrified her. He gripped her arms even more tightly. 'I didn't know. You must know that David stopped writing to me after – after he married you. I didn't know that he was dying until it was too late – believe me!'

There was an expression of such distress on his face that Gina could only whisper, 'I do . . .'

It was as if he hadn't heard her. He stared at her steadily, flintily, his grey eyes as dark as basalt, his face expressionless. She tried to pull her arms free but he tightened his grasp until she could feel his fingers gripping through the damp fabric of her jacket.

'Sam, you must let go – you're hurting me.'

He shook his head as if her voice had recalled him to the present. 'I'm sorry . . . I didn't mean to . . .'

He released her and she stepped back, rubbing her arms. I'll be lucky if I'm not bruised tomorrow, she thought.

She became aware that he was staring at her even more intently. 'I just hope that you made him happy.'

'Sam, listen to me – all that in the newspapers – it isn't true – you don't understand –'

26

'No, I don't. Oh, I can understand that you might have imagined yourself in love with David after – after I went away. After all, he was talented, handsome, rich . . .'

'Rich has nothing to do with it!'

'No? Well, perhaps not, at first –'

'Not at first, not ever!'

Sam ignored her interruptions and went on as if she hadn't spoken. 'Whatever your feelings for David when you married him, I know that you already loved Natalie – at least I thought that you did . . .'

'I did – I do!'

'Oh yes? If that's the case why did you persuade her father to leave her out of his will?'

'I didn't – it was David's idea – I tried to persuade him not to but he was so very ill and . . .'

She floundered. They were sailing on dangerous waters. David had not wanted anyone to know the whole truth.

'That must have made it easier for you.'

'What?'

'The fact that he was very ill.'

Gina felt sick when she realized what he was implying. 'Sam, no! Surely you don't believe all those lurid stories in the newspapers –'

'It makes good copy, doesn't it? Dying man alone in his luxurious villa in *Les Haute Pyrenees* with his beautiful younger wife and her even younger lover –'

'Not that much younger!' she couldn't help snapping. 'Juan is twenty-two and I'm only twenty-five!'

'Vanity, Gina, vanity!'

For a moment, there was a gleam of amusement in Sam's eyes and, without warning, Gina recalled how much shared laughter there had been between them. The memory brought anguish but it encouraged her to take a softer tone.

'Look, you said it yourself – it makes good copy. But you're a journalist – so how can you fall for it? Think, Sam! Even in the short time you and I had together, surely you got to know me well enough to realize that I would never behave like that!'

'I thought I did.' Sam stared at her uncertainly. 'Gina . . . ?'

He took a step towards her and she flinched. An expression of pain drew his brows together. 'Don't be frightened . . . I won't hurt you . . . how could I . . .?'

Gina held his gaze as Sam took hold of her shoulders, gently this time. He looked at her for a long, long moment and then his face drew nearer. She felt herself begin to tremble with long-suppressed emotion. She saw his lips part and she raised her own.

He was so close now that she could barely focus . . . she closed her eyes. In the silence she could hear the wind soughing through the leaves of the trees in the nearby woods . . . the faint crackling of the fire in the hearth . . . Sam's breathing as his face drew nearer. She imagined that she could hear her own heart beating as she waited for his kiss . . . it never came.

Suddenly, brutally, he pushed her away from him. Gina opened her eyes and stared at him. The expression on his face appalled her.

'Sam . . . what is it?'

He was staring at a point beyond her. His eyes had glazed over with contempt. She spun round.

Juan stood in the doorway. He looked disorientated, baffled, bewildered – the expressions that flitted across his handsome, mobile features would have been funny if Gina had felt remotely like laughing.

Finally, he spoke. 'Gina, what is happening? You said we would be alone here. Who is this man?'

Before she could answer him, Sam leant forward and murmured something that only she could hear. 'Now try to convince me that I'm mistaken, Gina. If you can.'

CHAPTER 3

'Gina, are you OK?'

Juan hovered in the doorway.

'Yes, I'm fine, really.'

'The door was open – I came to find you – I heard raised voices. You need my help, yes?'

'No – it's OK – really.'

She hurried towards him and laid a reassuring hand on his arm. She had the crazy idea that Sam was going to hit the young Spaniard – he certainly seemed angry enough – and she wanted to place herself between them.

'Gina – you are quite white – and you are shaking – what is the matter?'

Juan put his hand over hers. He was almost the same height as she was and she found herself looking into his expressive brown eyes. They were full of concern.

'How touching!'

Gina spun round. In spite of what she had feared, Sam had stayed exactly where he was. But she didn't like the splintered ice in his eyes.

'I beg your pardon?' Juan, unsure about what exactly was happening, remained polite.

'I said how touching.'

'I do not understand you.'

Juan's inborn courtesy was being tested to the limits but Gina could see that he was growing angry.

'Sam, please don't . . .' she began, but he interrupted her.

'Don't worry, Gina, I was only remarking how moving it is to see that you have found a friend to – support you.'

Sam's slight pause before the word support and the unmistakable hint of sarcasm infuriated her. She knew it would be no good pleading with him to be reasonable and she came close to losing her temper.

'For heaven's sake, stop this!'

Sam raised his eyebrows and, behind her, she heard Juan gasp softly. Gina, frightened at how close she was to losing control, made an effort to lower her voice. 'Sam, it's late and Juan and I are tired . . .'

'Of course. Forgive me. You'll be wanting to get to bed. Sorry if I've ruined your plans.'

His words and their implication sickened her but, before she could make any kind of answer, Juan cut in, 'Gina, please tell me what on earth is going on. Who is this man and what is he doing in your house?'

He moved away from her but she restrained him. 'This man is Sam Redmond, Nadine's brother. As you probably know, he used to be a friend of David's.'

She knew it was cruel to stress the 'used to be' but Sam had driven her to the edge.

Juan's eyes widened for a moment and then he smiled warily at Sam. 'Ah, yes, I have heard of you but, of course, I have never met you. The last time you came to visit the Villa Des Pines was before I came to study with David.'

There was no response from Sam and Gina wondered if he was still torturing himself with guilt because he had not known his friend was dying until it was too late.

Juan tried to fill the uncomfortable silence. 'You are a reporter, yes? For television?'

Still Sam remained silent so Gina cut in, brusquely. 'Yes, he is. But to go back to your previous question as to why he is here, I'm as puzzled as you are.'

She turned to face Sam. 'Well, are you going to tell us?'

She looked away from him and deliberately let her gaze linger on the desk and on the table where the computer, the files and the bottle of whisky demonstrated all the signs of established residence.

'And, furthermore, I think I'd like to know exactly how long you've been here – and who gave you the keys.'

Sam answered only the last part of her question. 'David did.'

'You're lying!'

'Why should I lie?'

'I have no idea – but if David really had given you permission to stay here, he would have told me.'

'It probably didn't even occur to him to tell you. After all, our arrangement goes right back to our days at university together. Remember your husband and I have – had – been friends for a very long time. We were friends even before he met my sister whereas you are – were – a very new wife.'

Gina ignored the barb in his last words. 'Are you telling me that you have been coming to Northmoor Hall for years?'

'That's right. David gave me a set of keys to the place when we were up at Oxford together. He knew I needed to hole up and work on my private projects every now and then and, as he hardly ever came here, he said I could come whenever I liked. I didn't have to check it out with him. Satisfied?'

'I suppose so.'

There was no reason to believe that Sam was lying. It was just the kind of thing that David would do, she thought. All his life he had been generous and kind and would go out of his way to help those he loved.

He had told her once that Sam and his younger sister, Nadine, had had a difficult time since their father had died when they were still quite young. She imagined that he had taken them under his wing like so many other troubled souls. Like Gina herself . . .

So, Sam's story sounded entirely plausible. She would have to accept it – and his presence here – for the moment. There were other questions that she wanted to ask – must ask – before she told Sam Redmond that his long-term arrangement to use

David's house was finally over, but they would have to wait until later.

Now, there was something else she had to see to, something she ought to have remembered sooner, if the shock of finding Sam here had not driven just about everything else from her mind.

She turned to Juan and said, urgently, 'Where's Natalie?'

'Don't worry, Gina. I did not leave her in the car. She is here . . . still sleeping . . . see . . .'

She glanced at Sam. He had his back to them. He had stooped to pick up the bottle of whisky from the low table and he was pouring himself a generous measure. He didn't say anything or attempt to follow them as she and Juan left the room.

They hurried across the entrance hall to one of the deep sofas beside the stone fireplace. Her stepdaughter was lying amongst the cushions, her soft, even breathing indicating that she was not in the least disturbed or distressed by the tiring journey.

Juan had covered her with the car rug but one small arm had been flung upwards, the fingers of her hand gently curling. Her cheeks were flushed with sleep. The dark blonde crescents of her eyelashes and her almost silver blonde hair, spread out around her face, gave her the appearance of a sleeping cherub.

Gina unbuttoned her jacket and shrugged it off. She dumped it on a chair along with her scarf.

'Juan,' she said quietly, 'we'd better organize rooms for ourselves before it gets much later. I'll take Natalie upstairs if you'll bring the overnight bags from the car. We can unload the rest of the stuff in the morning.'

'Of course,' Juan, too, kept his voice low, so as not to awaken the sleeping child, 'but what about this man – Sam Redmond? Can he be trusted?'

'I think so. After all, he's Natalie's uncle. Surely he wouldn't do anything that would result in her being hurt.'

'But it was not part of your plan to have anyone else staying here.'

'Don't worry. He won't be here much longer. I'll sort that out tomorrow.'

'Are you sure you will be able to do that? He seems to think he has a right to be here.'

'That may be so but, legally, he has no rights. No matter what the previous arrangement was, I have no intention of letting it carry on.'

He still looked doubtful so Gina made the effort to smile and whisper confidently, 'Go on, get the bags.'

Juan shrugged his acceptance and Gina watched him go, albeit reluctantly. Then some instinct made her turn and look behind her.

Sam stood in the doorway of the study, outlined in the warm rectangle of light. He was leaning against the door jamb, one hand in the pocket of his jeans, the other grasping his whisky tumbler.

How long had he been watching them? Watching and listening? Had he heard any part of her whispered conversation with Juan?

Nothing about his manner betrayed his thoughts. When he saw her looking at him he smiled and raised his glass to her before taking a long drink. She turned from him and gathered her stepdaughter into her arms.

'Where are you going?' Sam broke his silence and spoke low and urgently.

She didn't answer him, she just nodded towards the staircase. Surely he isn't going to create any difficulties now, she thought. We're all tired and Natalie needs to sleep out the night in a proper bed. She watched him anxiously, and was relieved to see him shrug and vanish back into the study.

She had only reached the foot of the wide staircase, however, when she heard him striding after her. She turned to find him at her side without his glass of whisky.

'Here, let me,' he said quietly. 'I know the house, you don't, let me carry Natalie up.'

He held out his arms and Gina made no protest. She was bone weary and it made sense. She allowed him to take the child and lead the way.

As they mounted the stairs, she was aware of Juan bringing their bags into the hall. She expected him to follow them, but he went out again. He must have decided to bring everything in now, she thought. That made sense, too. He would have to get away early in the morning.

Gina realized that, even when they had moved away from the fires, the house was warm. There must be some sort of central heating, she thought, but, even so, the place feels well-aired and lived in. She wondered how long Sam had been here.

When they reached the first landing she followed him along a richly carpeted, oak-panelled corridor. When he stopped outside one of the doors he nodded, indicating that she should open it.

Gina found the light switch and flicked it on. She surveyed the room briefly. It was attractively, but fairly anonymously, decorated in apple green, white and yellow. A guest-room, she guessed. But it was warm and ready for occupation.

Sam entered and laid Natalie gently on one of the two divan beds. The child sighed and they both held their breath in case she should awaken, but then she rolled onto her side and went on sleeping as deeply as before.

Sam gazed down at her. Gina was shocked at the depth of feeling he revealed in that long glance. But why should I be? she wondered, after all, Natalie is his late sister's child.

He looked up at her and Gina looked away, quickly. She found herself embarrassed to have witnessed such strong emotion. Especially in a man whom she had come to believe had no finer feelings at all.

When Sam moved away, he beckoned to Gina to follow him. He stopped just outside the door. 'You were right to bring Natalie to her father's childhood home. I thought, at first, that you'd left her at the villa with Madam Bernat.'

'I would never do that!'

A ghost of a smile played across Sam's features. 'Why not? You could trust her, surely? As far as I can remember, Florence Bernat is honest, cheerful, homely and a wonderful cook!'

Gina looked up into his eyes, trying to judge whether he was being serious or just teasing her.

'Of course Madam Bernat is trustworthy – and she adores Natalie. It's just . . . just that I would never willingly be parted from my stepdaughter. I love her too much.'

'Yes, I think you do.'

They looked at each other searchingly and, for a moment, Gina thought she saw a hint of the warm, endearing man that she used to know. The man with the infectious smile and the off-beat sense of humour. The man she had fallen so deeply in love with nearly three years ago.

But the smile that had begun to soften the hard line of his mouth vanished completely when they heard Juan's voice.

'Gina – where shall I put these?' He had struggled upstairs with most of the luggage.

Sam crossed the landing and opened a door immediately opposite to the one where he had placed Natalie. He switched on the light and revealed a large, grandly furnished room with a double bed. It was not made up.

'I suppose you'd better have this room,' he said. 'I'm not sure what your sleeping arrangements are, but . . .'

'That will do nicely for Juan,' Gina interrupted. 'I'll stay with Natalie.'

Sam looked at her coolly. She could feel herself

flushing. It was not because she was embarrassed. She was very angry. But, by now, Juan had joined them and, for his sake, she controlled her temper.

'Well then,' Sam said. 'The clean bed-linen is in that cupboard, just there. The next door along is a bathroom. I'll leave you to sort yourselves out.'

He strode away but at the top of the stairs he paused and looked back at them. 'I should have asked. Are you hungry?'

'No.'

'Well, if you want a snack or a hot drink or anything, I'm sure you can find your way down to the kitchen.'

He went downstairs and Gina watched bleakly until he was out of sight.

He was still behaving as though he were the host and she and Juan were visitors, she thought. What's more, a very reluctant host to very unwelcome visitors!

The only time the ice had melted a little was when he had carried his niece upstairs and laid her on the bed. But she was too tired to challenge his attitude tonight. She would feel better able to do that after a good night's sleep.

Gina collected the clean bedclothes from the cupboard and left Juan to look after himself. She had to see to Natalie. She decided simply to slip off the child's shoes and outer clothes rather than disturb her too much.

As soon as she had eased her into bed, she went to see how Juan was getting on. The bed in the room across the corridor was made up. Gina turned to see Juan coming back from the bathroom.

He had stripped to his jeans and had slung the towel around his neck. The white terry cloth contrasted sharply with his tanned, golden skin tones.

She watched him raise one end of the towel and dab at his face. The action revealed more of his upper body, the tightly-muscled planes of his chest, the soft covering of dark curls arrowing downwards.

Gina smiled wanly. Juan was so . . . so beautiful. That was the only word that seemed to fit. It was hardly surprising that people who saw them constantly together assumed that they were lovers.

'Gina? Are you OK?' He looked anxious again.

'Fine, I'm fine. Just totally bushed, that's all.'

His sensitive face immediately expressed concern. 'Are you sure you don't want a warm drink, Gina? I will come downstairs with you, if you like.'

She could see that he was uneasy at the prospect of further friction with Sam.

'No, that's all right. I just want to crash out.'

He smiled his relief. 'Me too. Goodnight, then . . .'

'Goodnight.'

He paused before closing his door. 'I will set the alarm on my watch for three a.m.'

'But that will give you only about five hours' sleep!'

'That will have to do,' now, his smile was rueful, 'if I am to get back to Toulouse before midnight tomorrow.'

'The hire car won't turn into a pumpkin if you don't return it by the stroke of twelve!'

'I beg your pardon?'

Gina was suddenly too weary to explain the details of her favourite fairy story. 'Sorry, forget it, just a silly joke. But seriously, there was no deadline for returning the car, was there?'

'No, it is just that I want to be able to phone Gerard and get back to the villa in time for a few hours' sleep, then perhaps a swim and breakfast on the terrace.'

'But, why . . . ?'

'Well, I think we must have fooled that rat pack of reporters by sneaking off the way we did. There has been no sign of any of them following us, has there?'

'No – and, as far as I can see, nothing in the papers about our escape.'

'Yes, but if one of us, at least, doesn't make an appearance at the villa very soon, they will start to get suspicious.'

Gina sighed. 'But, whatever you do, they'll realize that we've fooled them, sooner or later.'

'Of course they will – but I'll be there to lay a few false trails! Eventually, they will go away and find a hotter story, no?' He grinned.

'Yes, I suppose they will. You know, Juan, you should have been a secret agent, not an artist. Your true talents have been wasted. Goodnight, 007.'

'007? That I do understand. You think, perhaps, I should be the next James Bond?'

'When Pierce Brosnan's ready to retire we'll put your name forward!'

Gina hugged him but, before she broke away, Juan cupped her face with gentle, long-fingered hands and kissed her, briefly, tenderly, on her brow. 'Goodnight, *querida.*'

She couldn't sleep.

After a perfunctory wash, she had discarded her clothes, letting them lie where they fell, and had pulled on her night-dress before crawling into bed.

Firmly putting out of her mind all thoughts of Sam and the things she must say to him in the morning, she had tried to relax and concentrate only on the fact that she had reached her refuge without mishap.

But, as often happens after long periods spent travelling, she found herself reliving the journey in her mind. It hadn't been easy.

Juan had done most of the driving in France, during the channel crossing the seas had turned rough as they often did at this time of the year, then she had taken over in England because Juan faced the long drive back alone.

After he had gone she would be left here with Sam . . .

Gina glanced at the small travel clock which she had placed on the bedside table. It was after midnight.

She lay and listened to her stepdaughter's even breathing for a while and then, some instinct made her get up and pad softly over to the window. She parted the curtains and looked out.

The rain had stopped but the wind was still quite strong. In these northern climes the autumn leaves had already started to fall and some had been blown against the window, where they clung wetly to the glass.

The room Sam had chosen for them was at the back of the house; part of a small wing that jutted out at right angles. So Gina had a view both of the wooded hills beyond the walled grounds and of much of the main body of Northmoor Hall.

A light was burning in a downstairs room. The curtains were open and Gina stared down curiously. It was the study. Even from this distance she could make out the shelves lined with books and a pool of light illuminating the desk. Sam was working there.

What exactly was he doing? she wondered. And did he always work into the early hours of the morning or couldn't he sleep either? She hoped it was the latter.

She leaned her head against the cool glass and closed her eyes . . . she was so tired . . . so much had happened that she could never have expected when she first became Natalie's nanny.

She had been so happy to get the job. After the fiasco that had brought her previous position to an end, she had almost decided that she would have to find some other kind of career.

But a good friend had intervened. Mr Hargreaves, David's solicitor at the time, had interviewed Gina in London and he told David what had happened, but David had been prepared to judge for himself.

It hadn't taken long, apparently, for him to be happy with his choice. He had been a wonderful employer. He had been interested in everything she did for his daughter and totally supportive of her aims.

The kind of life he was trying to provide for his motherless daughter had been so different from her own bleak situation after her mother had died.

But, even more important, Gina would never forget the way David had been there for her when Sam had dumped her so cruelly. She didn't know how she would have survived that agonizing time without him.

So she had been more than willing to do anything she could when he'd told her that he needed her help, although at first she could not believe what he was suggesting. But he had been capable of great charm and powers of persuasion when he wanted something and he'd soon convinced her.

The first part of his plan had been that they should get married. He could have had no idea how much grief the rest of his plan would cause her . . .

Gina opened her eyes with a start. She felt stiff and disorientated. How long had she been standing here? Had she fallen asleep on her feet? She blinked and looked out, her eyes instinctively drawn downwards.

The study window was dark. Sam must have gone to bed. Now he must be upstairs somewhere . . . perhaps just along the corridor . . . Gina shivered convulsively and she knew it wasn't just because of the cold.

She let the curtain fall and, after a quick glance at

Natalie, she went back to bed. But proper sleep was as elusive as ever. For now she had something else to worry about.

It seemed that Sam Redmond still had the power to disturb her.

CHAPTER 4

She was back in the same old dream . . .

The night was warm and full of the scents of summer flowers . . . the stars were blazoned across the sky above the mountains . . .

She was walking alone, down the narrow road that led to the village. Her full-skirted, cotton dress was bleached white by the moon. Her bare arms welcomed the slight breeze.

She passed the first row of shuttered houses and she could hear laughter coming from the small café where *he* would be waiting for her. She must hurry . . .

In the village square, golden light spilled from the open doorway of the café into the blue shadows. Some tables were placed outside the café and couples sat there, leaning in towards each other, speaking softly; their faces illuminated by the flickering candles set in old wine bottles.

Her footsteps struck against the cobbles and the conversation stopped. Everyone turned to look at her, curiously, pityingly . . .

Then the pity turned to scorn. The people who

46

had once been her friends stared at her over hostile shoulders.

Her eyes were drawn to one of the tables, set apart from the rest. No one sat there. On the red and white checked cloth, propped up against the wax-encrusted wine bottle, there was a large white envelope. She knew that her name would be on it.

She reached for the envelope and it seemed that the watchers held their breath while she opened it. Their eyes were greedy, their smiles expectant . . .

She drew out the single sheet of paper. It was blank. She stared in puzzlement but, suddenly, she realized that no words were needed. She knew what it meant.

He had gone. Sam had left her without a word or an explanation and, as she stared at the piece of white paper, her tears began to fall.

The watchers left their tables and drew nearer. Their faces surrounded her, their eyes were huge and bright with malice. The laughter began again, softly at first, behind raised hands, but then it grew louder, more overt.

Gina turned and pushed through the circle of her tormentors. They gave way immediately, their bodies as insubstantial as twisting smoke.

The laughter grew louder and louder, filling the village square and following her as she hurried away through the narrow streets, out of the village and up into the sharp, cool air of the mountain road.

But she couldn't escape. Now the laughter echoed round the bowl of the mountains from peak to peak.

She began to run – not looking where she was going, nor caring. She only knew that she had to get away from that hateful sound . . .

Gina awoke with an aching lump of misery in her throat. Tears scalded her eyes. Her pillow was damp and she raised herself up wearily and turned it over.

The disturbing images of the dream were still vivid and they were so unsettling that she knew she would not be able to sleep again. She was even more tired than she had been before.

Every now and then, she glanced at her clock. When it was almost three she put the alarm off in case it should waken Natalie, and got up.

How she wished she had unpacked before she had gone to bed. Now, in the dimness she rummaged in her case for clean underclothes, jeans and a cotton-knit top.

The colours all looked faded in the pale, starlight filtering in between the curtains, but she thought she'd chosen the red top. She pulled it over her head and ran a comb quickly through her tangled curls.

Leaving the door ajar, in case Natalie should wake up and be frightened to find herself shut in a strange room, she crossed the landing to Juan's door.

She could hear him moving about and she knocked softly. The door opened immediately.

'I'm ready to go,' Juan whispered, 'but I have a few more of your things to unload from the car.'

'OK, while you do that, I'll make you some breakfast.'

48

The house was quiet and even the slightest creak of an old floorboard made her nerves twitch. The last thing she wanted to do was to awaken Sam. But, thankfully, she and Juan made it down the stairs without one of the bedroom doors being flung open angrily.

She hadn't actually said anything, but Juan must have read her mind for, when they reached the entrance hall, he put his overnight bag down on the floor and took hold of her shoulders. She was shaking slightly. They grinned at each other like naughty children who had just outwitted the grown-ups.

'Whew!' Juan breathed and then placed his finger on his lips, making a pantomime of saying, 'Ssh!'

Gina gasped with the effort to check the laughter his gesture had caused. I'm near to hysteria, she thought. Juan grinned ruefully and then picked up his bag and headed for the front door.

It didn't take her long to find the kitchen. It was a large room with old-fashioned units and a deep, white sink, but it was clean and warm. The heat reached out comfortingly from an Aga stove set into a tiled recess.

Gina soon found orange juice, eggs, bread, butter, apricot jam and coffee. Not too different from the kind of breakfast they used to eat on the sun-warmed terrace at the villa.

I'll have to reimburse Sam for all this, she thought, and as soon as I can I'll have to lay in some provisions of my own.

That problem was on Juan's mind, too. He questioned her about it as he ate his scrambled eggs on toast while they sat together at the scrubbed pine kitchen table. Gina had not made anything for herself but she had poured herself a large cup of strong, black coffee.

'What are you going to do about buying in food?' he asked. 'This house is pretty remote, isn't it?'

'Well, it's not too isolated. According to the map, there's a village, Brackenburn, it's only a two or three miles further north. And remember, David keeps – kept – a Range Rover here permanently. I'll be OK wherever I want to go. Then, of course, the caretaker and his wife live in the grounds somewhere.'

'That is something, I suppose. You know, I would not be too happy about leaving you with that man if I thought you were going to be completely alone.'

'For heaven's sake, Juan. He's unlikely to rape me.'

When she saw the look on his face she regretted her snappish outburst. 'Look, I'm sorry, but –'

'I wasn't thinking of rape, Gina.'

'I know, I shouldn't have said that.'

'I was thinking how difficult it will be for you if you have to face his hostility without me to support you. I wish that I could stay longer, but . . .'

'Don't worry, I'll cope – and you know I need you to go back. There's no one else I could trust to look after everything. It's not just the villa, it's the studio, the gallery, David's paintings . . . You're the only one I can trust.'

'And you know I will never let you down.'

'Oh Juan, I feel so guilty. I feel that I've betrayed David by running away and leaving it all!' Gina's eyes filled with tears.

'You have not betrayed him. You must never think that. David was ill. He just didn't think things out. He should have known what you would have had to face. In the circumstances, I am sure he would approve of your coming here.'

'You think so?'

'I know so!' Juan clasped her hands over the table. 'I won't let you down, Gina. Remember, I loved David, too.'

'Yes, everybody loved David, didn't they?'

She realized how cynical that must have sounded when she saw Juan's surprised look – and she hadn't meant to be cynical. It was just that she knew the man she had married so much better than his adoring students. He had been a much more complex character than they imagined.

'He – he couldn't help it you know . . .' Juan sounded hesitant.

'What do you mean?' Gina's eyes widened.

'Attracting people. He was so kind, so patient. He made young people believe in their own talent.'

'Oh, that. I know that, Juan, and I didn't mean to sound jealous. It's just that it took some getting used to – sharing my husband with so many other people!'

Gina hoped that her smile softened any critical implication that her words might have and she was relieved when Juan smiled too.

'But at the end, when his health deteriorated,

David sent all the others away, didn't he? He just wanted you and – and me and –'

The young Spaniard was finding it hard to control his feelings so Gina finished the sentence for him, 'And his friends the Bernats.'

The others had gone regretfully but willingly, she remembered. They assumed that David and Gina, so recently married, had wanted to spend as much time together as fate would allow them. They thought it was natural that David should ask Juan, his most brilliant student, to stay and take care of the studio and gallery.

Gina didn't think that any of them had guessed the truth of the situation.

She sighed and tried to look positive. 'Juan, I'm going to be all right here, trust me. But, now you really must go. You've a long drive ahead of you.'

Gina saw him to the front door and then closed it as quietly as she could behind him. Returning to the kitchen, she poured herself another cup of coffee and sat nursing the mug for a while as she tried to empty her mind.

It was no good. Too many thoughts and emotions were crowding to the forefront of her consciousness, demanding attention.

Gina stared into the dregs of coffee in her cup. She knew she ought to go back to bed and try to get some more sleep but, for the moment, she was just too exhausted to move.

Eventually, she pushed her coffee cup aside and, resting her elbows on the table, she dropped her head into her hands. Alone in the kitchen, in the sleeping house, she allowed her guard to fall. She began to weep.

'Gina?'

She raised her head, wiping the tears from her face with her fingers. Sam was watching her from the doorway.

'Are you OK?'

'Yes, I'm fine – just a little tired. But, I'm sorry. Did we disturb you?'

Sam was wearing a midnight blue silk robe, his dark hair was tousled. His expression as he studied her was guarded but somehow vulnerable – accessible, even.

For a long moment they looked at each other and Gina felt that if only she knew the right words, the right gestures, she would be able to reach out to him – bridge the yawning, terrifying chasm that had opened up between them.

But she could only stare at him helplessly and, eventually, he spoke. 'I heard a car start up – I looked out of my window just in time to see the tail lights vanishing down the drive. I waited for a while but the house was so quiet that I thought perhaps you'd . . .'

'Did you think your hostile reception last night had driven me away? Is that what you wanted?'

The vulnerable look vanished and Gina knew that it was her words and the tone of her voice that had made it vanish. Sam watched her warily, but he made no answer.

She sighed as she continued, 'No, I'm here to stay, I'm afraid. It's only Juan who has set off for the villa.'

A muscle twitched in Sam's jaw-line. 'So that he can let you know when the coast is clear?'

'Meaning?'

'I'm not stupid, Gina. Soon the newspapers will get tired of the scandal and move on to something new. Then your boyfriend will let you know that the reporters and photographers have all decamped and you'll be off to join him as fast as you can.'

'Is that what you think?'

'It's obvious, isn't it. Juan drives off into the dawn and I come in here and find you crying your eyes out. What else am I supposed to think?'

'Nothing else – if your imagination is so limited!'

'Tell me that I'm wrong!'

'Why should I?'

Gina glared up at him. He had advanced into the kitchen and, in her exhausted state, it seemed that he towered above her. But no matter how hostile he appeared, nothing prepared her for the shock of his next words.

'Well then, let me make it quite clear, when you do go back to France, you go alone. I won't allow you to take Natalie with you.'

Gina jerked to her feet, eyes blazing. 'You can't stop me!'

'Yes I can. Her mother was my sister. I'm a blood relative. You're only her stepmother and I don't think you're fit to have charge of her – and I could probably prove it.'

'Why, you –'

Gina took a step round the table towards him but, suddenly, she faltered, gasping for breath. Her heart began to pound painfully against her ribs. She took another step but her knees began to buckle. It seemed as if her legs were not able to support her . . .

What was happening to her . . . ?

The room began to revolve . . . she could feel herself swaying as if the floor beneath her feet were tilting. Her eyes were still open but all she could see was a red mist . . . she was falling . . . falling into a dark red abyss . . .

Sam caught her before she hit the floor.

CHAPTER 5

Gina opened her eyes to find a strange face hovering above her – a woman's face. The pale blue eyes were narrowed and the lips pursed disapprovingly.

Unwilling to confront the puzzling apparition, Gina turned her head to the side. She stretched her limbs tentatively and registered that she was lying on her bed in the guest room. Someone had slipped off her shoes and covered her with a blanket.

She was warm. The sun was streaming through the window and across the bed – but it had been dark when she and Sam had confronted each other in the kitchen, hadn't it?

She remembered his shocking words and the effect they had had on her. It had been like a body blow, leaving her breathless . . . weak. She'd started to fall. Sam had come striding angrily round the table towards her. He had reached out . . .

Had he caught her in his arms? Gina moved her limbs again experimentally. She had no sensation of being bruised and tender as she surely would have been if she had hit the floor. So Sam must have saved her. But she had no memory of what had happened since then.

She tried to work it out. Someone must have brought me upstairs, she thought. Could it have been this fierce-looking, woman who's giving a good imitation of a prison guard?

Gina sighed and decided to confront her fate. Reluctantly, she turned her head, at the same time trying to raise it up a little.

Mistake! Her heart began to thud and a giant hand squeezed her head. She gasped.

'Don't sit up too quickly,' the wardress in the flowered overall ordered.

'What? How?' Gina began. But she sank back into the pillows, grateful to obey the command.

'You fainted, Mrs Shaw.' The woman had a soft Northumbrian accent which gave lie to the sharp face.

'I know that.' Gina frowned. 'But how did I get here?'

'Mr Redmond carried you up to bed and watched over you until Jock and I arrived.'

'Watched over me? Uh-huh . . .'

Without warning, Gina found herself giggling. She was trying very hard to imagine the extremely angry man she had confronted just a few hours ago in the role of guardian angel. She failed but, before hysteria took over, her custodian's eyebrows rose alarmingly, and the fit of giggles ended in a gulping sob.

'What is it, Mrs Shaw? What is it that you find so funny?'

'Nothing! Please forgive me. It isn't funny at all. I seem to have caused you all some trouble.'

The woman's manner eased slightly. 'No, no trouble. Now, how are you feeling?'

'A little better I think. I was probably just very tired.'

And that's true, Gina thought. Sam's threat to take Natalie away from her, coming after the grief and stress of the last few weeks, had been enough to make her lose consciousness. And then, after he had brought her up to bed, her body must have sought the sleep she so desperately needed.

'That's what Mr Redmond said.' The woman was looking at her critically. 'That you would be tired after your journey. But he told me that I must call the doctor if you think it's necessary.'

Her last statement ended on a questioning note and her voice had softened considerably. Her expression, although still austere, had a hint of something else . . . curiosity? Excited speculation?

But why on earth should she be excited? No, it must just be plain curiosity, Gina decided.

'No, there's no reason to call a doctor.'

'We-ell, if you're sure, but you don't have to be embarrassed with me, you know.'

I'm not really awake yet, Gina decided. This is a dream – a nightmare – whatever. This woman is really an alien who's escaped from the *X-Files*. She, or should I say it, is only pretending to be human and it hasn't mastered the rules or the nuances of conversation yet. That's why she's talking nonsense . . .

But alien or not, the outwardly human female who was standing over her, had raised her eyebrows as though she were expecting some kind of response.

'Embarrassed? Why should I be?' Gina asked.

For an answer, the woman shrugged and suppressed a small smile. But the knowing look she shot from under half-closed lids gave the game away.

I know what she's thinking! What she suspects! Gina was shocked.

'I'll just put this on the bedside table,' the woman said.

Gina noticed for the first time that she had been holding a cup of tea.

'Mr Redmond told me to put sugar in. He says you need it. Now drink it up as soon as you can, but mind, it's scalding hot.'

'Thank you –' Gina glanced at the wedding ring on the woman's finger, 'Thank you, Mrs . . .?'

'Robson, Agnes Robson. My husband, Jock, is the caretaker here. I keep the house in order and help out if anyone's in residence.'

'Have – have you and Mr Robson worked here long?'

'Years. Since David – since your husband was a boy.'

'I see.'

The woman's features were suddenly pinched with sorrow and Gina realized how much she must have loved David. But then everyone had loved

David. He had inspired lifelong devotion and loyalty in everyone who strayed into the charmed circle of his life.

No, not everyone, Gina suddenly remembered with pain. There was one person at least who had betrayed him badly . . .

'I'm sorry, Mrs Shaw.'

Gina looked up and saw that Mrs Robson was regarding her uncertainly.

'Sorry?'

'I've upset you.'

Gina felt the wetness on her cheeks and her hands flew up to find that she was crying. Agnes Robson pulled open a drawer in the bedside table and took out a pack of tissues.

'Here you are.'

'Thanks.'

'I can see the very mention of his name is still too much for you.'

Mrs Robson's words were kindly but she sounded surprised. And so she would be, thought Gina, if she believes with the rest of the world that I married David only for his money.

Gina finished dabbing at her eyes and, still clutching the soggy tissues in her hand, she found herself blurting out, 'I did love him, you know.'

'Well, then,' the housekeeper's tone was noncommittal, 'I'd best be getting back to Natalie.'

Natalie! Gina's eyes flew guiltily to the other bed and she saw that it was empty.

'You needn't worry about your stepdaughter, Mrs

Shaw.' A certain asperity returned to her voice. 'She's having her breakfast with her uncle and they're getting on like a house on fire.'

And managing very well without you, she might as well have added, because that was the sentiment that hung in the air as she left the room and closed the door behind her.

Well, that was quite a welcome to my new home, Gina brooded as she sipped the hot, sweet tea. Mrs Robson has made it fairly obvious what she thinks about me. She's probably prepared to concede that I might have loved David, or at least been fond enough of him to be genuinely affected by his death, but, just like Sam, she thinks I've done Natalie out of her rightful fortune and she's ready to condemn me without a hearing.

It had not occurred to Gina until just now that the staff in the Shaw family home might be hostile. But that was perfectly natural, she accepted wearily. Not only would they be grieved and shocked by David's death but they would also be indignant that his new wife appeared to have stolen his daughter's inheritance.

Well, there's nothing I can do about that, she thought. It's just another problem that I'll have to deal with. I promised David that I would cope with everything – including taking care of Natalie.

Natalie . . . born so soon after his marriage to Nadine, Gina mused. Everyone had thought it was so romantic that the lovers had been forgiven any imagined misdemeanour. And now it seems that Mrs

Robson, at least, suspects that my own hastily arranged marriage might have been for the same reason.

She thinks that I could be pregnant and that's why David married me. That's what all that nonsense about calling the doctor and not being embarrassed was about.

And what if Sam thinks that too?

Gina heard her teacup rattling against the saucer and looked down to see that her hand was shaking. She reached over carefully and set it down on the bedside table.

Why worry, I'm not pregnant, couldn't possibly be pregnant, so I don't have to say anything at all. She smiled ruefully. The passing of time will take care of that speculation.

So that's not a problem, she told herself as she picked up her handbag from the floor beside the bed. But there were other things that were. She opened the bag and reached inside.

The day that she, Juan and Natalie had fled from the villa, a letter had arrived from David's solicitor, Robert Hargreaves. Gina hadn't even read it, she had stuffed it in her bag to be dealt with when she was in England.

Mr Hargreaves had responded personally when David had requested that someone from his office should come out to France and draft a new will. He was a kindly man who had become David's friend over the years.

She looked at the letter. Robert Hargreaves started

by stating his outrage at the way Gina was being treated by the media and offering his sympathy. He wrote that he would do anything he could to help her. And then he made a puzzling reference to David's will:

— as you know, David's will is pretty straightfor-ward; it was all explained to you at the time.

However, since David's death, I have had a con-versation with Jane Richards who made the final trip to France to tie everything up, and I have discovered that there may be something you do not know about.

Let me stress that there is nothing for you to worry about but I feel that I ought to talk to you in person, therefore I would be grateful if you would get in touch with me.

Mr Hargreaves ended with another request that Gina should try not to be too upset by the vindictive press campaign.

But then, he knows the full story, she thought as she put the letter back into her bag, I'm glad some-body does. I'll phone him and find out what it's all about.

David had trusted the elderly solicitor utterly, and he had told her that the firm he worked for had been handling the Shaw family's affairs for most of this century.

When Robert Hargreaves had started handing over some of his work to his junior partners, he had hinted that he might retire soon in order to look after his wife, Anne, whose failing eyesight had become a problem.

David had said that they must come to stay at the villa whenever they pleased. But the final acceleration of his own illness had put paid to this plan.

Once life gets back to normal, Gina thought, I'll repeat the invitation.

She wasn't too worried about whatever it was Mr Hargreaves had discovered. In fact she thought she knew what it would be. After drawing up his will, but before signing the final draft, David had decided to make Juan's position more secure.

He wanted it written into the will that Juan was to live at the villa and work in the studio and gallery as long as he wished to. And he was also to have a choice of David's own paintings.

David had told Gina that he was going to add a codicil to his will to that effect; she assumed that that was just what he had done when Jane Richards had come to the villa for the final time . . .

'Gina, here's your breakfast! I made it, didn't I, Sam?'

The door had opened and Natalie ran into the room with Sam close behind her. He was dressed in dark slacks and an Aran sweater. Gina suppressed the memory of him in his blue silk robe and concentrated on the fact that he was carrying a tray.

'Good morning, Natalie,' Gina said. 'I didn't hear you get up.'

'Sam said I mustn't make a noise and wake you because you were very tired.'

'That was kind of him.'

'I changed into my clean clothes myself. Sam got them out of the case for me.'

Gina looked at her stepdaughter. She was wearing a warm, peach-coloured sweater and blue cord dungarees. Most suitable for a small child who had just travelled from a country where it was still very warm to one where, at the end of summer, it was already turning cold. Clever Sam.

'Sam's my uncle, you know?'

It wasn't a statement, it was a question and Natalie's eyes were round with wonder and a hint of something elsc . . . concern?

Gina realized that the child could hardly be expected to have remembered her uncle very well, if at all. She had only been a baby the last time he had visited the Villa Des Pines – stayed there so briefly – and then walked out of their lives.

'Yes, I know.' Gina smiled reassuringly at Natalie and the concerned look vanished.

She trusts me, Gina thought. If I accept Sam, then he's OK. She trusts me and she loves me, she knows that I love her. I'll never do anything to break that trust. If I let Sam take her away from me, she and I would both be heartbroken.

Natalie hurled herself across the room and on to the bed. Her eyes were shining with excitement. Gina enfolded her in her arms but, after bestowing a hasty kiss, the little girl wriggled out of her embrace and slid down on to the floor again.

'Look – I made your breakfast! Come on, Sam!'

'Ooh, what a treat!' Gina smiled with exaggerated surprise and delight as Sam placed the tray on the bed before her. On it there was a plate with two slices of toast and marmalade and yet another cup of tea – but this time it was black with a slice of lemon.

'I told Sam that you liked your tea like that and I made the toast myself!'

'Under strict supervision!' Sam smiled. All the bitter antagonism towards Gina had gone for the moment – or was well hidden.

'Can I go and help Mrs Robson now, Sam? She said I could.' Natalie looked up at her uncle.

'You must ask your – you must ask Gina's permission.'

'May I, Gina? Mrs Robson's making cakes.'

'Are you sure you won't be in the way?'

'Agnes likes children,' Sam replied for her. 'She'll enjoy having Natalie in the house.'

'All right then, off you go. But wait a minute, what's all this "Sam" business? Have you asked your uncle if it's all right to talk to him that way?'

Sam laughed. 'That's entirely my own fault. I told Natalie that I was much too young to be an uncle! Now off you go, love.'

Natalie flew out of the room without a backward glance and Gina reflected ruefully that both the forbidding Sam and the dour Mrs Robson seemed to have made quite an impression on the child, and vice versa. But then it was easy for Natalie to win hearts, she was enchanting, just as they said her mother had been.

Sam had remained in the room and Gina looked up at him cautiously but, so far, the hostile expression had not returned. He was looking in the direction of the door; when Natalie was out of sight, he turned to face her, still smiling.

'She takes after David, doesn't she?'

'What makes you say that?'

Sam's eyes widened with mild surprise. 'The fair hair – the blue eyes – it's obvious. My sister was dark like me.'

'Yes, of course. I never met her, as you know, but I've seen David's portrait of her. It's one of his best works.'

'It is, isn't it?' Sam's face became animated with pleasure 'Nadine was very beautiful, wasn't she? But, even so, the portrait is breathtaking. David must have loved her very much.'

'Yes, he loved her . . .'

Gina looked away uncomfortably. There was so much she could have told Sam about his younger sister's marriage to his friend, but she didn't think that she ever would. It might break his heart . . .

'And, you know,' Sam sighed, 'I think Natalie might turn out to be every bit as beautiful as her mother – and, Gina, she does you credit.'

'Why's that?' Gina hid her smile. She could guess how unwilling Sam must be to praise her.

'She's confident, well-behaved and bright – and remarkably articulate!'

'She's never stops talking, you mean.'

They both laughed and then Gina added, 'And

she's just as much a chatterbox in French and in Spanish!'

Sam studied her face before he spoke. 'I know she has you to thank for that. One of the job specifications was that you could speak both those languages, wasn't it?'

'Mmm, David thought that as he was living in the High Pyrenees we ought to be able to converse with all our neighbours – not just rely for company on the English ex-pats.' As my parents do, she thought.

Her face clouded. When her father and step-mother had moved to Marbella on the Costa Del Sol, they had hardly changed their way of life at all. All they had wanted was have a good time with the same kind of people as themselves. Gina had been in the way.

She glanced up and saw that Sam was studying her. He looked puzzled and she forced herself to push the gloomy memories out of her mind.

She smiled. 'But I didn't have to teach Natalie very much at all. She seemed to be able to pick up any language from the word go. I think it's because she can't bear to be left out of any conversation!'

'You're genuinely fond of her, aren't you?' Sam's voice was subdued.

'*Fond* of her? I *love* her as though she were my own child. Why should you think otherwise?'

Gina felt her anger rising and she fought to control it. After all, why should she be surprised at his question?

She saw the doubt reflected in his eyes and was

miserably reminded of all the things that had been written about her in the last few weeks.

He thinks I'm the wicked stepmother, the nanny who married the boss and set out to steal a defenceless child's inheritance. Well let him think it. I'm not going to tell him any different!

Gina picked up her cup and sipped her tea. She didn't think she could eat anything and she pushed the plate of toast aside.

'I'd rather you ate that toast – both slices.'

'Why?' She looked up in astonishment.

'I wouldn't like to answer to Natalie if you leave it!' He grinned and then his brows furrowed. 'Besides, I've noticed that you've lost weight.'

'Have you?'

'You're too thin; it doesn't suit you.'

'Thanks a lot!' Gina muttered but, nevertheless, she picked up a slice of toast and began to nibble at it.

Sam still hovered. 'Gina –' he began.

'It's all right. I promise you I'll eat every scrap; you don't have to stand over me.'

'It's not that. Look,' he said, 'I'm sorry about what happened earlier this morning. I shouldn't have behaved the way I did when you were obviously so tired and upset. It's no wonder you passed out.'

Gina flushed. She remembered Mrs Robson's speculative look. 'That's all right,' she murmured. 'Thank you for bringing me back to bed.'

'Oh, well . . .'

Sam stood uneasily by the door. Clearly he didn't know how to take his leave. It's as though he's surprised at himself for actually being pleasant to me, Gina thought.

A surge of bitterness overwhelmed her. How dare he think badly of her without giving her the chance to explain anything! After the way he had behaved, he was the last person who should be acting righteous.

'Don't let me keep you.'

Her sudden coolness took him by surprise. Any trace of a smile vanished. He frowned and looked for a moment as if he were going to say something but he obviously changed his mind. Without a word he turned and left the room.

Gina finished her breakfast but hardly tasted it. She pushed the tray aside. She was fuming. No matter how pleasant Sam had been just now, she realized that it had probably been for Natalie's sake. He wouldn't have wanted to upset her.

But the challenge he had issued just a few hours ago was very real. He intended to prove that she wasn't fit to look after her stepdaughter – he intended to take Natalie away from her.

She couldn't let that happen. It wasn't just because she loved Natalie as if she was her own daughter and, God knows, that was reason enough. She had made a solemn promise to David before he had died that she and only she would be responsible for Natalie's upbringing. And she always kept her promises.

CHAPTER 6

By the time she had showered and washed her hair Gina felt revived. She was exasperated to find that her French hairdryer would need an adapter to fit the English three-pin socket, so she dried her hair with a towel and then brushed it into shape.

She pulled on the same pair of jeans and red cotton sweater that she had worn earlier that morning and then glanced in mock despair at her half-emptied case and travelling bags. I'll sort this lot out later, she thought. But right now, there are other, more important, things that need seeing too.

The house was quiet, but it felt warm and lived in and appetizing smells of baking wafted across the hall and up the stairs to meet her. A log fire burned in the old stone hearth and Gina thought how welcoming it looked.

She remembered how apprehensive she and Juan had felt as they'd crept down in the dark a few hours earlier, but it was daylight now and, with any luck, Juan would be almost half way to Dover. And even after the pitifully short amount of sleep she'd been able to snatch, her confidence was growing. Now, instead of being wary of encountering Sam, she was ready to confront him.

No matter how long he had been coming to Northmoor Hall, things were going to be different in future. I own the house now, Gina thought, David left it to me and even though he might have made certain promises in the past, he wouldn't want anyone to threaten my guardianship of Natalie now. Not even his oldest friend. Sam will have to go.

But how on earth am I going to tell him?

She made her way to the kitchen. She could hear Natalie chattering and she wanted to make sure that Mrs Robson was not tiring of the child's company.

She needn't have worried. Her stepdaughter was wearing a pinafore made from a couple of tea towels safety-pinned together at the shoulders and at the waist and she was kneeling on a chair at the table absorbed in the task of cutting scones. There was a smudge of flour on her cheek and her expression was rapt.

Mrs Robson was busy adding ingredients to a huge mixing bowl. The kitchen was redolent of warmth and baking and there was already an impressive array of fruit and savoury flans cooling on wire racks on the bench tops.

'Oh, Mrs Shaw,' Agnes Robson looked up and saw her standing in the doorway. 'Is there something you want?' Her tone was polite, no more.

'No, thank you. I just came to see if Natalie was OK. I don't want her to bother you – to get in the way.'

'She's no bother at all. We're getting along fine together.'

'Mrs Robson said I'm a big help, Gina.' Natalie's eyes were shining.

'Did she, poppet?' Gina responded to her step-daughter's smile, pleased that the rigours of the last few days did not seem to have had an adverse effect.

'May I stay and do some more baking?'

'If Mrs Robson doesn't mind.'

'Of course I don't mind. The child is company for me.'

The housekeeper went on pouring the mixture she had been making into a greased and papered cake tin. Gina felt herself dismissed.

'I'll go and find Mr Redmond, then . . .' She hesitated but no help was forthcoming so she asked, 'Do you know where he is?'

'Mr Redmond's gone to town.'

'Town?'

'Into Berwick to do some shopping. Mainly news-papers I think. The village paper shop carries orders only and doesn't have many to spare. He'll be an hour or two but he said he'd be back for lunch.'

'I see.'

Gina shut the kitchen door behind her and leaned back against it for a moment. So Sam had gone to buy all the latest papers. She could guess why.

On one level, it might have been puzzling that he was bothering to follow the scandal. After all, he had dumped her, walked out on her and, if it had been left to him, she doubted whether she would ever have seen him again. So why the interest in what she was supposed to have been doing?

She knew the reason, of course, and it wasn't straightforward. It was twofold. Firstly, it's about David, she thought. Sam feels guilty that he didn't know his friend was dying. He probably thinks that if he had been there, he would have been able to protect him from getting involved with me. So, by finding out everything bad he can, he's trying to justify his own angry guilt.

But secondly, and more worrying, it's about Natalie. Perhaps Sam's hoping to find enough evidence to build up a case against me. A case to prove that I'm not fit to look after her. Then, he thinks that because he's her uncle, a blood relative, he'll be able to take her away from me.

Well, that can't be allowed to happen. Gina sighed and pushed herself away from the door. I'd better see what evidence he thinks he has. She crossed the hall to the study, opened the door and walked in.

She stared around her. No one could ever have guessed that Sam had been working here until very late the night before. Agnes Robson had obviously been in here already. The room smelled of lavender polish, everything was neat and tidy and a small fire crackled in the hearth.

There was no sign of the whisky bottle and, worryingly, the pile of newspapers and magazines had also vanished.

Had Mrs Robson thrown them out? No, Gina thought cynically, Sam's probably filed them all methodically. Where had he put them? She conquered her distaste at going through someone else's personal papers and began to search.

The desk drawers, all left unlocked, revealed only the usual collection of notebooks, boxes of paper clips, pens, pencils and typing paper. The solitary filing cabinet, standing against the wall, contained folders that were full of facts and figures and some long passages of text. A cursory glance showed that they were nothing to do with her. There were no newspapers or cuttings.

So perhaps Mrs Robson had been instructed to throw the old newspapers away and the misinformation was now only filed in Sam's mind. No – surely if he were trying to build up a case for the courts, he would keep a documentary record somewhere.

Gina glanced over to the desk again. Was everything stored in the computer? She knew that with a machine as sophisticated as this one seemed to be, it would be possible to scan both text and photographs into its memory.

She laughed weakly at the idea of her life being processed into orderly data files, to be called up at the touch of a computer key. If she switched it on would she be able to find the files and erase them?

Holding her breath in case the computer was alarmed, she sat at the desk and pressed the on/off switch but no warning sounds disturbed the silence of the study. A fairly normal-looking screen blinked into view.

Gina was used to computers. David had used one

for personal correspondence and household accounts, also for any business connected to the gallery. It hadn't been long before she had begun to help him with these matters and, as his illness progressed, she had taken over entirely.

Sam's computer was more sophisticated, however. Gina soon discovered that his files were all password protected and she sat back resignedly. It could take hours, days to find the right password – in fact she could go on guessing forever.

And if she was successful with one, she might then find that every separate file had a different password. No, it was impossible. She switched off the computer and got up.

She stood gazing into space for a moment. So, if Sam was keeping a file on her, there was no way of having a look at it – not for the moment anyway.

When her eyes re-focused, she found herself contemplating a neat pile of manuscript paper that lay on a small table next to the printer. This couldn't be what she was looking for, could it? There was too much of it, it must be Sam's own work.

But, what was he working on here in the peace and quiet of the old house in the border country? She began to leaf through the pages. Then her eyes returned to the first sentence . . .

He crouched low amongst the rubble as another missile cruised overhead seeking its predestined target. The acrid smell and the lung-searing fumes from the fires that had broken out made him gag repeatedly.

Tears were streaming down his face and he wiped them away angrily with the back of his hand – trying to forget that, only last night, this smoking heap of broken masonry had been a children's hospital . . .

A moment later Gina picked up the entire document and walked over to the chair beside the fireplace. She sat down and continued to read. She was so engrossed that she didn't notice time slipping by.

When she had finished, she laid the stack of papers on her knee and rested her head back against the chair. Sam was writing a novel.

She realized that the story was unfinished; these pages represented only a part of what was obviously going to be a major blockbuster. And, even to Gina's inexperienced eye, it didn't look like a final draft. But there was more than enough to show what a powerful writer Sam was.

So powerful that, while she had been reading it, Gina had found herself living in the world he had created, a world of danger and courage and heartbreak. She had been taken away completely from this safe, solid house on the Scottish borders and had even forgotten, for a while, all her own problems.

It was not the kind of book she usually read for it was about war and its consequences, but she had found herself deeply moved, disturbed even. Sam's book was not just a tale of action and adventure. The story was told from the viewpoint of a young and idealistic man who left university to become a reporter – a war correspondent.

At the beginning he was elated by the exciting nature of his work and determined to report the truth at all costs, even if this involved him in personal danger.

Then, instead of becoming hardened by the horrors that he witnessed, he gradually lost his self-protective shell of cynicism. Even though he fought against it, his deepest feelings became involved. He began to fear for his sanity.

She wondered how long Sam had been working on it. Some pages of notes had obviously been typed on a simple portable typewriter and there were scribbled references in the margins to real news events that had taken place over the years.

He must have come here to David's house whenever he could, in order to pull it all together, she thought. And now I've arrived to interrupt his work. Gina gripped the pages of the manuscript and lifted them up to hold them against her body. After what she had just read would she still be able to tell him to go?

Somewhere in the house a door slammed. Gina rose from the chair. She heard Sam's voice questioning and Mrs Robson's answering. She hadn't been able to make out the words but she could imagine them.

She walked quickly over to the printer table to replace the manuscript. Gina turned towards the door as it opened and Sam walked in. He was carrying a thick bundle of newspapers.

'What are you doing in here?' His eyes narrowed.

She felt like a thief caught in the act and her cheeks

burned with a mixture of chagrin and anger at her own reaction.

'I don't have to answer that question.'

'No?'

'No. This is my house, now.'

Sam nodded, almost imperceptibly. His small smile of acknowledgement tinged with irritation. Then suddenly he looked beyond her in the direction of his manuscript.

Gina hoped that she had replaced the pages in order. She sensed that his work was not just important but also intensely private to him. She could imagine his reaction if he thought she had been snooping.

Suddenly, he walked towards her and, in spite of herself, she flinched. But he merely dumped the pile of newspapers onto his desk.

'These are for you.'

'Thanks, but I'm not in the mood for reading fiction.'

Almost before the words were out of her mouth, she found herself flushing as she recalled the fiction she had been reading a moment ago. But if Sam noticed the way her complexion had darkened, he must have taken it for anger.

'Humour me. Read them.'

She stared at him. His expression was inscrutable. 'Thank you for taking so much trouble to get the latest instalment,' she said, 'but I have no intention of reading a pack of scurrilous lies.'

Gina began to walk away but Sam grabbed her

shoulder and then spun her round to face the desk. 'Look at them, damn you!'

With his other hand he fanned the papers out on the desk top.

'I don't understand . . .'

Gina looked at all the front pages he had revealed by his action. There were no photographs of her and Juan – no sensational headlines – nothing at all.

Mutely, she turned over the pages of the newspaper which lay on top of the pile. It wasn't until she got to about halfway through that she found any mention of the supposed scandal.

'Try the next one,' Sam said.

It was the same, tucked away on an inside page was a few column inches of the story. She closed the paper and backed away.

Sam put out a restraining hand. 'And the next,' he said.

'Why? What's the point of making me read the same old rubbish over and over again?'

'You've said it yourself – it's the same old rubbish. There are no new facts in any of the papers and the story has slipped from the front page. With you and Juan safely out of sight they may even give up soon and let you alone.'

'Do you think so?' Gina faced him her eyes widening with hope.

'Well, don't count on it, but it looks as though the newspaper editors decided that there's no more mileage left in the story.'

Gina put both her hands on the desk in front of her and sagged forward. She closed her eyes. Was it true? Were they really going to leave her in peace now, so that she could try to start building some kind of life for herself and Natalie?

Sam moved round behind her and took hold of both her shoulders. With sure fingers and thumbs he began to massage the knotted muscles at the base of her neck.

'You can relax for a while,' he murmured.

'Yes.'

'You didn't really think I'd gone to get the papers just to torment you, did you?'

'I did. I'm sorry. I should have trusted you.'

What on earth had made her say that? she thought. Sam was the last person she could trust.

'I suppose you had every right to think the worst after the way I greeted you last night. But, Gina . . . ?'

'Mmm?' She was having difficulty in concentrating on anything except the movement of his thumbs and fingers as he went on massaging her.

Sam had pulled her close against his body and all the old, familiar feelings of longing flooded through her. In this moment of closeness was he remembering too . . . ?

Then suddenly, he let go of her shoulders and stepped back. When she turned to face him she saw his expression was bleak.

'Sam, what is it?'

'So it might work out for you, Gina. You can hide out here with Juan until the coast is clear just as you

81

planned. It would all be just perfect, wouldn't it, except –'

'Except what?'

'Except that you didn't expect to find me here, did you?'

'No.' Gina stared at him, levelly.

'So now, I suppose you want me to go?'

Sam observed her cheerlessly as he waited for her answer

What's the matter with me? Gina thought. This is the opportunity I've been waiting for. I didn't know how on earth I was going to broach the subject of asking Sam to pack up and leave his old friend's house – the house that's become a second home to him.

And now he's making it easy for me – the trouble is, I don't want him to go.

CHAPTER 7

They stared awkwardly at each other. The atmosphere in the room became oppressive. Gina felt enclosed – hemmed in. For the life of her, she couldn't find the words to reply to Sam's question.

At last he said, 'You *do* want me to leave, don't you, Gina?'

'I . . . I . . .'

'I mean, Northmoor Hall belongs to you now, and if I'm unwelcome here – what's the matter? You're bristling like an angry wild-cat!'

'When I arrived last night,' Gina said, 'it was me who was made to feel unwelcome. You made me feel like an intruder in my own home!'

'I'm sorry, truly I am. I was taken unawares. I had no intention of staying on in your property, believe me. I knew that I would have to pack up and go but I thought that I would have a little more time. I didn't think that you would come here so soon.'

'And if you had known?'

'I would have been long gone.'

'I see.'

83

Why did she feel so disappointed? Why should the fact that Sam wanted nothing to do with her cause her such anguish? She'd been through all this before, hadn't she? She'd already experienced the bitter humiliation of rejection. She thought that she'd learned to let go . . .

'So-o,' Sam sighed and, for a moment, Gina imagined that he sounded as dejected as she was. 'I'll start packing up my things, but –'

'What is it?'

'I have a favour to ask you.'

'A favour'

'Look – let's get out of the house for a while – walk in the grounds – bring some colour back into your cheeks.'

Instinctively, Gina raised a hand to her face. 'Do I look dreadful?'

Sam smiled faintly as he reached for her hand and held it in his own. 'No, not dreadful. Just tired and anxious and a little sick of life.'

Sam's sympathetic tone brought an ache of longing to her throat. She was conscious of his fingers curling round her own, the warmth, the comforting feel of being enclosed in his grasp.

He let go of her hand and propelled her gently towards the door. 'So go and put a jacket on and we'll go for a walk before lunch.'

'I can't leave Natalie.'

'Yes you can; with Mrs Robson. The last time I saw my young niece she was up to her elbows in a big mixing bowl making currant scones.'

'I'll just go and make sure . . .'

Sam stared at her searchingly for a moment and then said, 'Don't be long.'

The leaves had barely started to change to their autumn colours of yellow, red and gold, but the heavy wind and rain of the night before seemed to have started the autumn fall.

The air smelled of fresh, damp earth and there was a keen, heathery tang from the not-so-distant hills. The grass was still wet so they stuck to the gravel drive as it curved away from the house between the graceful avenue of trees.

Sam thrust his hands into the deep pockets of his green waxed jacket and, as he strode ahead, Gina had to make an effort to match his long stride. His shoulders were hunched slightly; whether against the freshening breeze or some inner turmoil, she had no way of knowing. Every now and then she glanced up at his strong profile. It told her nothing.

Could she assume that he wanted to be friends? Well, if friendship was too strong a word, at least he had called a truce. He wanted to talk to her, wanted to ask her a favour.

But she couldn't help remembering the scene in the kitchen very early that morning and the things he had said, about her not being fit to be Natalie's guardian. She felt uneasy.

They reached a point where the drive curved round so far that the house behind them could no longer be seen – and neither could the gate ahead.

The trees on either side were tall and the growth was dense; it was like walking through a primeval forest, just Sam and her alone. They could have been the only two people in the world.

'We'll go that way. Don't worry, you won't get your shoes muddy.'

Gina looked to where he was pointing. A footpath veered off from the drive and headed through the woods. A wooden walkway had been constructed about a foot above ground level; to reach it they had to cross a small bridge over the ditch at the side of the road.

Sam crossed first and held out his hand. She took it wordlessly, but relinquished it as soon as she had reached the other side.

They walked on in silence and she began to wonder just how far they were going to go – how deep into the forest he was going to lead her. And then the trees began to thin out and Gina kept catching glimpses of a stretch of water.

'Here we are,' Sam said at last.

They had reached a clearing where there was an old summerhouse. The back of the building was solid stone but it was open-fronted. Sam led the way round and nodded towards the wooden bench inside.

'We can sit and talk in peace and enjoy a view of the lake too, if you like.'

Gina didn't sit down straight away. She stood and looked out across the bright water. The lake seemed to be completely private. Woodland hugged the reedy shore right round to where the hills began to rise quite steeply at the other side.

There was enough of a breeze to ruffle the surface of the water and to chase the clouds across the pale blue sky. From where they were standing, the ground sloped down to a pebbled shore and an old, wooden jetty reached out across the water.

Gina walked towards it. 'But this is marvellous!' She turned towards Sam and smiled.

'Yes, isn't it.'

'I can see why you like to come here, after – after the kind of life you lead – I mean your job – it must be stressful.'

'It is. If I can get a couple of weeks here, now and again, I can unwind, get my thoughts together and –'

'And?'

'Go back to the fray renewed in mind and body.'

Gina had thought for a moment that Sam had been going to tell her about the book he was writing. But he hadn't and she didn't feel that she could mention it.

'So how long do you stay when you come here?'

Sam glanced at her oddly, but he must have decided to take the question at face value. 'As long as I can. But it's usually only about a week or two. Three if I'm very lucky.'

'Do they call you here? The people you work for?'

'I don't work for anybody, as such; I'm a freelance, so I call my contacts at set times to see if there's anything they want me to do.

'No one has this number. When I'm here, I like to

feel completely free. The only other person I call is the guy in the apartment next door to mine in London. He keeps an eye on the place, waters my plants, collects my mail, you know the usual neighbourly kind of thing. His job takes him away, too, so I do the same for him whenever necessary.'

Gina tried to imagine Sam's life in London, tried to picture his apartment. It was strange that they had once been so close and yet she had never met any of his friends and had no idea what the place he lived in looked like.

She walked slowly forward on to the jetty. The water slapped against the posts and glinted through the gaps between the timbers. Near the end, a metal ring was set into a wooden bollard.

'Is there a boat?' Gina asked, turning towards Sam and grinning.

'There used to be,' he responded wistfully. He had followed her along the jetty. 'When David and I were younger. Those were great days for me, you know. Of course David was used to all this – he'd grown up with it – but my background was quite different – as you know.'

He stared out in the direction of the hills and Gina watched him thoughtfully. Not long after they'd met, just over three years ago, Sam had told her a little about his family background – what had happened and how it had affected him and his younger sister, Nadine.

It was surprising how quickly they'd grown close – how intense their relationship had become. At first

Gina had thought that it couldn't be happening to her – that it was almost too wonderful to be true – but she had allowed herself to be carried along on a miraculous tide of emotion. She had fallen completely, utterly in love.

She knew now that she should have trusted her first instincts. Her love affair with Sam had ended abruptly, almost as soon as it had begun. And he had never told her why.

He was looking at her. 'You do understand that this is all yours too, don't you?'

'What do you mean?'

'These woods, the lake, even some of those distant hills. The solicitors have explained to you the extent of David's estate, haven't they?

'Yes, although seeing it – or part of it – is different from looking at words on paper.'

'Oh, I'm sure those words looked good to you, Gina.'

'What do you mean?' Stung by the cynicism in his voice she glared up at him.

He shook his head as if he were angry with himself. 'Look, I don't want to fight with you –'

'I don't suppose you do. After all, you brought me here because you wanted to ask me a favour, didn't you?'

Gina blinked; she was dangerously near to tears. Why had everything suddenly gone wrong again? It seemed Sam couldn't free himself from the notion that she was calculating and mercenary.

'Gina, why did you do it?'

'Do what?'

'Why did you marry David? Why didn't you wait for me?'

'Wait? But you left me. I was alone . . .'

'Not for very long, it seems.'

'How can you say that! You walked away without a word of explanation. Are you telling me that you expected me to be waiting for you whenever you decided to return?'

'I realize now it was too much to expect, but you didn't wait very long, did you? You didn't even answer my letter.'

'Letter?'

Sam hurried on, ignoring her interruption, 'Had you already decided that David was a much better bet – far richer than I would ever be?'

'Sam, no, you're so wrong. Listen, we've got to talk . . .'

'Too late, Gina, it's much too late for talking. What a fool I was.'

'Fool? Why?'

'I once thought that you loved me.'

'But I did. I d–'

She stopped herself just in time, horrified at what she had just been about to say. But Sam hadn't noticed.

'Then why did you marry David?'

'I've told you! I thought you'd walked out on me – and I married David because . . . because . . .'

'Well?'

'He asked me to.'

Gina was defeated and she knew it. She ought to have said, straight away, that she had loved David – and it wouldn't have been a lie – not really. She had loved David – in a way.

But the moment had gone. Sam wouldn't believe a protestation of love for her late husband if she made it now.

'How sick was he when he asked you to marry him?'

The shock made her stomach cramp. 'What are you suggesting?'

Sam remained silent and Gina stared at him angrily. 'Are you implying that David was coerced into marrying me? That he didn't know what he was doing? That he wasn't in his right mind?'

'No – I don't know – I don't know what I'm suggesting . . . But I want you to know that I intended to seek you out once all the commotion that followed David's funeral had died down.'

'Did you?'

'Yes – look – let's go and sit down – I'll explain.'

He looked at her questioningly. The sun vanished behind a cloud and the wind grew stronger. Gina didn't know whether the spots of moisture on her face were rain or spray from the lake.

'Gina?'

'OK.' She was glad to follow Sam and sit down in the shelter of the old summerhouse.

He wasn't looking at her. He was staring down at some leaves which had been blown in and were circling aimlessly in the breeze.

Eventually, she prompted, 'You were really going to come and see me?'

'Of course I was. Why do you sound so surprised?'

'I shouldn't have thought there was any "of course" about it. Not after – not after some of the things you've said.'

'Gina, I –' he turned to look at her, 'I can't go on apologizing for last night –'

'I know, I'm sorry, but please tell me –'

'The fact is, however badly I phrased it, Natalie's welfare is paramount now.'

'Natalie. Of course.'

'Yes, Natalie. Whatever kind of a mess you and I have made of our lives, I couldn't just forget my sister's child, could I?'

'No . . . I don't suppose you could.'

'So-o.' He sighed and then smiled uncertainly at her. 'As I said, I would have waited until things had calmed down a little –'

'Good of you.'

'Don't be bitter, Gina. I'm not trying to antagonize you.'

It was Gina's turn to sigh. 'OK, go on.'

'And then I would have come to see my niece.'

'To take her away from me, you mean.'

Gina said it without rancour but her accompanying smile was wintry. Sam looked wary when he saw her expression.

'To be honest, that had crossed my mind.'

'But now? There is a "but", isn't there?'

'You're right. I've seen you together. You've

looked after her since she was a tiny baby. I can't believe it's possible that she could remember her own mother. And you say that you love Natalie –'

'I do!'

'But what's even more important, I think she loves you.'

'So?'

'So I want to stay round here for a little while longer –'

'To check up on me? To judge me?'

'To get to know my niece, not just for my dead sister's sake but for my own sake, too. Surely you can understand that?'

Gina stared into his face trying to gauge his expression. The request sounded reasonable enough but could she trust him?

Suddenly he reached for her hand. 'That's all it is, Gina, believe me.'

'And do you swear that I'm not on trial?'

He looked uncomfortable. 'I wouldn't put it quite like that – but –'

'But if you thought I was a corrupting influence you would take her from me?'

'No – no – I just want to make sure . . . can't you accept that?'

'Yes, of course I can. Furthermore, I think it would be good for Natalie to get to know you. I don't mind if you stay until – I don't mind if you stay for a while.'

'Do you mean it?' Sam looked astounded.

'I do. Now let's get back to the house.'

'Look – I'll try not to interfere with the way you're bringing her up –'

'You'd better not!

'No, I mean, I'll just fit in with whatever you decide to do.'

'Good. Well, right now, I feel that I've been away from her for long enough. She's had a sad and confusing time of it, lately, and no matter how kind Agnes Robson is, she's still a comparative stranger. Shall we go?'

On the way back it was Gina who took the lead. Her thoughts and emotions were in turmoil. For a crazy, wonderful moment she had thought that Sam had been going to declare that he couldn't keep away from her and, knowing that she was widowed, he had intended to find her again.

Crazy, crazy, crazy! Why on earth would he do that when he had walked off and left her in the first place!

But, much as she hated to acknowledge it, his request to get to know Natalie was more than reasonable. And how could she deny the little girl the chance to make contact with her uncle – her only remaining blood relative?

She imagined that divorced mothers must feel like this – not wanting their children to suffer by being denied access to the absent father, even if it meant a certain amount of pain for themselves.

No, she'd had to agree to Sam staying here for a while, it would have been cruel not to. But she and Natalie didn't have to stay if she had the remotest hint that Sam had found something out that would go against her – the slightest premonition that things might go wrong.

She'd already escaped one intolerable situation – outwitting half the world's press, it seemed, in order to do so. If it came to the crunch she could bolt again – taking Natalie with her.

Then, if Sam wanted to challenge her guardianship in the courts, he would find that he had a fight on his hands.

CHAPTER 8

South West France

Marco Doyle went downstairs as quietly as he could. He paused on the last step, instinctively moving back into the shadows, and watched and listened for a moment.

Even though it was very early in the morning, the day's work had already begun in the Hôtel Lion d'Or. Marco could hear the clattering of pans in the kitchen and the animated conversation and laughter of the maids.

Soon they would begin cleaning up in the dark, smoky, little bar and the dining-room, where one glassed wall gave a breathtaking view of the mountains, before moving on to the bedrooms. For the moment, they would not expect any of the guests to be out of bed.

But when Marco was on an assignment, no matter how late he had stayed up enjoying himself the night before, he liked to be up and about before any of the other journalists and photographers. He made it a rule to be one, if not several, steps ahead of the pack.

The foyer was deserted and Marco relaxed. It did not seem as though any of the staff were about to come hurrying through and there was no sign of the *concièrge* at the desk. He moved swiftly towards the entrance; it had become a habit to come and go as unobtrusively as possible.

He reached forward to push the half-glassed entrance door and couldn't resist pausing briefly, and glancing at his own reflection. He had always been vain and he knew that his dark blond hair combined with the olive-tinted skin he owed to his Italian mother made him very attractive to women.

He could have wished that he was taller but otherwise he was satisfied with what he saw. He was still trim and hard-muscled – in spite of the punishing workload he gave himself and the rackety way he lived.

As he stepped down from the worn stone step on to the pavement outside the hotel, the warmth of the morning sun hit him and he grinned appreciatively. Summer lasted longer here.

The town square was already suffused with golden light and the mouth-watering aroma of newly baked bread drifted from the *boulangerie* to mingle with the robust smell of freshly made coffee coming from a couple of cafés.

The double doors of the larger of the two establishments, a *bar-tabac*, were hooked open. A row of men, probably on their way to work, were propped up against the zinc counter enjoying a breakfast of coffee and brioches as they read their newspapers and exchanged pleasantries.

Marco wondered if they were relishing the local scandal as much as the rest of the world seemed to be doing. It had certainly put this part of France on the map.

So far the story of Gina Shaw, the nanny who had married her very rich boss just before he died and then inherited everything, had been very profitable for Marco. He had sold the pictures he had snatched of her and Juan Sanchez to newspapers and magazines world-wide – and for top prices.

Marco was one of the most successful paparazzi in the business. He made his living by seeking out news stories that could be sensationalized and then taking the best and the most intrusive pictures – often risking life and limb in the process. He was good at what he did and his talents had made him a fortune.

He headed across the square to buy the morning's papers. There was a small queue at the *kiosque à journaux* and, rather than stand in line, he made for one of the benches set in the shade of the old trees near the fountain and sat down for a moment.

He could phone home while he was waiting. He frowned slightly and stared into the mid-distance as he tried to marshal his thoughts. He would have to work out very carefully what he was going to say.

A yellowing leaf detached itself from one of the trees and began to drift slowly down. It landed in the ornamental pool of the fountain and bobbed about in the spray for a moment before escaping to the calmer water under the stone rim.

At last, Marco took his mobile phone from the inside pocket of his leather jacket and punched in the international number. He frowned as he listened to the phone ringing in the lonely, old mansion in County Waterford.

Come on, Emma, pick up the phone!

He knew it was early in the morning – even earlier in Ireland because the clocks in France were an hour ahead – but Emma hardly slept. She went to bed late and she rose early, even when he was at home and sharing her bed.

She must be out with the dogs, he thought, but, just as he was about to break the connection, the call went through. There was a slight pause before she spoke.

'Emma Doyle here.' The voice was cool, impersonal.

Damn you, Emma, Marco thought, you know it's me, I phone you every morning, couldn't you sound a little more welcoming – even pleased to hear from me!

He controlled his spasm of irritation before he said, 'Are you OK?'

'Why shouldn't I be?' At least she didn't pretend that she didn't know who it was.

'You took your time answering.'

'I was out – walking. The phone was ringing as I opened the back door.'

Marco could imagine her now, standing in the kitchen, the two dogs waiting patiently at her feet. Dressed casually in slacks, a shapeless sweater and old wellington boots, his wife would still look sensational.

Emma Doyle, small and slender with her soft, light-brown hair tied back carelessly into a pony tail, had more class than many of the film stars and society beauties who were his professional prey.

'Oh, Marco it's such a lovely morning –' her voice suddenly warmed '– the mist rising from the fields, the Michaelmas daisies in full bloom at the bottom end of the garden, the apples ripening in the orchard – this place is – is as near heaven as I'm ever going to get . . .'

She faltered and Marco could imagine the shadow that had clouded her fine-boned features.

'I wish I could make it perfect for you.'

'Don't, Marco.'

He could hear the fear in her voice. She was frightened that he was about to open up old wounds. Normally, he would have changed the subject quickly but, this morning, he couldn't stop himself saying, 'But maybe I can.'

The silence went on for so long that he wondered if she was still there. Perhaps she had just put the receiver down on the kitchen counter and wandered off – he knew that she was becoming increasingly eccentric and, deep within him, he acknowledged that it was probably his fault.

But then she spoke; she was quite calm. 'If you're

talking about adoption, Marco, we've been through that before. The powers that be don't approve of your lifestyle, or had you forgotten?'

'Forget that, Emma, there may be another way –'

Suddenly he balked at what he had to tell her. Maybe he should present the whole thing as a *fait accompli*. But she hardly noticed his hesitation as she interrupted him. 'I couldn't bear to go through all that again, Marco. Let's just – let's just get on with our lives.

'You've bought me this lovely, crumbling mansion, you've given me *carte blanche* to restore it any way I want to and the means do it. I'm not ungrateful,' she said.

But you're not happy either, Marco thought and no matter how much you pretend, you'll never accept what happened . . .

'Will you be coming home, soon?' Emma's tone was brisk; the subject had been changed.

'Do you want me too?'

There was a pause that showed how taken aback she was before she replied, 'We-ell – of course.'

'I will soon, I promise, but, would you mind if I stayed on here just a little longer?'

'Of course not. It's your job. I understand.'

Marco grinned cynically. Emma was always more than prepared to understand – to believe every flimsy excuse he ever offered. Could a woman really be so trusting? So gullible? Or did she simply not care what he did?

The notion that his wife had long ago decided that

the best way to defend herself from further hurt was to pretend nothing out of the way was happening simply did not occur to him.

'The others are packing up and leaving,' he said, 'they believe the story has run its course, but I think there may be a little more mileage in it.'

'Oh?'

Marco knew that she never followed any of his stories closely. She preferred not to think too deeply about the way he made a living. In fact she never read the sort of newspapers or magazines that published his pictures and she very rarely questioned him about his assignments.

If ever she did she was inclined to say things like, 'Oh, the poor girl, how awful for her family!' or, 'Poor foolish man – this publicity will surely cost him his job – and what about his children?'

Marco had never been able to make her understand that the kind of people he pursued with his cameras were legitimate targets and they usually deserved everything they got.

This time it suited him very well if she wasn't too interested, so he went on, telling her things that he knew she would find distasteful, that would make her close her mind to what was going on.

'Yeah, I think that something may have happened in the girl's past,' he said, 'something that she may want to keep hidden – something not too savoury. If so that would jack it all up again.'

'I see.' And then she surprised him. 'Marco, don't you think you've done enough harm?'

'Harm?' He was so unused to her criticizing him that he was caught off-guard. 'What do you mean?'

'Well, the girl, Gina, David Shaw must have loved her – I mean surely she can't be all bad –'

'The man was ill – who knows what state he was in when he married her – made her his heir.'

'Very well. I don't want to argue with you.'

'Emma –'

'No, I'd better go. The dogs are wet from running through the stream and they need drying off and brushing up a bit. Take care, now.'

She had already returned to her own domestic world and Marco heard the line go dead almost before he had finished saying, 'Goodbye.'

He put his mobile phone back into his pocket and sat staring at the ground for a moment. So Emma had followed the story enough to know who was involved. He would have to be careful.

He had breakfast on *la terrace*, which sounded grand but was really just a few mis-matched tables set out under a striped awning on the pavement in front of the hotel.

He had returned from the other side of the square with an armful of newspapers and he dumped them on a vacant chair next to him. He gave his order to the waiter; a world weary sallow-faced man with a glass-cloth folded over one arm and a pencil behind his ear.

Marco had bought not only *Le Monde* and *Figaro*, but also as many English language papers as he could find. He scrutinized each paper carefully.

There was nothing new – no further revelations – it

seemed as though the reporters were just rehashing the same old facts.

The story was on the way out. After all, there was nothing much to be gleaned by hanging round outside the Villa Des Pines and trying to communicate with the close-lipped Madame Bernat or her equally taciturn son.

Of Gina, Juan or the child, Natalie, there had been no sign for two or three days. Not since Marco's own shots of the three of them round the villa's swimming pool had appeared splashed all over one of the more down-market tabloids.

Marco wasn't surprised that they were keeping out of sight inside the villa – if that was all it was . . .

He glanced up from his papers and grinned at what he saw. The press pack were beginning to abandon the story. Some were coming out from the doorways of the small hotels round the square and the little streets leading from it to dump their luggage on the pavement.

For a while they had brought their generous expense accounts and spent them equally generously in the hotels, cafés and bars – especially the bars. But, by now, they had probably outstayed their welcome and the inhabitants of this small town on the French side of the Pyrenees would be relieved to see them go.

While they waited for the taxis and hire cars which would take them to the airport, they chatted, cheerfully. They'd probably already dismissed Gina Shaw from their minds and were eager to move on to the next assignment.

Then, at last he saw what he had been half-expecting. A pick-up truck was making its way around the town square. It was driven by Gerard Bernat.

Marco raised the paper he was holding and concealed himself behind it as the truck rolled past. He moved his head very slightly so that he could see round the edge of the paper.

Gerard pulled up outside the small supermarket on the corner of the block, just a few yards beyond the hotel. Marco kept the paper in front of his face as he watched the young farmer get out and help his mother down from the bench seat in the cab. There was someone still sitting inside, it would be Gerard's wife Céline.

Marco smiled. Céline hardly ever let Gerard out of her sight. She gave every indication of being violently jealous and whenever one of the female reporters had tried to question her husband, Céline had appeared as if from nowhere and hovered nearby, scowling furiously.

He noticed that the younger woman made no move to help her mother-in-law. Madame Florence Bernat, the housekeeper from the Villa Des Pines, went into the supermarket and her son leaned back against his vehicle and surveyed the square through half-closed eyes.

One or two of the reporters who had got to know him while they were besieging the villa waved and shouted cheery goodbyes to him as they climbed into their taxis. Gerard's handsome, Gallic features arranged themselves into an expression of contemptuous disdain and he ignored them, as he had done from the start.

Eventually, his mother reappeared in the doorway of the shop and he pushed himself away from the door of his truck and went to help her carry her shopping.

Marco wished that he could have risked moving near enough to examine the contents of her wide-mouthed basket but he didn't want any of the Bernat family to see him. Let them think that all the press pack were leaving town; that way they – and anyone else who was at the villa – might relax their guard a little.

The basket was heavy, Marco could tell that from the way Florence Bernat gave it up gratefully to her son and at least he could see that there were four or five long French loaves laid carefully across the top of the shopping.

So, she's shopping for a full house then, Marco thought. Or she wants people to think so. There was a chance that the provisions were meant for the farm but he didn't think so, Céline usually saw to that.

No, this could be a scam – she could be play-acting – particularly as she doesn't usually buy bread in town; she usually gets it at the *boulangerie* in the little village that was just about a kilometre down the road from the villa.

Since Marco had started work on this story he had got to know the daily routine at the villa very well. As far as he could see, everything had gone on pretty much as usually over the last few days – but perhaps that could all be part of a plan to fool everyone . . .

'Still here, Marco? Not packing up and going like some of the others?'

Marco glanced round in exasperation. Chrissie Drake, a young reporter from one of the English tabloids, was standing behind him.

'Oh, hi, Chrissie.'

'Well, you could sound more enthusiastic – particularly after what happened last night.'

'And what was that, now?' From the corner of his eye he had seen the farm truck leaving the square and he relaxed his guard a little. He also turned on the charm.

'Marco, I can't decide whether it's all Irish blarney or whether it's just compulsive with you – like an illness.'

'What are you talking about now?'

'The way you respond to people – well, to women – old or young, they all seem to come in for the treatment – the Marco Doyle charm treatment.'

Marco laughed. 'Sit down. I'll order you some breakfast. Coffee and croissants?'

'What else?'

While they waited for the order, Chrissie looked through the newspapers that Marco had bought and came to the same conclusion.

'There doesn't seem to be much point in hanging around here any longer, does there?'

'No.'

'So what are you going to do?'

'I'm not sure. I may take a few days off – have a holiday.'

'You never have holidays, Marco. What are you really going to do?'

'As if I'd tell you. But you, Chrissie? What are you going to do?

'I suppose I'd better get back to London.'

'Seems sensible.'

'Will you miss me?'

'I'll be heartbroken.'

'Oh, sure.' She sighed.

Marco picked up the cafetière and concentrated on pouring them each another cup of coffee. He was aware that she was watching him wistfully. He was worried by that look in her eyes.

She was attractive as well as smart. Small, shapely and naturally blonde, she had been fun to be with during this time in France. But that was all – fun. Marco didn't even consider that an interlude such as this was on the same level as a proper affair.

According to his own lights, he played fair. For the short time a relationship lasted, he gave the woman all his attention. But when it was over, they had to understand that he had no more to give.

He had never made any secret of the fact that he was married and that he had no intention of leaving his wife. And now here was Chrissie staring at him like a wounded kitten. It was time to make things clear.

'I hope we meet again one day, Chrissie.' He pushed her cup towards her, deliberately not looking up into her face.

There was a soft intake of breath and then she replied, 'Bound to. We cover the same ground a lot of the time.'

He looked up and grinned, but now Chrissie was looking down as she stirred sugar into her coffee.

'You've had some good by-lines on this one,' he said.

'Yeah, the editor's pleased with me.'

'So what do you make of it all?'

Chrissie looked up. She was puzzled. 'What do you mean?'

'Gina Shaw . . . what do you think of her? Is she really a mercenary gold-digger or have we all jumped to the wrong conclusion?'

'Why are you asking me this, Marco? Surely you're not having an attack of conscience over the way you've hounded her!'

'No. Hard as it might be for you to believe this, I do respect women's judgement – female intuition if you like and I'd like to hear the woman's angle on this story. Even a hard-bitten little hackette like you might have noticed something about the girl that a mere male would miss.'

His smile and the look in his eyes took away any sting there might be in his words and Chrissie frowned as she considered her reply.

'No-o . . . I think we've been right to take this story at face value. Except . . .'

'Except, what?'

Chrissie shook her head and took a sip of coffee. 'Oh, I dunno. Nothing, really. It's just that the girl wasn't as angry as she should have been.'

'What do you mean?'

'Well, she was shocked – horrified – wounded – everything you would expect when all the world's press turned up on her doorstep, but she was also frightened.'

'Wouldn't you be?'

'At first, yes, but she had the dashing Juan and the Bernat family to protect her. No, it was something else. I think she's covering something else up. Something we haven't found out about yet'

'So what are you going to do about it?'

'Me?' Chrissie grinned at him. 'Nothing. There's no way I could persuade my paper to let me stay on here unless I had something definite to offer them. So unless the local gendarmes suddenly announce that she bumped her husband off, I'm heading back to London.'

She looked at Marco as if she expected him to say something and, when he didn't, she gave a crooked smile. 'Well, I guess I might as well go up and start packing now.'

Before she left she leaned over and kissed Marco, lingeringly. Her breath was sweet and the musky scent she wore stirred memories of the nights they had so recently shared. He was almost tempted to ask her to stay one more night but he suppressed his surge of desire.

'I meant it when I said that I hoped we'd meet again,' he called after her.

Chrissie paused in the doorway of the hotel and raised one hand above her shoulder in acknowledgement. She didn't turn her head.

Marco lit one of the slim cigars he favoured and leaned back, angling his face to catch the sun. He closed his eyes. Chrissie's suspicions had confirmed what he had been thinking. But he hadn't just been going on intuition.

He was sure he had heard the nanny's name mentioned before in some other context but, of course, she hadn't been married then. She had been Gina Rowlands. He wished he could remember exactly what it was . . .

Never mind, he could always call a contact or two, make some discreet enquiries. For people like Marco there were always ways of finding out things.

But meanwhile he had to discover exactly what the situation was at the late David Shaw's villa. He stubbed out his cigar. It was time to head for the hills.

CHAPTER 9

'Where are you going?' Gina faced Sam across the entrance hall.

He paused in the doorway, smiling; he was holding Natalie's hand. 'Just out for a while. Is that OK?'

'Where?'

Sam's smile vanished. 'I'm not a kid, Gina, I don't have to tell you all my plans, do I?'

Gina made every effort to hang on to her temper. The last thing she wanted was to upset Natalie by quarrelling in front of her.

'No, it's just that she's not – she's not supposed to be here, remember?'

Natalie was beginning to look anxious but Sam's frown cleared. 'I haven't forgotten, don't worry. I'm not going to take her anywhere she'll be noticed.'

They had spent the day before in the house or walking in the grounds, all three of them together, acutely aware that if they were seen in the village, any resulting gossip would destroy Gina's cover.

'But you are leaving the grounds?'

'I want to take Natalie to meet a friend of mine – and don't worry – I trust her discretion totally.'

'Do you?'

'Do you think I would risk bringing any reporters here to hound my little niece?'

'No, of course not.' Gina realized that as far as Natalie was concerned, Sam would be more than protective. 'But, you should have asked me.'

'I'm asking you now.'

Only because I happened to walk through into the hall at this moment, Gina thought, but she didn't say it out loud because Natalie looked so worried.

'I won't go if you don't want me to,' the little girl said and Gina cursed herself for not being a better actress.

Natalie had sensed her tension and was trying to put things right. No child, especially one so young as Natalie, should have to play the peacemaker between two adults.

Her stepdaughter looked from one grown-up to the other, her eyes round with worry. When Gina spoke again her voice was reassuring. 'It's all right, poppet, I just need to speak to Sam for a moment, OK?'

It was Sam who answered. 'Of course. Natalie, why don't you go and see what Mr Robson is doing? Look, he's in the garden.'

Natalie slipped her hand from her uncle's and ran out into the autumn sunshine. Sam watched her go.

'Now,' he breathed as he turned back to face Gina, 'you're not convinced – what's bothering you?'

'Nothing, it's just . . .' Gina didn't know what to say. How could she tell him that the moment she had seen him and Natalie in the doorway her stomach had cramped with fear?

'Did you think I was going to snatch Natalie and run off somewhere?'

'N-no . . . of course not . . .'

But for one frightening moment that's exactly what she had thought. After everything Sam had said – everything he had hinted at, about her not being a suitable guardian for his sister's child – how could she not have allowed that possibility – and her flush betrayed it.

'So there's no objection to my taking my niece out for a while?'

Gina didn't want to voice her fears. It was as if putting them into words might make them come true. She settled for a half-truth. 'It's just I thought that Natalie might be too tired to go anywhere, yet . . . it was such a long journey . . . she may need to rest some more . . .'

She knew that sounded feeble so it was all the more galling when Sam began to laugh. 'Too tired?'

'Yes. What's so funny?'

'Come over here.'

'Why?'

His answer was a smile and, reluctantly, she walked over to join him in the doorway. He moved aside to allow her to look out. 'Tired, you said? Just look at her.'

A brisk breeze was swirling through the early fall

of leaves, driving them across the broad sweep of lawn towards the house.

Agnes's husband, Jock, a small, wiry man in wellingtons and working overalls, had started sweeping the leaves from the wide path and Natalie was shrieking with laughter as she chased a black and white puppy round and round the tidy piles he had made.

Gina smiled. She was grateful that the child, after the grief she had had to bear, could still find innocent pleasures in a world that was more threatening than she knew.

'Tired is she?'

Gina turned and glanced up at Sam. Any hint of antagonism had drained away and he was regarding the scene with genuine pleasure.

At that moment, Natalie looked up and saw them. She raced up the wide stone steps with the puppy lolloping after her. 'This is Mr Robson's new puppy, Gina. He's called Rebel. Isn't he lovely?'

'Yes, he is, sweetheart.'

Sam went down the steps to join them then he kneeled down to fondle the puppy's head. Rebel jumped up and licked Sam's face energetically and Natalie shrieked with laughter as her uncle tried to fend the puppy off.

Suddenly, seeing Natalie and Sam together, Gina realized how much the child must be missing David. David had been a good father and, when he had become too ill to spend time with her, the child had never complained.

She suddenly knew that she had made the right decision in bringing Natalie here. Sam had not been part of the plan and all kinds of trouble lay ahead but, just for the moment, Gina allowed herself to hope that her problems would be resolved one way or another.

It was this unexpected lifting of her spirits that prompted her to ask Natalie, 'Shall I come too?'

She was totally thrown by the answer.

'Oh, no! I asked him but Sam says you can't come with us, because –'

'Hush, little tell-tale!'

Sam laughed and scooped the child up in his arms. Gina was plunged back into a state of panic. Why didn't Sam want her to go with them? He couldn't really be planning to run off with his niece could he?

'Don't worry, Gina.'

She looked up and found that he was regarding her humorously. 'We'll let you into the secret, eventually – and I promise you that we won't be long.'

He swung Natalie up on to his shoulders and began to walk down the steps.

'Wait!' Gina followed them down but Sam was already striding away.

'Where . . . ?' she began.

'My car's round behind the house in the garage block.' Sam turned his head and spoke over his shoulder. 'Jock has already fitted the child seat for me. We found it with the other things that your boyfriend dumped in the hall.'

'Juan's *not* my boy –' Gina started to say, but it was

116

too late. Sam and Natalie had vanished around the side of the house in the direction of the old stables.

Moments later a sleek, blue Audi estate car eased into view and headed down the drive. Natalie, secure in the child seat in the back, didn't even turn to wave. Gina was left with cheeks flaming and a desire to scream with frustration.

The car disappeared as the drive curved into the avenue of trees and Gina's rage subsided into a nagging anxiety.

Was Sam hiding something? After lunch, eaten informally at the kitchen table, she had helped Mrs Robson with the dishes. She hadn't really been aware of the moment that Sam and Natalie left the kitchen but now she knew that if she hadn't come into the hall at just this moment, Sam would have taken his niece out without asking her.

And who exactly was this friend that Sam was taking Natalie to meet? This *female* friend whose discretion Sam could rely on so utterly. She must be close to him, Gina thought and was horrified to discover how much pain that possibility caused her.

'Woof!'

She looked down and had to blink away a tear. The puppy was sitting at her feet, looking up at her with velvety, appealing eyes. Absent-mindedly, she hunched down and began to fondle its silky ears, taking comfort from the young animal's trust in her.

'Aye, he likes that.'

Jock stopped sweeping the leaves and leaned on his broom whilst he observed her. 'It's my wife's dog,

117

really,' he went on when Gina remained silent. 'Now that our bairns have grown up and gone, she likes to have a wee creature to make a fuss of. She's a real softy, is Agnes.'

'Really?' Gina was so startled by this description of the dour, disapproving housekeeper, that she almost lost her balance.

She covered her confusion by getting to her feet, then she flushed when she saw Mr Robson's raised eyebrows. The awkward moment didn't last long. The caretaker smiled, wryly. 'Aye, I can imagine what kind of greeting my wife gave you, yesterday morning, and you can't really blame her,' he said.

Now it was Gina's turn to raise her eyebrows. 'Can't I?'

'Neither of us liked what we read in the newspapers, Mrs Shaw.'

'No, I don't imagine that you would, but I –'

'There's no need to say anything. You don't have to give any explanations to us. Agnes and I will make up our own minds – and I can tell you, she's beginning to change hers already.'

'Is she?' This time there was no hiding Gina's amazement and he laughed outright.

'Oh, she may not have said anything to you – and she probably never will, but it hasn't gone unremarked how well you've brought up Master David's daughter – and how much you really seem to care about her.'

Then, as if he believed he'd said too much, the caretaker began to sweep the leaves again.

Gina felt anguished. She knew how much these people had loved and respected David and she felt that they, at least, deserved an explanation of why things had turned out the way they had. But she had made a promise . . .

She sighed; well, at least Jock and Agnes seemed to be prepared to make their own judgment of her character – and so long as Sam did nothing to spoil things, she wouldn't let them down.

The puppy, obviously bored while she and Mr Robson had been talking, had wandered off to rummage amongst the nearest pile of leaves. He had found a stick and, now, he brought it back and dropped it at Gina's feet.

She bent to pick it up, she guessed that he wanted her to throw it for him, but Rebel immediately grabbed the other end and began to tug, growling at the same time. He wanted to play.

Jock looked up from his task. 'Here, boy,' he called, 'come away and stop bothering the mistress.'

'Oh, he's not bothering me,' Gina said. 'In fact, I wonder if you would lend him to me for a while?'

'Lend him to you?'

'I'd like to go for a walk. Rebel would be good company.'

The caretaker smiled. 'He would that. But it will be more like a run if you don't control him. He's not properly trained yet. Here,' he fished a leader out of his pocket and as soon as Rebel saw it he dropped the stick and began wagging his tail.

'Take this,' Mr Robson said, 'and make sure you

put it on if you get anywhere near the road. He's got a mind of his own and he can clear a seven-foot wall, no bother.'

Rebel had a mind of his own all right and he knew the terrain better than Gina did. She found herself running headlong through the woods that bordered the estate, whilst the determinedly mischievous puppy ran circles round her – literally.

There had been quite a heavy fall of leaves, but the winding paths were still reasonably clear. But, here and there, brambles reached out to trip her up or catch at her hair.

Soon, Gina's cheeks were flushed and her eyes were sparkling. She found herself laughing at Rebel's antics and she realized ruefully that it had been a long, long time since she had felt so carefree.

At the same time she marvelled at herself for being able to forget her cares and give in to the pleasures of the moment. She wondered if here, in this peaceful part of the world, the healing process had begun already.

Rebel darted in and out of the bushes and long grass on either side of the path, backwards and forwards, round and round until Gina began to worry that she might lose him in a moment of inattention.

She soon realized, however, that he was playing a game with her. He never went so far away that she couldn't hear his sturdy little body crashing through the undergrowth and he always came back to check that she was still following.

Gina had come out in order to forget her troubles and, for a short while, she succeeded. But soon, the wild beauty of the countryside began to evoke a deeper kind of sadness.

She wondered when David had last enjoyed these woods and if he and Sam had ever walked along these twisting paths together when they were students on vacation. Had Sam's young sister, who was later to become David's wife, ever joined them at Northmoor Hall?

There was so much she didn't know about her late husband's past, Gina realized and yet, there were things that he had told her about his first marriage that she wished he hadn't. It would only bring grief to the living if she were ever to divulge certain facts.

She wondered how much she would be forced to tell in order to fulfil the promise she had made to David and keep the guardianship of Natalie to herself. Abruptly, she forced her mind away from the consequences of revealing such knowledge and what it would mean to Sam.

The path she had been following, or rather the path that Rebel had chosen for her, ended in a sheltered glade. What a perfect place for picnics, I must bring Natalie here, she thought.

And then she was overcome by the feeling that she had been here before. But that was impossible. And yet, the place seemed so familiar . . .

In the stillness of the woods, with only the faintest rustlings betraying the presence of unseen, small creatures, Gina gave free rein to her imagination.

She had the strongest feeling that David had visited this very place many times as a child. And later through the years . . .

In fact, there was a small water colour that he'd painted years ago . . .

David had never exhibited his early pictures, the ones he had painted before moving to France, and only Gina and Juan had been allowed to see them. It was as if he had wanted to keep his childhood home completely private.

The picture she was reminded of now had hung in his bedroom, at the Villa Des Pines; it showed a wooded glade, just like this. Even the colours were the same, the reds, golds and yellows of autumn. Surely that was the same gnarled tree with branches perfect for small boys to hide in.

It was the same place, Gina was sure of it, and that was why it had seemed so familiar. She felt it was a sign that David approved of her decision to bring Natalie here and she was disconcerted to find how moved she was.

And then she was wrenched back to reality. 'Rebel! Don't you dare roll in that mud! Come here, you little monster!'

Gina laughed at the hurt look the puppy gave her but, a moment later, she lunged out desperately as the rogue ignored her command and rolled in the mud anyway. Her wild lunge forward caused her to lose her balance and she tripped and landed in the puddle that lay right across the path.

They were eye to eye in the middle of the mud

patch. Gina's hair had fallen forwards and she peered at Rebel through a tangle of curls. The black and white puppy, now a uniform sludge colour, seemed comically surprised to find Gina down at his level.

'Oh Rebel, what have you done!'

The puppy responded to her reproach by leaning forward and licking her nose. How could she stay angry? Deciding to forgive him, she was just about to give the puppy a hug when, for no apparent reason, he lurched to his feet and took off again through the trees.

'Rebel! You bad, bad, dog!' She screamed as she began to run after him but her orders to 'come back at once!' were mixed with laughter. For the first time in many months, Gina was enjoying herself.

CHAPTER 10

'For heaven's sake, Henry, get our bags and let's get out of here.'

'We have to wait, Sandra, like everybody else.' Henry Rowlands, bland and unruffled as ever, was a navy-blazered island of calm as he stood amidst the mêlée waiting for their luggage to appear on the carousel at Newcastle International Airport.

Sandra turned her head away before her husband could glimpse the flash of irritation that marred her perfectly made-up face. Even after the early morning flight from Spain, in an aircraft full of boisterous returning holiday-makers, Sandra knew that she looked cool and elegant.

Her model training had never left her, thank goodness. Now, dressed in an expensively casual, light-weight dress and jacket in pale ivory, gold jewellery glinting against her understated tan, she stood out from the common crowd like a celebrity who had lost her way to the VIP lounge.

She caught at a wayward tendril of Nordic blonde hair and smoothed it into place in her chignon as she glanced around at the families, men, women and children; they were all dressed in brightly coloured, uni-sex clothes.

Some of them clutched holiday souvenirs, giant fans, sombreros, donkeys and Spanish flamenco dolls too big to go in their suitcases. They were the kind of 'craft' goods meant only to be mementoes for undiscriminating tourists. Sandra certainly wouldn't have had any of them in her luxury apartment in Marbella.

I might have ended up like this, she mused. Just like my two sisters I might have believed that the sum of earthly happiness was an annual package holiday to anywhere the sun shines, the music is bone-shaking and the booze is cheap. And, for a moment, Sandra had the grace to be thankful to Henry for providing the escape route.

But then, she had always been different from her older sisters, she thought with satisfaction. Henry would never have noticed her in the first place if it had not been for her spectacular looks.

Her face and her figure had won her first place in a magazine modelling competition while she was still at school in Salford. In turn, this led to a contract with a top model agency in Manchester and, after that, her own intelligence and ambition had taken over.

She had never transferred to a London agent and she'd never been a 'name', capable of demanding £10,000 before she got out of bed for one day's toil on the catwalk. But she had made a good living, mostly from catalogues, until she was nearly thirty. And she'd learned a lot about life along the way.

But there had come a time when the better assignments started going to younger girls with modern, boyish figures. Sandra, not knowing what else to do with her life, had found herself accepting the kind of jobs that she would never have considered in the past. She'd already decided that it was time to get out of the modelling game when Henry came along.

They'd met at Manchester airport. She'd just returned to the UK from a job in Tangier and had been waiting for her luggage to appear on the carousel, just like today.

An unmannerly crowd of youths, football fans, straight off a flight from Milan, had pushed in front of her and, by the time she could see the revolving procession of cases and travel bags again, her own case was off on its second circuit.

Henry had heard her gasp of dismay and seen her half-hearted attempt to grab her case. He reached out and rescued it for her.

'It would have come round to this very spot again, you know.' He smiled at her indulgently.

'I know that.' Sandra didn't like to appear an unsophisticated traveller, so she snapped at him. Then she flushed.

Oh no, she thought. I must have sounded rude – and he's not bad looking in spite of his age – and, from the cut of those clothes, he's obviously not short of money.

After registering all this, she had summoned up a

126

grateful smile and effusive thanks. Henry's offer of a drink had led to dinner at his hotel. He wasn't returning to his home on the outskirts of York until the next day.

Henry was impressed when he learned that Sandra was a model. She'd discovered early on that a certain type of man always is. She'd shown him her portfolio; she always carried it with her on assignments in order to show it to the clients, artistic directors and their photographers. This could often lead to another job.

Henry looked at the beautifully presented collection of tear-sheets from magazines, studio portraits and prints from shoots she'd been on. These prints had to be begged from the photographers who could often be persuaded to send some on.

'You don't seem to have any of your recent work represented here?' Henry had queried and Sandra had cursed him inwardly for being so observant in spite of the amount he appeared to be drinking.

'The portfolio can never be bang up to date,' she'd parried. 'You know, the magazine and catalogue shoots are sometimes done months in advance and as for the photographers, they promise everything but a lot of the time they don't bother to send any shots on to you.

'But, that's enough about me. I'm dying to know what you do with your life!'

Henry told Sandra that he and his business partner had a property development company that was expanding in Spain and the Balearics. She'd been interested to learn that he was recently widowed, but less keen to hear that he had a teenage daughter.

'Poor motherless, little Gina,' he'd said. 'Only her sad, boring, old father to look after her. What she needs is an attractive, lively, young woman in the house.'

The way he'd looked at her, significantly, over his after-dinner brandy persuaded Sandra that Henry had already imagined her in that role. So when he invited her up to his room, she took a calculated risk and allowed him to think that what followed was a grand seduction.

In truth, although Henry's spirit had been more than willing, he had drunk too much over dinner and, as a result, his flesh had been weak. It had taken more than a little erotic skill on her part to bring about the desired result. Sheer gratitude had convinced Henry that he was in love.

And, all in all, in spite of having to take on his miserable, toffee-nosed daughter, she hadn't done too badly over the years. She couldn't help it if it was becoming a trifle wearisome . . .

'Penny for them?'

Sandra re-focused to find Henry standing in front of her. He had retrieved their luggage and was smiling, tiredly. And, was she imagining it, or was he a little unsteady on his feet?

All this fuss about Gina has taken it out of him, she thought, but of course, he's twenty years older than I am; he's over sixty, now.

It might have been better if we'd booked in at the

airport hotel for one night and then resumed our journey tomorrow – but that would have meant the waste of almost a whole day – and I want to find Gina and her lover before anybody else does.

'What is it, Sandra? Are you tired?'

She realized that she hadn't responded to him. 'No, of course not. I was just wondering if I ought to go and buy a map of Northumberland and the Borders whilst you go and hire a car.'

'Oh, sure, good thinking. But, now we have to go through customs. Have you got your suitcase keys handy?'

'For goodness' sake, we've got nothing to declare, have we? Follow me.' Sandra headed for the green channel, Henry carrying the baggage and following obediently, and soon they were out in the main airport concourse.

The crowds were even worse here, as people queued at the various airline desks to check in for their flights. Most of them looked like holiday makers.

Sandra looked with distaste at the young couples, some of whom had very badly behaved children, and she couldn't imagine why they would want to tie themselves down like that. It had been bad enough being landed with a teenager.

Luckily, she had been able to persuade Henry that it wouldn't be fair to his precious daughter for them to have any children of their own.

As she negotiated the queues of people and the baggage strewn on the floor, she glanced at her husband anxiously. Was she imagining it or was he having to concentrate on every step he took? Henry was good at covering up.

Even though she was keen to get on with the quest to find the Shaw family home, and thus the errant lovers, she decided it might be expedient to find the coffee shop first and make Henry drink several cups. Luckily, he agreed to her suggestion.

On the way to the restaurant on the first floor, she made a detour into the news stall and bought a road map of the area. Then, whilst Henry queued for their coffee, she opened the map and studied it.

When he arrived at the table with the tray, she looked up briefly and smiled. 'It seems to me that there are three possible routes into Scotland from here,' she said, 'but David's house is at the eastern side of the Borders if that crazy old woman is right.'

'Crazy old woman?' Henry drew his brows together and Sandra sighed.

'Maud Cavanagh,' she reminded him.

'Ah, the artist.'

'Well, that's what she calls herself,' Sandra sniffed, 'although I've never met anyone in Marbella who would give any of her daubs house room.'

'Poor old thing, she may be batty but she's harmless,' Henry said mildly, as he placed the coffee pot, cream jug and cups on the table.

'I suppose so,' Sandra agreed, 'and quite useful too, considering she's probably the only person to have worked out where Gina has gone.

'Look,' she stabbed at the map with a scarlet talon,

130

'that must be the lake Maud went on about, not far from a village called Brackenburn.'

Henry leaned over his wife's shoulder to look at the map. 'If you say so – I didn't see the pictures, did I?'

He moved back but not before she had smelled the whisky on his breath. Oh Lord, she thought, I should never have allowed myself to have that nap during the flight. Heaven knows how many drinks he ordered while I wasn't awake to keep an eye on him. I should have had a word with the air hostess but sometimes it just gets too much for me.

She watched him stir two sachets of cane sugar into his coffee and she noticed that he was taking it black.

'So it looks as though we'll be taking the A1, then,' he said. 'Straight up the coast for most of the way.'

Sandra folded the map and sipped her coffee. She wished she could drive. She had no way of knowing whether Henry was over the limit; if she asked him he would just be evasive. So the responsibility was hers alone.

Damn that daughter of his, she thought. He's always felt guilty, ever since we took her away from that fancy school. I never really convinced him that higher education is wasted on a girl, and he feels that everything that's happened to Gina since we said she couldn't go to university is his fault – or mine. She stared gloomily into her cup.

'Why so pensive, Sandra?'

She looked up to find Henry looking at her, levelly.

'Pensive, darling?' She pinned on a smile.

'Yes. What were you thinking about?'

'Gina of course.'

She had made her decision. If Henry was alert enough to notice her mood, then he was alert enough to drive.

'Were you?' Henry looked anxious. 'I'm sorry she's caused you so much trouble, Sandra.'

'Caused *me* trouble?'

'All that gossip amongst our friends, once the story broke – it can't have been pleasant for you. Spoiled the old social life somewhat, didn't it?'

'No, Henry, not really.'

'Bless you, but you're just trying to make me feel better. Just think of the way the conversation stopped whenever we walked into the bar at the golf club – remember the way they all got into a huddle again the minute we made for the door.'

'Well, yes, there has been a lot of gossip but it hasn't all been bad you know.'

In fact some of Sandra's women friends amongst the English expatriate community had congratulated Sandra on having such a clever stepdaughter. They joked that they wished their own daughters might find ailing millionaires to marry!

In Miguel's beauty salon, just the other day, Barbara Samuels had wisecracked, 'We all thought Gina was so clever to marry her boss in the first place – but to manage to be widowed so soon afterwards and then to inherit all the loot! Congratulations, Sandra, you've taught her well!'

Sandra had taken the teasing in good part and they had all laughed. And when Miguel had insisted on doing her hair himself and he had been particularly attentive, Barbara had gone on to suggest that taking younger Spanish lovers must run in the family!

Of course there had been a touch of envy in remarks like that but, on the whole, the scandal that Gina had caused wasn't going to lose them any friends amongst the fast set that they socialized with.

She could never tell Henry any of this, of course. He'd always been under the impression that his wretched daughter was nothing short of saintly and this, along with the trouble that had ended her previous employment as a nanny, had hit him hard.

He was looking at her hopefully. 'You're right, it hasn't all been bad, has it. Some of our friends have been very sympathetic. More than one of the chaps at the club has shaken my hand and told me that, if I need help of any kind, all I have to do is ask. Loyal friends, eh? Makes life worth living, don't you think?'

Sandra stifled the urge to snap at him. Could the old fool not see that the expressions of sympathy had been prompted by the fact that his daughter was now an extremely wealthy woman? A lot of them must be wondering what was in it for her dear old Dad.

Just as I am, Sandra thought. Or more particularly, I'm wondering what I can screw out of her once I remind her about what I know – and what I might do if she isn't extremely nice to me.

'And you too, Sandra,' Henry said. 'You've shown

what you're worth. You know, sometimes over the years, I imagined that you've never really liked Gina and yet, look at you now, insisting on grabbing the first possible flight and coming to look for her, just because you think she might need help . . . a mother's help . . .'

Henry's voice had risen. Drink and emotion, Sandra thought and she reached across the table and squeezed his hand. 'Hush, darling, people are looking.'

It was true, heads had turned and faces at the nearby tables looked curious. Sandra hoped that they hadn't heard Gina's name and put two and two together.

She lowered her voice. 'Some of the passengers on our plane had English newspapers a few days old. Gina's exploits were splashed all over them. The story's been pretty big here. It won't be long before some bright reporter starts wondering where she might have run to–'

'They can't be sure that she's not still at the villa in France –' Henry interrupted.

'If *we* think she's bolted, I'm sure other people do – Maud for a start – that's why she came round to see me – asked me to go to the tip-heap she calls her studio.'

'But are you sure that it wasn't just some crazy delusion of hers – that she didn't just want to make herself feel important? You know how she's always name-dropping – likes people to think she's on first-name terms with famous artists?'

'Well, of course I was sceptical, but she was so persistent. And once I'd seen the pictures . . .'

Sandra had known at once that Maud hadn't painted the two small water-colours herself. She'd watched in amused fascination as the sun-weathered, eccentrically dressed old woman had unlocked the cupboard and reached for the box on the top shelf.

She'd put the pictures on the cluttered table, almost reverently. 'There you are,' she sighed.

After a few puzzled moments, Sandra had asked, 'Maud, what exactly are these two pictures supposed to tell me?'

'He painted those when he was very young.'

'Who?'

'David – your stepdaughter's husband.'

'So?'

'The house is his family home – look, the name is on a label on the back – and the lake is in the grounds.'

Sandra smothered an urge to scream at the dotty old woman; she had the beginnings of an inkling that this conversation might be leading to something useful – eventually!

'I think Gina has taken David's daughter there to get her away from those awful reporters.'

In that instant Sandra thought so too, although her hopes subsided a little after the next question she put to Maud. 'But David Shaw has lived in France for years – how do you know that he still owns – I mean still owned this place?'

'I don't.'

'For goodness' sake, then, what's the point of showing me these pictures!'

'I just have this feeling – when I talked to David he was very reluctant to talk about his past – he said that he'd only started truly living when he came to live in France and set up his studio and gallery – and yet . . .'

'And yet what, Maud?'

'I got the impression that he hadn't cut his ties completely – that the house on the Scottish borders was still useful to him, otherwise why be so protective about the place – why hide away all his early paintings?'

'Oh, come on, Maud, perhaps he didn't want people to see them because they're not very good!'

'But they are good, aren't they?'

And, even though Sandra knew very little about painting, she had realized that they were . . .

'. . . did she ever tell you how she came by them?'

Sandra realized that Henry had asked her a question. 'Sorry, what did you say, dear?'

'How did Maud get hold of the pictures if David didn't like anyone to see them?'

'Oh, she told me that when she went to study with him in France he actually invited her to stay at the villa – can you imagine – and that she found them by chance. It's my bet that she was having a good root around out of sheer nosiness!'

'And?'

'He was a bit upset but he didn't evict her. Told her a few sparse details and then changed the subject.'

'But that doesn't explain how she got the pictures.'

'She pinched them.'

'What!'

'Yeah – oh, she says she knew that he would never sell them and yet they were hidden away out of sight so that no one could enjoy them – so she just took them when she left.'

'I can't believe it – our old Maud a thief!'

'Well, not exactly – later she arranged to send a banker's draft to the Shaw Gallery – you can do that quite anonymously. She hoped David would think it was a contribution to the work he was doing with young artists.'

'Do you think David ever missed those pictures?'

'Who can say? And that's the point of all this. It's been on Maud's conscience ever since. She couldn't even bring herself to hang the pictures up on her wall – so no one got to enjoy them after all. And that's why she wanted to help us – she hopes that we'll square things with Gina for her.'

'And so we will,' Henry said, 'and I'm sure Gina will be sympathetic.'

'Yes dear,' Sandra smiled, humouring him, 'but, remember we've come here because I want to help her. She must be out of her mind with worry, she needs her family to support her. So drink up your coffee and go and arrange a hire car – nothing too flash – we want to keep a low profile, right?'

'Low profile?'

'The last thing we want to do is attract attention

and arrive at her door with the entire press pack following.'

Henry looked stricken. 'Oh, goodness no! Right, you stay here and try to relax and I'll come and get you when everything's arranged.'

Now that he'd been told what to do, Henry looked happier. Thank goodness I can still talk him out of his moods, Sandra thought, but it's very wearing. She watched in exasperation as he dutifully cleared the table and put the coffee cups on the service trolley.

She resisted the temptation to scream after him that there was no need to do that – more than half the other customers simply got up and left their dirty plates and assorted litter behind them.

But Henry was ever the polite, well-trained, gentleman; the trouble was that Sandra was sick and tired of being a lady. But, with any luck, it won't be for much longer, she thought.

With money of my own I could leave Henry while I'm still young enough to enjoy life. Miguel flirts with all his clients, but if one of them was prepared to finance his plans for expansion in return for his undivided attention, he'd be willing to do his duty – I'm sure of it.

Henry would have to find someone else to look after him in his dotage – his daughter for example. Sandra's smile was superior, Gina was just stupid enough to do that.

The girl would be loyal to her father, Sandra could count on that. She would tell Gina that she had been worried about Henry for some time – and that was true – the fact that he was beginning to drink too much was an ever-increasing cause of irritation.

She would make sure that Gina understood how the recent headlines had affected him and hint that any more bad publicity about his daughter might even send him over the edge – turn him into an alcoholic.

And there *was* more – so much more that Sandra could tell the press if she chose to – and then the press interest in Gina would be even more intense, the publicity much, much worse.

Gina might be persuaded to pay her – and pay her very well – to keep quiet.

CHAPTER 11

How long had she been away from the house? Gina wasn't wearing her watch and in the sheer joy of having no one but herself to consider for a while, she had lost track of time.

Would Sam and Natalie be back from wherever they had gone to? When she remembered how happily her stepdaughter had gone off with Sam, she gave way to a momentary feeling of pique.

But then she told herself not to be so childish – Natalie loved her and she should be glad that the child was confident enough to respond so well to her uncle.

She looked down at the puppy who had come to sit at her feet. 'Rebel,' she sighed, 'I think we'd better go home.'

When she attached the leader to his collar Rebel made no protest. It was as if he knew he had stretched the bonds of friendship to the limit, she thought, and he'd decided that from now on he'd better behave himself.

'Or are you just tired?' she asked him and laughed

when he put his head on one side and looked up at her with intelligent eyes as if he was trying hard to understand her words.

'Come on, rascal, see if you can lead me home.'

They retraced their way through the woods and Gina began to feel apprehensive. She wondered what Agnes's reaction would be when she saw the state of her 'wee creature'.

'I'm hardly her favourite person and this might be the final straw, what do you think, Rebel?'

And what about her own bedraggled condition? She looked down at the mud caked on her jeans and shoes and grimaced ruefully. She knew it would brush off as soon as it was dry but she had no wish to have Sam – or anyone – see her in such a state.

She wondered if there was some way of sneaking into the house through a back door?

She was almost out of the woods when the sky suddenly darkened. Gina peered up through the branches of the trees and felt drops of moisture landing on her face. It had started to rain.

She frowned and began to hurry. She had to cross a large expanse of open grassland punctuated with small clumps of trees not large enough to give much shelter before she would be safely home.

Rebel seemed to sense that good behaviour was now obligatory and he ran ahead of her without straining the leader. He made no attempt to make interesting detours.

Gina paused just before committing them to the open terrain. 'Wait, Rebel.' The dog looked up at her obediently, pathetically eager to please. She looked up into the glowering skies; the drizzle had turned into a steady downpour and there was no sign of a gap in the clouds.

'Come on, then,' she said to the puppy, resignedly. 'We'll have to make a dash for it!'

They raced across the parkland through the driving rain and Rebel began to bark with sheer enjoyment. By the time they drew near to the smoother contours of the lawn, Gina was laughing again and out of breath.

Suddenly she stopped. There was a car parked on the drive, near the entrance to the house, just where she had drawn up the night before. A nondescript, grey saloon. It wasn't Sam's. Then whose?

She told herself that it was probably someone come to visit the Robsons – or a friend of Sam's. After all they all had a life here which was nothing to do with her. And yet she felt uneasy.

By now she could see that the car was empty. When she reached the drive, she walked across and peered inside. The interior was curiously impersonal, no private possessions, no bags, or gloves or tapes for the cassette player. No hint or clue to who might be the driver, only a touring map folded and left lying on the front passenger seat.

'Are you all right, Mrs Shaw?'

Startled, Gina turned to find Jock staring at her. He was wearing a waterproof coat over his overalls and his bony features were wet and shining with the rain. He looked concerned.

'All right? Why shouldn't I be?'

'Don't take offence. It's just the state of you – and the dog. It looks as though you've had a fall.'

'Yes, nothing serious. It was Rebel . . . he rolled in the mud and I –'

'I can guess.' Mr Robson reached for the leader. 'Here, I'll take him.'

'I'm sorry about the state he's in. What will Mrs Robson say?'

'She won't even see him until I've cleaned him up. Don't worry.'

His grin made them conspirators and she smiled gratefully. 'Thank you, Mr Robson.'

'Don't mention it – and call me Jock, why don't you. Now you'd better get in out of the rain, the door's open, just push. By the way, your visitors are in the morning room.'

'*My* visitors?' Gina glanced at the car again, and her stomach turned over. Had some reporter, brighter than the rest, tracked her down?

'I thought you weren't expecting them.' Jock was watching her shrewdly.

'Not expecting who?' She was aware that she sounded foolish, repeating Jock's words like this, but her mind was spinning.

'Your parents.'

'Oh.'

'They've travelled a long way to see you.'

'Yes.'

And now she could hardly speak at all. At first she had suspected that her hide-away had been discovered by the media. That the car belonged to an advance member of the press pack and that the rest would follow.

Well, it wasn't as bad as that but it was bad enough. Trust Sandra to find my hiding place, she thought, for she had no doubt that it would have been Sandra who had made the decision to come here. Her father had given up having a will of his own years ago. But what could her stepmother want?

Jock raised his eyebrows at her reaction but he didn't probe. 'They've not been here long.' he said levelly, 'and Agnes has made them welcome with a cup of coffee and a plate of her home-baked short-bread.'

'And Sam – Mr Redmond . . .'

'Not back yet.' The caretaker began to lead the puppy away and then turned and said, 'Just a word of advice, why don't you slip those shoes off at the door?'

'What . . . ?'

Jock grinned. 'If Agnes has any fault at all, it's her obsession with clean floors!'

The entrance hall was empty and Gina found herself holding her breath as she tiptoed towards the stairs, shoes in hand. It wasn't just that she would feel more confident if she washed and changed her clothes, she also wanted to postpone the meeting with her parents as long as possible.

Why had they come here, now? They had shown no interest in her for years. When she had written to ask if she could go home after the job with the

Harringtons came to an end so disastrously, Sandra's swift reply had made it plain that it would be too embarrassing for them to have her with them.

So, she'd stayed in London with a friend she had made at college until she found the job with David in France.

She had written to tell them about her marriage after the event, apologizing for not inviting them but explaining that they had decided to marry rather suddenly and that there had been no guests other than the inhabitants of the villa.

Sandra had sent a cheery note wishing her well and expressing the hope that she would keep in touch. All previous troubles seemed to have been forgotten.

At the time, Gina interpreted the letter as meaning that her parents were glad to be free of any further responsibility for her.

So why were they here now?

'Poor darling, what a dreadful time you've had!'

Gina paused in the doorway of the morning room, hardly able to cover up her surprise, as Sandra hurried towards her. She could not remember a single time in her life when her stepmother had expressed sympathy for her. She watched her warily.

'Disgraceful!' her father said and Sandra turned to look at him.

'What do you mean, Henry?'

He had risen to his feet but remained standing by the hearth, blinking in the watery sunlight that filtered through the rain-streaked windows.

'Henry, what do you mean by disgraceful?' Sandra's tone was sharp.

Gina noticed that he seemed to have to make an effort to concentrate. 'You know – those reporters, badgering Gina the way they have – even on the day she buried her husband. The scrum in the cemetery was shameful. No respect . . . no respect at all . . .'

'That's right,' Sandra said. 'Just for a moment I thought you were criticizing Gina's behaviour, when it's quite plain that she has done nothing to be ashamed of.'

Gina stared at her stepmother in disbelief. Why was she so ready to leap to her defence now, when in the past she had been only too eager to believe the worst of her?

'But, come in, dear, come and sit down beside me.'

Sandra, in her high-heeled court shoes, was almost the same height as Gina. She placed an arm around her waist and propelled her towards one of the small sofas near the fireplace. Her father sank back gratefully into the other, placed opposite to them. He's looking older, Gina noticed with a pang.

Embarrassed to find herself sitting so close to a woman she had come to detest, she glanced nervously around the room.

The walls were painted a soft, warm apricot and the sofas and chairs were covered with fabrics of delicate pastel shades. A fire burned in the Adams fireplace and, when she looked up at the gilt-framed mirror, she was amused to surprise her stepmother

146

gazing speculatively at the ormolu clock on the mantelpiece.

The sofas that we're sitting on, the clock, the paintings and the occasional tables are probably all valuable antiques, Gina mused. And she couldn't help thinking that her elegant stepmother might look more at home in this setting than she did in her hastily pulled-on slacks and striped, grandad over-shirt.

'Henry, why don't you pour some coffee for your daughter? The poor girl looks exhausted.'

Do I? Gina wondered. When I was tidying my hair just now, I thought that the walk with Rebel had brought the colour back to my cheeks. Perhaps she's just trying to say the right things. But why?

Henry had leaned forward immediately at his wife's peremptory tone and he busied himself over the tray that was set on the table between them.

Gina stared at his bent head. His hair was thinning now, and there were strands of silver amongst the dark brown, but he was still a handsome man. Perhaps it was just the long journey that was making him look a bit rough around the edges.

'There you are.' He handed her the cup and settled back with a smile. 'See, I remembered how you like it – black and no sugar.'

'Thank you, daddy.' From somewhere outside herself, Gina heard her own voice sounding just like a child again and, for a moment, she had to fight back tears. For the look in her father's eyes really had seemed to show that he cared.

'But, I don't understand,' she went on when she had managed to control the tremor in her voice, 'why have you come here?'

'Isn't that obvious?' Sandra asked.

Gina turned her head to look at her but it was her father who took up the conversation. 'When we read all that filth in the tabloids, Sandra said that you would need us to look after you.'

'Sandra said that?' Gina could hardly believe what she was hearing. Her stepmother had never been particularly caring in the past.

She looked from one to the other and Sandra was just not quick enough to mask the spasm of irritation that crossed her face, before she said, 'Yes, it was my idea to come, Gina. I know how unworldly you can be and I thought you needed help this time.'

This time, Gina thought. Why this time and not the other time when she had so desperately needed help? Sandra was acting out of character.

Or was she? Gina could think of a reason why *this time* might be different . . .

But all she asked was, 'What made you think that I'd left the villa?'

'When there were no new stories in the papers,' her father said. 'We can buy the English papers the same day, you know. Anyway, there were just different versions of the same old facts. No new revelations –

'And most of all, no new pictures,' Sandra added.

'That could have been because we locked ourselves in and refused to show our faces.'

'True,' her father agreed, 'but Sandra said that if you had any sense you'd have made a break for it – gone somewhere where the press couldn't find you.'

'OK, that sounds reasonable, but what I'd really like to know is how did *you* know where to look?'

CHAPTER 12

When Sandra told her about Maud Cavanagh and her pictures, Gina succumbed to a sense of unreality.

It wasn't the fact that the eccentric-sounding artist seemed to have feloniously appropriated a couple of David's water-colours; over the years David's generosity had made him an easy target. No, she had met others like Maud and she would deal with her fairly, as David would have wished.

But what was really strange was the fact that Sandra – and even her father – should put themselves out to find her.

'Well, anyway,' Sandra said finally, 'I thought the old girl was talking sense and that David's old family home would make the perfect bolt hole for you until the heat dies down.'

She's talking like someone in a cheap thriller, Gina mused, and it's almost as if she's enjoying the situation, as if she's excited by something.

'But if you've managed to work out where I am, then it may not be too long before some clever reporter does the same,' she thought out loud. 'I mean Maud might show the pictures to someone else.'

'I don't think so,' Sandra said. 'She seemed almost to worship your late husband – she told me that she would never do anything to hurt his wife and daughter. She approached me and revealed her guilty secret because she thought you might be desperate and need our help.'

Gina didn't feel reassured. She knew that David had never displayed his early pictures in the gallery but he had some strange house-guests over the years. He had told her once, sadly, that being a gifted artist, actor, or musician didn't always mean that you were a nice person.

She glanced at her father worriedly. 'Do you think there could be more of David's early pictures around that might give the game away?'

'That crossed our minds,' her father said. 'And some people would do anything for money – you know, give information to the press. That's why we had to make our decision so quickly. We had to get here first so that we could be with you if you need us.'

Gina stared at him in bewilderment. She was sure he was telling the truth. He probably meant it when he said he wanted to help her, and yet, she acknowledged sadly, he almost certainly would never have made the suggestion himself.

Left to his own devices Henry Rowlands would have settled for a gin and tonic on his balcony overlooking the Mediterranean, rather than an escapade that might turn out to be a wild goose chase.

Over the years he had given in to Sandra's wishes at almost every turn. Had he been so weak-willed when her mother was alive? Gina frowned, she suspected that he had, but the three of them had been so happy together that it had hardly mattered if Tricia Rowlands had been the stronger character.

Her father had put all his energy into developing his property company, secure in the knowledge that his wife would devote herself to making life run smoothly for them and their daughter, Gina.

Tricia Rowlands had been free to choose where they would live, a beautiful old manor house in North Yorkshire, and where Gina would be educated, a traditional independent school with an excellent reputation for encouraging girls to go to university.

When her mother had died after a frighteningly short illness her father had been a lost soul. It was his loneliness, of course, that had driven him to marry so soon after his first wife's death. Their lives had never been the same again.

'Gina?' Sandra was looking at her speculatively.

She dragged herself back to the present. 'Mmm?'

'You were wise to come here. It will give the two of you time to decide what you want to do – discuss where you want to live.'

Gina was perplexed. 'Well, I'll try to take her wishes into account of course, but it will be up to me to make the decision. Natalie is only four years old.'

'*Natalie*? Oh, I didn't mean your stepdaughter, I meant Juan – Juan Sanchez, the young artist. Your . . . your "partner" as they say these days.'

Gina fought to control a surge of rage. 'Juan is not my "partner" as you so delicately put it. Neither is he my lover, nor my boyfriend, nor my toyboy – nor any of the other choice labels that the gutter press has used to describe our relationship!'

'Uhum . . . Gina . . .' her father looked distressed. 'Sandra wasn't criticizing you, you know, but all the papers said that you and the young Spaniard were – ahem – an item.'

'And of course the newspapers always print the gospel truth!'

'Er . . . well . . .'

'I don't believe this! Surely it isn't too much to hope that my own father, of all people, would know that those stories are lies!'

Even as she said it, Gina knew that it might, indeed, be too much to hope for. After all, in spite of his assurances to the contrary, she had never been sure whether he had believed her the last time. The time that Paula Harrington had dismissed her instantly and thrown her out on to the street.

'Gina . . . I don't want to upset you, goodness knows you've been through enough . . .' her father looked distressed, 'but Sandra said that if you were having an – I mean, a relationship with the young man, there would probably be a very good reason for it.'

'Such as?'

'Well . . . your husband was so very ill. Juan was there to help you . . . he must have been a great comfort . . . it would be entirely understandable if –'

'Stop it! It wasn't like that!'

She felt instantly guilty for the way she had shouted at him but, before she could say anything, Sandra got to her feet. She placed a hand on his shoulder. 'Henry, why don't you take this tray and go and find the kitchen. Ask that nice little woman for a pot of fresh coffee. I think we could all do with some, don't you?'

It's as if she were speaking to a child, Gina thought but she was not surprised to see her father look up at his wife with relief in his eyes. It's just like he was with my mother, he likes someone to smooth things over for him

'Ah, yes, good thinking,' he said. He picked up the tray and walked purposefully out of the room, obviously glad to have been given something useful to do – and to have been extricated from an awkward situation.

When the door closed behind him, Gina turned to find Sandra regarding her through narrowed eyes as if assessing her.

'Let's spare your father all the embarrassing emotion, shall we?' Her dry tone was more like the Sandra Gina knew of old.

'Look, Gina,' she hurried on, 'I can understand that you don't want your father to know the truth of the situation, but you don't have to pretend with me.'

'Pretend?'

'I tried to put the best interpretation on the affair to spare Henry's feelings, he's a different generation, after all. But, as far as I'm concerned I can't think of any reason why you shouldn't have a handsome young lover. After all, you can afford it.'

'Afford it?'

'Of course you can. You're a very rich widow.'

'*Rich widow*?' Gina stressed each word, angrily.

'Don't play games, with me,' Sandra snapped. 'David Shaw was a multimillionaire and according to the newspapers he's left it all to you.' She suddenly faltered as a worrying thought occurred to her, 'I mean that's true, isn't it? You are the sole heir, aren't you?'

'Oh, yes, the tabloids were right about that bit.'

Sandra didn't notice Gina's look of contempt and she continued, 'Well then, as far as the young Spaniard is concerned, go ahead the two of you and have your fun. But just make sure that you keep the upper hand and he doesn't get control of your money, that's my advice.'

'Stuff your advice!'

'I beg your pardon?'

Gina rose to her feet and stared down at her stepmother's astonished face. 'You heard me. I've never heard anything so disgusting in my life – although I shouldn't be surprised, should I, coming from you!'

'Don't take that tone of voice with me. I – I'm your stepmother . . .'

'And I'm a very rich widow, you said so yourself,

155

and I don't have to put up with this kind of poison from anyone. If that's why you came here, to offer me advice like that, you've had a wasted journey.'

Gina was shaking with rage. The older woman had just revealed such a gulf in their moral codes that she knew they would never be able to walk on common ground.

'Now listen to me –' Sandra rose to her feet, her face twisting with fury. And then, to Gina's astonishment, her angry expression was replaced by a tender smile. Her stepmother held her arms out towards her and said, 'Oh, darling, don't cry . . .'

'What?' Gina raised a hand and found that it was true, tears were streaming down her face. She rubbed at her cheeks with the back of her hand.

Sandra stepped forward and enveloped her in her arms. Sickened by her nearness and her cloying perfume, Gina jerked backwards, only to have Sandra grasp her arms and hold on to them painfully.

'Leave me alone!' Gina gasped.

'Very well, dear, but please sit down and I'll pour you a fresh cup of coffee.'

Gina sank down on to the sofa as she realized the reason for the little scene that had just been acted out. She could pinpoint the very moment when her father had returned to the room – the moment that Sandra had seen the door open and hidden her true character behind a false smile of sympathy.

In fact her father had returned along with Agnes. It was the housekeeper who carried the tray laden with coffee, clean cups and a plateful of shortbread.

As she placed the tray on the table she shot Gina a keen glance.

'Is anything the matter, Mrs Shaw, dear?' she enquired.

Gina stared at her through her tears. Mrs Robson's show of concern was so unexpected that it seemed surreal. But, in Agnes's case, she decided, the concern might be genuine. Was this prickly little woman beginning to like her?

'Call me Agnes, do and, look, here's a clean handkerchief,' she took one from her apron pocket, 'you'd better wipe those tears away before Natalie comes in.'

'Thank you Mrs – Agnes.' She dabbed at her eyes obediently. 'Have Sam and Natalie returned, then?'

'Yes, dear, they're just tidying themselves up to come and meet your guests.'

Agnes left the room, closing the door behind her and there was a prolonged silence. Sandra was avoiding looking at her.

I could tell my father everything she said while he was out of the room, Gina thought, but she would just deny it – or say I had misinterpreted her words.

She sighed as she remembered the countless arguments she had had with her stepmother when she was a teenager. Sandra had always been too clever for her. She knew how to twist things round; without actually lying she could make whatever had gone wrong appear to be all Gina's fault when she reported the incidents to Henry.

More often than not, what had started as a trivial disagreement, became a great drama, and her father had always believed his wife's version of events. If it got too much for him he would slide off to his club and not come back for hours. Then Sandra would accuse Gina of trying to break up the marriage.

But surely it would be different now? Surely now that she was a grown woman, her father would give more credence to her words? Gina looked at him uncertainly, he had to go on living with Sandra, after all. She didn't want to do anything that would make life difficult for him – she would have to tread very carefully.

She watched as he poured the fresh cups of coffee; his hands shook slightly. Was that age or something else? And when had it started?

Sandra took her time stirring in the sugar and she took a long sip before she spoke. 'I think your Mrs Robson is what they call a "treasure". It's a pity we couldn't take her back with us to Marbella, isn't it, Henry?'

And your going back there won't be soon enough as far as I'm concerned, Gina thought despondently. I'll have to think of some way of getting rid of them.

'And, by the way,' her stepmother continued brightly, as though the angry scene between them had never happened, 'I know that Natalie is your stepdaughter, but who is Sam? Sam Redmond, wasn't it?'

'Sam Redmond . . . the name sounds familiar,' her father interjected.

'Sam – Mr Redmond – is – was a friend of David's, in fact, until fairly recently, you could have called him his closest friend,' Gina replied.

Sandra frowned and Gina could tell that her brain was working overtime to try and figure out what the situation was.

Then the frown cleared. 'Oh, I see, as a friend of your late husband's he must be helping you at this difficult time, is that it?'

Trust my stepmother to come up with that bunch of clichés, Gina thought. 'No, he isn't helping me,' she said, 'and you couldn't possibly begin to see.'

Both her father and Sandra put down their coffee cups and stared at her in astonishment. Gina realized that her denial had come close to hysteria.

Then her father astonished her with a flash of his old astuteness. 'What's the problem? Is he causing trouble?'

'You could say that.'

'He's not going to dispute the will, is he?' Sandra asked in alarm.

'As a matter of fact, I think he might.'

'Oh, no, Gina. You must fight him all the way. Your father and I will back you to the hilt.'

'I'm not sure that you will.'

'What on earth do you mean?' Sandra was vexed.

'You see, Sandra, Sam Redmond was not only David's oldest friend, he was also his brother-in-law. His younger sister, Nadine was David's first wife and Natalie's mother . . .'

Gina paused and Sandra said impatiently, 'Well, I don't see how that would give him any claim to David's money.'

'Don't worry, it doesn't, but it's not the money he's interested in.'

'Well, what then? Some of David's paintings? I know how valuable they are.'

'Valuable or not, I doubt if Sam has even thought along those lines.'

'Then what are you worried about?'

'He wants custody of Natalie – his niece.'

Sandra looked genuinely perplexed. 'Wants the child? But why?'

'He doesn't think I'm a fit person to bring her up, that's why.'

Gina watched the changing expressions on her stepmother's face. Her eyes widened and then narrowed again as she became thoughtful. Finally, she smiled and gave a slight shrug.

'Well that's probably for the best,' she said.

Gina was stunned, although she shouldn't have been. 'What do you mean? How can it be "for the best" that Sam Redmond thinks I'm not fit to bring up my own stepdaughter?'

'Think about it, Gina. Do you really want to be saddled with the responsibility for a small child? You're rich now, you can go anywhere, do anything. Having Natalie in tow could really cramp your style.'

Sandra had leaned towards her, earnestly and Gina found herself drawing away. She wanted to put as much distance between herself and this cynical woman as possible.

She glanced at her father. He was staring down at his coffee cup miserably. He couldn't meet her eye. Was he remembering what it was like when he married a glamorous model and presented her with a lonely, mixed-up teenage daughter to look after? Did he feel guilty because he'd cramped Sandra's style?

'Listen to me, Gina,' Sandra said. 'This young lov – friend of yours – Juan – I'm sure he's very sweet and good-natured but he could lose interest in you if there's always a child tagging along –'

'Stop it, Sandra –'

'No, listen to me, Natalie is just your stepdaughter. Why don't you let Mr Redmond have her if he's so keen? After all, her father hasn't left her anything, has he? Let her uncle have the expense of bringing her up.'

Gina stared at her stepmother in despair. She knew that she would be wasting her breath if she tried to explain that, quite apart from the fact that she loved Natalie as if she were her own child, she had made a solemn promise to David, that she, and she alone would care for her.

There's nothing I can say to her, she thought. And, although I'd like to explain things to my father, it's too late to upset his life with Sandra, now. It's obvious that he depends on her totally.

'Look,' she said to Sandra, finally. 'You said that you've come here to help me, right?'

'That's right, darling, and we will.' Sandra looked eager.

'OK, I'm not going to explain why, you'll just have to accept this. Nothing will persuade me to part with Natalie.'

CHAPTER 13

As if on cue, the door burst open and Natalie ran into the morning room with Sam close behind her. He was laughing as he captured her and scooped her up into his arms.

'I'm sorry, Gina,' he apologized, 'I told Natalie that you might want to be alone with your parents for a while.'

'No, it's all right.' She rose and walked towards them. Natalie immediately turned and hooked her arms round Gina's neck. Sam relinquished her and the little girl cuddled close and rested her head against Gina's shoulder.

'We've got ice-cream,' she said. 'Sam called in to the village store and bought lots and lots – all different flavours. We've put it all in the freezer.'

'Have you, poppet?'

Anxiously, she sought Sam's eyes and he shook his head slightly and smiled. 'Natalie looked after the car for me while I was in the shop – she didn't come in.'

'You're Sam Redmond, aren't you?' Henry Rowlands had risen to his feet and he was staring at Sam with a growing look of recognition in his eyes.

'Thought the name was familiar and, now that I see you . . .'

'Oh, I'm sorry.' Gina realized that she had, as yet, made no introductions but they weren't really necessary.

Agnes had already told Sam that the unexpected visitors were Gina's parents so, after a brief exchange of names, they all sat and made polite conversation.

Her father explained his remark. 'We have satellite television in Spain, you know – we keep right up-to-date with all the news. That's why I recognized you, Mr Redmond. But you've been away from our screens for a while, haven't you?'

Sam confirmed this but didn't say why. Gina knew that it was because he must have been gathering material for his book and then coming here, to Northmoor Hall to get on with the job of writing it, but she couldn't tell her father that because she wasn't supposed to know anything about it.

'I like your reports, you know, you always seem to get straight to the point – ask the right questions – not like some of the others. A lot of them seem to be more concerned with demonstrating how clever they are than in giving us the facts.

'It's kind of you to say so, but there are a lot of very good journalists – both men and women – working in television,' replied Sam.

'Really?' Sandra suddenly interjected, her expression and her tone of voice disparaging. Gina wondered what on earth she was going to say.

Sam turned to her politely. 'You sound as though you don't agree with me, Mrs Rowlands.'

'Oh, please call me Sandra – and I'm not disagreeing with you – it's just that it was journalists of the worst sort that turned up at the Villa Des Pines to make our poor little girl's life a misery!'

Our poor little girl! Gina squirmed with embarrassment. How can she talk such drivel!

Sam looked uncomfortable. 'Yes, it must have been very distressing. I'm not surprised that they – that she – decided to come here.'

Sandra frowned. Gina could see that her stepmother had sensed the temperature dropping and, although she couldn't have understood why, she rushed in to try and repair whatever damage she might have caused.

'Of course Henry and I were disappointed that Gina didn't think of coming to us but I'm sure it was because she didn't want to risk turning our lives upside down with all that media circus – she's always been such a considerate girl, hasn't she, Henry?'

Gina was amused to see her father completely taken aback but he pulled himself together when he saw Sandra's pointed glare. 'Er – yes, very considerate – but we'd have loved to have her with us in Spain – if it had been possible . . .' he managed.

Sandra, sensing the air of unease, changed the subject. She launched into an amusing account of life as an ex-pat.

'Of course Marbella isn't what it used to be,' she began, 'not quite the same class of people settling there, these days. But it's still possible to have a very good life style . . .'

Gina stopped listening. She wasn't sure what Sandra was up to and she didn't know what Sam would make of her. He was a very astute man but would he guess that Sandra was putting on an act for his benefit?

Gina groaned inwardly. What if he accepted things at face value and believed that Gina was close to Sandra . . . close to a woman whom he must have realized was a shallow pleasure seeker. He might think that she and Sandra shared the same values . . .

Finding herself too troubled to contribute to the conversation, Gina excused herself and stood up. She imagined that she caught a glimpse of panic in Sam's eyes as he realized that she was going to leave him alone with her parents and, was she being fanciful, or did his lips form the word, 'traitor'?

She concealed a smile and looked down at the drowsy child in her arms as if in explanation. Her father had moved the conversation around to Sam's work as a reporter again, and Sandra couldn't have cared less whether she stayed or not. She made her escape.

Natalie was very sleepy and Gina decided that an early night was called for. Natalie wasn't hungry – had she and Sam eaten somewhere? – so after her bath, Agnes brought a beaker of hot milk up to the bedroom. Gina read stories while Natalie drank it, settled down and closed her eyes.

Reluctant to leave the peaceful atmosphere of the

bedroom, Gina lingered there, sitting by the bed long after her stepdaughter was asleep.

When she came downstairs, the light beyond the tall windows near the door was fading fast and the hall was shadowy. The only illumination came from the log fire burning in the wide, stone hearth.

'Over here, Gina.'

She froze, waiting on the bottom step until her eyes became accustomed to the dim light. Sam was sitting on the deep sofa by the fire, his long legs stretched out across the hearth rug. He looked up, smiled and patted the seat next to him.

Gina walked over to join him but she sat as far away from him as she could, pressing herself into the corner cushions and the padded arm rest. For a moment they regarded each other cagily. Then, Sam leaned forward to place another log on the fire.

'Your parents are resting,' he said as he turned to face her. 'I've told them that they're welcome to stay here.'

'Thanks. Great. But it's my house, remember.'

'I'm sorry, I'm so used to acting the host.' Sam wasn't prepared to quarrel. 'Anyway, Agnes has prepared a room for them and, now, the kitchen is a scene of frantic dinner preparations.'

'Oh, I'm sorry . . . such short notice . . .' Gina was embarrassed.

'There's no need to worry about Agnes, she's enjoying every minute, emptying the pantry and searching every shelf of the freezer. She's got Jock preparing the vegetables.'

167

'But the expense – I'll repay you, of course.'

'Why on earth should you? I've been coming to David's house for years and in all that time he never sent me a bill. I even had to argue with him about settling for my own phone calls!'

'I see . . . well, then –'

'The subject's closed, Gina. Now, is Natalie OK?'

'Yes. She was simply tired. You kept her out a long time today – a very long time, in fact.'

'Is that a question?'

'Yes, I suppose it is.'

'Did you ask Natalie where we'd been?'

'Sure and apart from telling me that you went to get ice-cream, she wouldn't say another word.' But Natalie had giggled as if she had a secret, Gina remembered. It was exasperating.

'I hope you didn't give her a hard time trying to find out where.'

'Of course I didn't!' Gina was indignant, but then she saw that Sam was grinning.

'Gina, Gina . . .' he said. 'Don't take it all so seriously.'

'That's unfair. How can I not take everything you say very seriously indeed, considering that you've made your opinion of me so very plain?'

Sam didn't answer her. Instead he turned his head away and stared into the fire. Gina became aware of the logs shifting and settling in the hearth. The piny, resinous smell. The sound of an old clock ticking away the seconds came from some deeply shadowed corner.

After a while, Sam sighed and moved forward so that he was sitting hunched over his knees, his head supported by his clasped hands. Finally, he asked, 'I don't suppose we could try to forget the things we said last night, could we?'

'The things you said, you mean.'

'All right. The things I said.' When she didn't answer he turned to look at her. 'Could you?'

Gina stared at him. His head was outlined by the fire behind him but his face was in shadow. 'I don't know that I can forget, Sam and I doubt if you could – after all you haven't said you've changed your mind about me, have you?'

Without warning he reached for her hand and, at the touch of skin on skin, currents of shock rippled through her body.

'Gina, I was angry last night, for all kinds of reasons, but I shouldn't have spoken to you the way I did. Will you forgive me for that, at least?'

'I . . . I . . .' She couldn't speak. She was awash with sensations. Anger, longing, pain but most of all, and she almost felt ashamed to acknowledge it, she felt a growing excitement.

She stared down at Sam's hand as it covered hers in the space between them. Had that space shrunk? Had he drawn nearer to her? She tried to pull her hand away – a mistake – Sam tightened his grip and she only succeeded in bringing both their hands to rest on her upper leg.

The heat from his fingers seemed to burn through the fabric of her slacks . . .

'Sam – let go – please –' Her chest felt constricted, she began to tremble.

And then Sam did let go of her hand but only so that he could take hold of her shoulders. 'Gina – I've tried so hard to stop thinking about you . . .'

She heard him catch his breath and then they were in each other's arms. He brought his mouth down and his lips moved against hers, tentatively at first, then more confidently and then hard and demanding. Her lips parted to allow his tongue to slip inside and explore, caress, torment.

She couldn't breathe, she couldn't think, she couldn't have moved away from him if her life had depended on it. A sweet ache of longing was building up inside her. He gathered her closer into an intimate embrace that sent her senses spiralling out of control.

And then, just as suddenly as he had taken hold of her, he let her go. The pain of his sudden withdrawal left her breathless and disorientated.

'I'm sorry, Gina . . .'

She looked up in confusion. He was standing over her and he looked discomfited. Discomfited, God forgive him when I'm feeling bereft, deprived, totally confused. What on earth is going on here?

She stared at him in anguish and he had the grace to look contrite. But, a moment later, he was striding away across the darkened hall.

'Sam . . . where . . .?'

'I think we could both do with a cup of strong coffee,' he called over his shoulder. 'Stay there, I won't be long.'

Gina sank back into the sofa and pulled one of the cushions round to hug to her body. *Coffee*, she thought, viciously. Strong coffee, is that what he thinks we need? Oh, Sam, right at this moment I need more than coffee!

She lowered her head and wept silently into the cushion.

By the time he returned with a tray, she was composed enough to listen half-heartedly as he told her the arrangements for dinner.

'I told your parents that this was an informal household and not to bother to dress up.'

'Poor Sandra.'

'I don't understand.'

'She loves dressing up.'

'I don't. I hate unnecessary fuss.'

'Well, thank you, anyway.'

'What for?'

'For arranging everything.'

And she meant it. At this moment in time, it did not matter to her who was supposed to be the host or hostess here. All she wanted to do was finish her coffee, go upstairs and sleep.

In fact she might just go to bed and stay there until they all went away. Sandra, her father and Sam . . . but did she really want Sam to go away . . .?

She didn't allow herself to lie down, although she would have loved to have simply crawled into the bed opposite the sleeping child, pulled the bedclothes

171

over her head and stayed there until all her problems were solved.

But no one is going to solve my problems for me, she thought wearily, I'm on my own, I'm afraid. She realized that she had never felt so alone in her life.

Not even in the dreadful days immediately after David's death had she felt so low, so depressed. But, then, she had been surrounded by the other people who loved him, the small household at the Villa Des Pines. She and Juan had clung to each other, acknowledging the other's grief and sharing the pain.

She was beginning to wish that she had never left France – perhaps they should have just held out at the villa for a little longer. But life had been intolerable whilst they felt that they were under siege every day and they had been driven to take desperate measures.

It had seemed such a good idea at the time. She had thought that she and Natalie would be able to hide out and rest in David's family home for a time, while Juan went back to France to take care of the villa and gallery and put the press pack off the scent if necessary.

It had worked in one respect – no reporters had turned up on their doorstep – so far – but Northmoor Hall had not turned out to be the peaceful refuge she had hoped for. Instead of a haven it had become a battleground.

She left her clothes lying where she discarded them on the bathroom floor and subjected herself to the invigorating, needle-sharp spray of the shower. Soon she felt revived enough to even take pleasure in dressing for dinner.

When she entered the dining-room, she was relieved to see that her father, freshly shaved and wearing a clean shirt, looked more like his debonair old self and, as for Sandra, she was positively sparkling.

'I understand that we have you to thank for this hospitality, Mr Redmond?' Her stepmother extended one arm in a graceful gesture that encompassed the waiting dinner table.

Sam inclined his head and managed a small, tight smile; Gina concealed a grin. For all his *savoir-faire*, he hasn't placed her yet, she thought; he's not sure how to respond to her. At the moment, he's being courteous for my sake.

So he can't think too badly of me, can he, if he's trying to be polite to my family . . . my awful family . . .

In spite of the slight air of tension, Sam was obviously at ease in this setting, although he had told her once, that he and Nadine had had an impoverished childhood. But then you didn't have to be rich to know how to live in style, she thought.

He had warned her that he rarely dressed formally for dinner and, true to his word, he was now wearing dark slacks and a dark blue shirt, without a tie. But, even though his clothes were casual, they were obviously expensive.

Gina had taken her cue from Sam's words and was dressed simply in a long-line, button-through dress in redcurrant-coloured crêpe. Her only jewellery was an antique garnet pendant with matching drop earrings that had belonged to her mother.

Sandra was still slim and shapely and she looked good in classic black. Sam held her chair for her whilst they took their places at one end of the Victorian, mahogany dining table and Gina felt a rush of gratitude.

Sam could have no idea of what the true relationship between Gina and her stepmother was and so, the fact that he was prepared to tolerate Sandra, more than that, make her feel welcome, was oddly touching.

Agnes was also behaving well and Gina observed her with affection as she ladled soup into Sandra's bowl from a tureen that looked as if it might be a very valuable piece of eighteenth-century blue and white ware. But the housekeeper was more concerned about the contents than the value of the container.

'This old-fashioned broth may not be what you're used to, Mrs Rowlands,' she said, 'but the dinner preparations were all a bit hasty, you understand?'

'I'm sure it will be delicious.' Sandra was on her best behaviour. However, she shielded her soup plate with her hand after one ladleful, 'That's enough for me, thank you, Mrs Robson, it looks very filling.'

Henry Rowlands had no such reservations. As the meal progressed, he tucked in, quietly and enthusiastically, to each course.

Broth, poached salmon, game pie with a selection of local vegetables, fresh fruit salad and cream you could stand a spoon up in, were followed by cheeses, fruit and finally coffee and a very good brandy.

It was at this stage that Gina began to worry. Her father hadn't demurred each time Sam had filled up his wine glass with either the red or the white, and now he was on to his second large brandy.

She had seen Sandra lean forward and look at her husband across the table every now and then, but he had ignored the warning glances – either deliberately or because he was too preoccupied to notice.

He had been very quiet during the meal. But then, neither he nor Gina had been able to get a word in. Sandra had dominated the conversation from start to finish. Sam was beginning to look strained.

'So you've been coming here for years, then?' After the usual pleasantries about the food and the wine, it didn't taken her stepmother long to try establish what the exact situation was at Northmoor Hall.

'Yes, for years.'

'You and David must have been very good friends?'

'We were.'

'He married your sister, in fact?'

'Yes.'

Sam's answers had got shorter but he'd still managed to arrange his mouth into a smile. It was only when Sandra asked, 'And do you intend to stay here much longer, Mr Redmond, now that Gina has inherited the house?' that his eyes iced over and his voice became distinctly cool.

'That is something that Gina and I will decide.'

Sandra wasn't stupid, she knew that she had gone too far, she immediately turned the conversation to the traditional damask napkins, the crystal wine glasses, the silver rose bowl filled with old-fashioned, heady-scented blooms and, finally, the dining-room itself.

'I can just imagine this marvellous old room as it must have been a hundred years ago or more,' she said. 'Those family portraits lining the walls would be quite new, that chandelier would have held candles instead of electric bulbs . . .' Sandra paused, seemingly impressed by the powers of her own imagination.

And then she went on, 'The head of the Shaw industrial dynasty would be at one end of this enormous table and Mrs Shaw at the other – and each side lined with little Master and Miss Shaws.'

Gina surprised herself with a passing flicker of admiration for her stepmother; she acknowledged that Sandra knew how to be charming and, if her original education had been lacking, she had made up for it since. So, with her undoubted beauty, it was no wonder that her father had been attracted to her.

But if only he hadn't rushed into marriage so quickly . . . surely his judgement had been clouded by his loneliness . . .

'Yes,' Sam had recovered his poise and was prepared to join in Sandra's social banter, 'the Shaws were a large family but, tragically, at some stage, a hereditary blood disease was brought into the family.

176

It affected the sons – and, as if that wasn't enough, two world wars took their toll.

'David was the only son of this generation, I'm afraid the direct line has died out . . .'

There was an uncomfortable and lengthening silence. Without meaning to, Sandra had steered the conversation into very dangerous waters. The subject of inheritance would now be uppermost in everybody's mind. The heir to the Shaw property should surely have been Natalie . . .

She could see what Sandra was up to, of course. Her stepmother had decided that she, Gina, was a very rich widow and, therefore, she wanted to find out as much as possible about her situation.

An underlying note to Sandra's questioning of Sam had been to try to establish how much of a problem he was. Well, good luck to her, Gina thought bitterly. If my stepmother can figure out a way to deal with him I would be enternally grateful to her, in spite of what she's done to my father.

Where did that thought come from? Gina glanced at her father and a nagging worry took hold. He had always liked a drink . . . was he starting to drink too much? If so, why?

Was he unhappy? And yet he adored Sandra. But then, a lot of people indulged in things that weren't good for them.

It's the life they lead, Gina decided, suddenly. It's too fast for him and he'll never complain because he's terrified of losing her.

Suddenly her father yawned. 'Oh sorry,' he murmured and grinned self-consciously.

'Don't worry,' Gina said. 'I know you've had a long journey. We'll forgive you two if you want to go up to bed.'

Sandra shot her a poisonous glance but, before she could say anything, Sam had risen from the table – with great alacrity, Gina thought – to agree.

'Certainly, don't let us keep you up. Do you have everything you want? I asked Agnes to leave some extra blankets in your room – the temperature difference might be quite a shock for you.'

Before she knew it Sam had ushered them to the stairs. When he came back into the dining-room he grinned at Gina but she couldn't dredge up even the ghost of an answering smile.

'Don't close the door,' she said. 'I'm going up too.'

'But, Gina, I want to talk to you.'

'Do you?' Gina was standing behind her dining chair and she held onto it tightly as she looked at him. 'OK, but not now.'

'Gina –'

'Goodnight, Sam. I really am tired. I'll see you in the morning.'

CHAPTER 14

Gina hadn't lied to Sam when she said she was tired but, nevertheless, she didn't go straight up to bed. She had been feeling guilty about all the extra work she had caused the Robsons since she arrived, so she went to the kitchen with the intention of offering to help.

She found that there was nothing left to do. The pans and dishes were washed, stacked and put away and Jock and Agnes were sitting in easy chairs by the Aga, with hot drinks. Rebel was asleep on an old blanket on the floor beside them.

'Oh, Mrs Shaw . . . we're just relaxing for five minutes before we go back to the cottage.' Jock started to get up but Gina motioned for him to stay seated.

'Is there something you want, dear?' Agnes asked her.

'No, I came to see if I could help –'

'It's all done –'

'I can see that. And I also wanted to thank you very much for the dinner you prepared for us tonight.'

'Och, there's no need to make a fuss.' Jock grinned. 'Agnes enjoyed herself. She often says that the only thing wrong with Mr Redmond is that he never wants anything special.'

'Aye, that's right,' his wife agreed. 'He keeps telling me that all he wants is good plain fare. He thinks he's doing me a favour – making things easy for me. The poor man doesn't understand that I *like* fancy cooking!'

'But don't just stand there, lass,' Jock said. 'Draw up a chair – no have this one,' he started to get up again. 'Would you like a cup of hot chocolate?'

Rebel, disturbed by the voices, or perhaps by the word 'chocolate', opened one sleepy eye and thumped the floor with his tail.

'No, really,' Gina said, 'please don't disturb yourself. I couldn't manage anything after that wonderful meal.'

'Very well,' Agnes smiled kindly at her. 'But any time you want to join us, you're welcome, I'd like you to know that.'

It seems as though I've been accepted, Gina thought, by the Robsons at least. She glanced back before closing the kitchen door and almost changed her mind. They looked so cosy and secure sitting by the stove, that she would have liked to have become part of their world for a moment.

But she didn't think she would have been very good company. There was so much on her mind – so much to worry about – most of all the turmoil David had caused by marrying her and leaving everything to her in his will.

Finding that Sam was here and having to reconsider all the unresolved problems of their brief romance, only added to her present predicament.

Quite apart from the fact that her love for Sam had never died and was threatening to cloud her judgement, there was the added threat of his wish to take Natalie away from her.

And then there were her parents. She had already worked out that the probable motive for her stepmother wanting to 'help' her was her new status as a wealthy widow. But there was something more than that, something underlying the surface charm, she was sure of it . . .

Sandra's presence here was unnerving her and she would have to find some way of getting them to leave without upsetting her father. Although why she should care about his feelings she just didn't know.

As she crossed the hall, Gina noticed that the dining-room door was closed. Was Sam still in there? Sitting at the head of dining table with a glass of brandy? Was he brooding over the fact that she had refused his request to talk things over? She forced herself to banish him from her mind and went upstairs.

Natalie was fast asleep so Gina didn't put the light on. She grabbed her robe and hurried to the bathroom; when she came back, she tossed her clothes carelessly on a chair. I'll sort them out in the morning, she thought, I'm just too tired to care tonight.

Before she got into bed, something drew her to the window. She moved the curtain a little and looked out.

The light was on in Sam's study. Gina stared down into the room, expecting to see him working at the computer but, although he was sitting at his desk, the computer screen was dark. Sam was sitting back in his chair reading a newspaper.

She was suddenly overwhelmed with fury. She recognized the tabloid shape of the paper – not the kind of newspaper that Sam would usually read – and knew what it would contain.

She left the room swiftly and, tightening the belt of her robe as she went, flew downstairs in bare feet. She had barely opened the door when she found herself shouting at him, 'You can't leave it alone, can you?'

'Gina . . .' Sam looked shocked by her sudden entrance. He stood up, the paper falling from his grasp.

She hurried over and snatched at it, catching it almost before it had settled on the floor. She rifled through the pages and found what she was expecting to see.

It was one of the photographs of her and Juan at David's funeral. The shot that had been taken just after she had placed the flowers on her husband's new grave.

'Why, Sam, why?' She faced him over the paper, her eyes blazing. 'Why have you kept this filth? Is it to support your twisted theory that I would actually go with my lover to my husband's funeral?'

'No . . . it's not you, not Juan . . . it's the photograph . . .' Sam's voice was uncharacteristically uncertain.

'What do you mean?'

Gina glanced down. She had been gripping the paper so tightly that the page was creased and rumpled. She pulled it straight.

'Look at it.' His voice was still strained, subdued.

Gina stared at the photograph, uncomprehendingly. The sharp lines and the colour seemed to leap off the page. The day it had been taken came back, all too vividly.

The twelfth-century church that seemed to cling precariously to the side of the mountain, the cemetery sloping steeply down away from the church, making the headstones look as though they were about to topple over.

David's many friends amongst the artistic community crowding in between the marble angels and ornamental headstones.

She remembered the heat of the day and the way she had almost collapsed after she had placed the wreath of lilies. The way Juan had leapt forward to support her . . .

She tore her eyes away from the page and raised her face to look at Sam. 'So, what about the picture? If it's not Juan or me that you're interested in, is it because the scene gives you some sort of sadistic pleasure? Do you enjoy torturing yourself with the knowledge that you weren't there when your best friend was dying? That you failed him?'

'Gina, no!'

Sam flinched and the grief on his face was unbearable to watch. Gina was appalled at the effect of her words.

'I . . . I'm sorry . . . I shouldn't . . .'

But the moment had passed. Sam, still looking strained, but more in control of himself stepped forward and took the newspaper from her. He turned round and spread it out on his desk.

'I meant it when I said it was the photograph that I was looking at. The photograph itself, not its subject.'

'The photograph . . . ?' Gina took a step towards the desk and stared down at the picture.

'It's good, isn't it? Look how sharp it is. In spite of the fact that the photographer must have been some distance away, perhaps as much as half a mile, it's well composed and completely in focus.'

He was standing next to her and she glanced up at him in angry astonishment. 'I don't understand you! How can you go on about how technically perfect the shot is, when the unscrupulous rat who took it was flouting all the laws of decency – invading my privacy – and on the day of my husband's funeral of all days!'

'Don't get me wrong, Gina, I'm not revelling in anybody's misery, but as a reporter I can't help recognizing that this shot was taken by someone at the top of his profession – the very top. In fact I think it can only have been taken by one man . . . Marco Doyle.'

'So?' The name meant nothing to her.

She watched as Sam leaned down and drew out a briefcase from the kneehole space under the large mahogany desk. He took out one more newspaper. So that's why I couldn't find them the other day, Gina mused, I missed the briefcase. But it doesn't look as if he has any more newspapers in there, just these two.

'Look,' Sam said.

The paper he was holding was folded open at a spread of photographs of the Villa Des Pines. The most prominent shot was of Natalie and Juan and herself relaxing by the pool.

Juan was actually in the pool and he was holding Natalie up above the water, the child was laughing and obviously enjoying herself. Gina was looking up at Natalie's happy face and smiling.

This picture had been quoted in the press as 'evidence' that Gina and her lover were having a thoroughly good time so shortly after her husband's death.

The truth was that she and Juan had been doing their best to provide a moment of happiness for Natalie – Gina's own happy smile had been in pure relief that her little stepdaughter could laugh again.

Sam was staring at the photograph intently and, this time, Gina knew that he was not censuring her. 'You think that was taken by the same person? This Marco Doyle?' she asked.

'I'm sure of it.'

'I don't understand . . . you're talking as if you know him.'

Sam folded the paper and put it in his briefcase. After putting the briefcase back under the desk, he walked over to table near the fire and picked up his bottle of Johnny Walker.

'Sam! Aren't you going to tell me about it? I think you owe me an explanation, don't you?'

'Explanation?'

'Yes, for goodness' sake! After all, whoever took the damn shots and whether you know him or not, I'm the one in the pictures, aren't I? It's my life that's being ruined by all the libellous publicity!'

Sam poured whisky into two glasses. 'Come over here.'

He held out one of the glasses. Gina clutched at her robe in an unconsciously defensive gesture and walked over to the fireplace. She reached out hesitantly and took the glass.

Sam motioned for her to sit in one of the easy chairs near the fire and he took the other one, facing her. For a while he just stared into the flames and then, eventually, he said, 'Yes I do know Marco Doyle,'

Gina kept quiet. There was so much she wanted to ask him but she sensed that she would learn more if she let him begin in his own way.

'I've known of his work as a photographer for years, of course,' he said, 'but once I knew him personally. We met at university. In fact, he was the first friend I made there. We had so much in common.'

'You and this – this poisonous snake, had things in common?'

Sam smiled. 'Oh, I didn't know he was a snake at first. I was drawn in by his charm, seduced by his warmth . . .'

'Charm . . . warmth?' Gina was confused. The person Sam was describing didn't sound like the kind of person who could make his livelihood by destroying other people's lives.

'He could be utterly charming, believe me. He could make you feel as though you were the most interesting person he had ever met.

'I didn't find out until much later that it was all superficial; that the most interesting person in Marco's life was Marco himself.'

'But you said that you had something in common?'

'Yes, we had. We were both from relatively poor backgrounds. The other guys in our set were mostly ex-public school – moneyed families – whereas Marco and I had got there by dint of scholarship.'

Gina remembered Sam telling her something of the story once. It was when Sam had come to visit David in France and they had first become romantically involved.

He had said that although David and he had come from entirely different backgrounds, it had never made any difference to David; he had never been at all snobbish. But that was all he'd said at the time.

Now, he was prepared to tell her more. 'My parents weren't exactly poor to start off with, but the trouble was that my father had no head for business. He trusted the wrong people and when, one day, he realized that there was no money left, he committed suicide.'

'Sam, I'm so sorry.'

He continued as if she hadn't spoken. 'My mother was left to care for Nadine and me – my sister was nine years younger than I was –'

'Yes, I know.' David had told her something of the story but not the details. He had simply said that after their father's early death, their mother had had a hard time caring for Sam and Nadine and that had probably been a contributory cause of her own death a few years later.

'I was just about to go up to university when my father died,' Sam continued, 'luckily I got a full grant but I never had much money to spare – it was pretty tough – and it was the same for Marco.'

'Oh, yes, Marco.' Gina had almost forgotten why Sam had started telling her all this.

'In a way it was even worse for him. Perhaps I shouldn't have been so surprised when I discovered what his true character was.'

'Don't make excuses for him!'

'Oh, I'm not. We all have free will – we can all choose how we behave. But Marco never even knew his parents. His father was an art student, studying in Italy when he got his landlady's daughter pregnant.

'He married her and took her back to his home in Ireland and then ran off. She went back to her parents leaving the baby with his grandparents. I don't think Marco ever saw either of them again.'

'But his grandparents? Weren't they kind to him?'

'They were very strict with him. They were probably terrified that he would grow up to be like his father so, as a consequence they were very harsh.'

'Did . . . did David know Marco Doyle?'

'Oh yes, David was drawn to him too and, for a while, the three of us were inseparable. It was one of those carefree friendships that only students can have.'

It was strange, Gina thought, that David hadn't told her about Marco. As his final illness progressed, he had talked a lot about his past life, the good times he had had at university and the people he had been fond of.

So why had he never mentioned Marco? David had always been soft-hearted, Marco's cheerless upbringing would have made him feel protective.

'But the friendship didn't last long.' Sam was smiling cynically. 'In fact it came to an end when Marco got married.'

'Why? Did the girl – Marco's wife – come between you?'

'You could say that. You see it was almost like history repeating itself. Marco got a fellow student, a brilliant girl, pregnant but, unlike his father, he refused to marry her.'

'Refused? But I thought you said . . .'

'Emma was frantic . . . suicidal . . . she loved him, you see . . .'

Sam sipped his whisky and, for a moment, Gina thought that he was not going to say any more.

'So Marco did the right thing then?' she prompted. 'He married her?'

'He was persuaded to.'

Suddenly Gina thought she knew the rest of the story. 'It was David – David who persuaded him, wasn't it?'

'Yes.'

'But you said that was the end of the friendship? Why?'

'Before David had his little talk with Marco, Emma had been driven to find her own solution – an abortion.'

'So why did the marriage go ahead?'

'Emma was – her mind was affected – she was near to total breakdown . . . even Marco knew that it was his responsibility to care for her.'

'Oh, how awful . . .'

'It gets worse, I'm afraid.'

'How could it?'

'The abortion – something must have gone wrong – it sometimes happens, unfortunately. It was only after the wedding, when Marco and Emma had dropped out of college and gone back to Ireland that she became physically ill as well as mentally – and then she discovered that she could never have any more children.'

Gina stared at Sam, aghast. 'Poor Emma. And – and they're still married?'

'I've heard so. That's about the only point in his favour. He nursed her back to health and since then, whatever his lifestyle, he's tried to protect her.

'For a while I thought that once the worst was over he might abandon her – in fact, I prayed that he would.'

'Prayed that he would? But she loved him! Sam, that's cruel!'

'Cruel? Maybe, but you see I thought that if he abandoned her she would come back to me. I was still head over heels in love with her.'

'In love with her?' It came out as a whisper.

'Oh yes, like my poor father, I sometimes trusted the wrong people. Especially when I introduced Marco Doyle to Emma, the girl I loved and wanted to marry.'

CHAPTER 15

Gina had barely touched her whisky. She put her glass down on the table and moved forward to kneel on the floor by Sam's chair.

'You never told me.' She looked up into his face. He was holding up his glass and staring into the liquid, made golden by the reflected firelight.

'Told you, Gina?' At last he looked at her and the trace of a smile lifted the corners of his mouth.

'About Emma – when you and I were . . . close.'

'When we were in love you mean?'

Sam leaned forward and put his glass beside hers on the low table. Gina moved back but she wasn't quick enough. He caught hold of her shoulders and pulled her towards him.

'I know it happened quickly – took us by surprise – but you did love me, didn't you, Gina?' His voice was low, urgent.

'Yes . . . you know I did.'

Suddenly, Sam eased forward and slid down on to the floor beside her. He leaned back against the armchair and pulled her round into his arms so that they were sitting on the hearth rug.

'Here, make yourself comfortable.' He eased a cushion down behind her back and settled her head into the crook of his shoulder. 'There was no need to tell you about Emma – it had happened ten years or more before I met you and I was "over it" as they say.'

'But you loved her – very much . . .'

'Loved her and lost her – it happens. That's life. Oh, it's true that it took me some time to get over her, but I did – and I have to admit that there were other women over the years.

'But perhaps getting my heart broken when I was young made me wary of getting too involved – until I met you.'

Gina closed her eyes and tried to control her breathing. Sitting next to Sam like this, with his arm holding her close to his body was almost more than she could bear.

She longed to surrender herself to the sensations of the moment, the feel of his fingers through the silk fabric of her robe . . . the lemony tang of his after-shave . . . the sound of his heartbeat . . .

She wondered if Sam could tell that her heart was racing . . .

But she forced herself to hold back. There was too much of the past that was unresolved and too many present problems forming a barrier between them.

'I suppose I would have told you about Emma eventually.'

'Would you?'

'We didn't have long together did we, you and I? But, if . . . if it hadn't ended when it did, if we had got to know each other better, eventually, we would have reached the stage of confessing our past lives and loves. Lovers usually do – not that you would have had much to confess.'

Not much to confess. Gina felt a prickle of alarm. There had been something she should have told Sam and she had tried her very best . . .

Gina remembered that evening when they had been sitting on the terrace of the Villa Des Pines. Night comes swiftly in that part of the world and the sky was ablaze with stars; the earth was suffused with the scent of summer flowers.

There were lanterns in the gardens of the villa and scented candles in holders placed along the stone balustrade and one in the centre of the table.

David, Sam and she had just finished their evening meal. Florence Bernat had already cleared the dishes away and David had gone into the villa to check on Natalie, his baby daughter . . .

'I'll go, David,' Gina had said.

'No, you work too hard, Gina. Stay there and talk to Sam. You know how I like to look at her when she's sleeping. She's so innocent . . . so adorable . . .'

'OK, but don't forget to come back.'

After he had gone into the villa she smiled sadly at Sam. 'You know, some nights I find him in Natalie's room, just gazing down at her. He loves her so much.'

'And he misses Nadine dreadfully, doesn't he?'

'Of course. The shock – the pain of losing her – it hasn't left him yet. I'm not sure how long it will take . . .'

'Thank God that he has their daughter.' The grief was clearly etched on Sam's face, too. 'And you to take care of her. He told me that, young as you are, you'd brought blessed calm and peace of mind to their lives.'

'If that's true, it's a two-way thing . . .'

'What do you mean?'

'I've found peace here – David's been good to me –'

'And so he should be – your being here has allowed him to start working again, to start teaching, to function like a normal human being.'

Gina smiled gently. 'He's good to work for, you know, in the short time I've been here he's become more like a friend than an employer.'

Sam reached across the table for her hands. 'When David wrote to me and told me that he'd found an English nanny for the baby, I don't know what I was expecting – a fierce old woman or Mary Poppins.'

Gina laughed. 'So which one am I?'

'Neither – or perhaps a bit of both.'

'Explain, please.'

'Well, you're firm and practical and full of common sense like the fierce old woman, but you're also sweet and kind and even a little magical. But then there's something else . . .'

'What's that?'

'You're very, very beautiful . . .'

Gina tried to pull her hands away but Sam held on to them. The jasmine-scented candle on the table between them was flickering in the glass container.

When the light wavers, everything that it illuminates seems to waver, too. Sam's face was shadowy, his expression uncertain, but there was no denying the emotion in his voice.

'Gina, the world I move in is full of hardened, self-seeking people who seem to have lost the ability to care. But you . . . you're so different . . . so innocent –'

'Sam, stop. There's something you should know . . . something I should tell you . . .'

'There's no need, I can guess.'

'No, you couldn't possibly –'

'I'm moving too quickly for you, that's it, isn't it?'

'No, I –'

'It's all right, sweetheart. I can wait. But meanwhile . . .'

Before Gina could say any more, Sam rose from the table and pulled her up into his arms. When he kissed her, all thoughts of what she had been going to tell him were driven from her mind.

He held her close to his body and feelings that she had never experienced before exploded within her. One hand moved up and down her back, bringing her even closer; the other moved up under her hair to caress the nape of her neck.

The circling movement of his fingers on the soft skin made her sigh and cling to him as if she were drowning and only he could save her. She began to tremble.

'Gina,' Sam whispered and she felt his sweet breath fanning against her cheek as he brought his lips down on hers.

She closed her eyes and returned his kiss, hungrily, and for a while she lost all sense of time and place.

There was a soft cough from the doorway behind them and they sprang apart. David had returned.

How long has he been there, she wondered, how long has he been watching us?

Gina found that she was still trembling. She was embarrassed to have been discovered in Sam's arms so soon after she had met him, she half-expected some rebuke, but David didn't say anything at all.

The two men stared at each other awkwardly and, perhaps it was because of her heightened emotional state, Gina imagined that she saw an expression of pain tug at David's sensitive features.

It was Sam who spoke first. 'Is Natalie OK?'

'Yes, sound asleep.' David stepped forward into the candle-light and his smile seemed genuine. 'Do either of you fancy a night-cap?'

The awkward moment was over and the two men relaxed as they sat at the table and David poured the wine.

Gina, still too abashed to say anything, moved her chair slightly back into the shadows. She looked at them, savouring the contrast: David, tall, rangy and blond, and Sam, raven-haired, equally tall but with a more powerful physique.

Both of them attractive men even although they were so very different . . .

'Gina, are you crying?' Sam's voice shocked her out of her reverie.

She raised her hand and discovered that her cheeks were wet . . .

He gripped her shoulder more tightly and dipped his head towards her, trying to read her expression. She moved away from him and was horrified to see that her tears had left a damp patch on his dark, blue shirt.

'Sam . . . I'm sorry . . . your shirt.'

'There's no need to apologize. But why are you crying?'

'I didn't realize that I was. Fatigue, I suppose. Emotionally drained by all that's happened lately. Sitting here alone with you, I just . . . I just . . .'

'I know. Me too.'

Sam turned his head away and stared into the fire. She wondered what exactly he had meant by that. Had he been remembering what they had once meant to each other as vividly as she had?

Or rather what they were just beginning to mean to each other before he walked out on her. Their love affair had ended before it had really started. They had never had a chance . . .

'I wasn't keeping those newspapers to taunt you with them, you know.'

Gina frowned. She had almost forgotten why she had come storming into the study in such a rage. 'Then why do you keep them?'

'There's something that bothers me about Marco Doyle's involvement in all this.'

'Why should it bother you? He's a – what do you call it? – a paparazzo, isn't he?'

'One of the best. So why is he pursuing you? His usual victims are mega-celebrities – world-famous rock stars, royalty, the kind of people who are always in the news –'

'David was a respected artist –'

'Sure, but unless he was one of those weird individuals who call a pile of bricks, or a bin bag full of slaughtered animal entrails, a work of art, an artist doesn't usually have the same pulling power for the media as, say, a cabinet minister, a top footballer or a supermodel would.'

'I should imagine someone like Marco Doyle would simply go anywhere that was profitable. After all, he sold the pictures, didn't he?'

'You're right. And I hope that's the explanation. I'm probably just being paranoid.'

'Well, get rid of those newspapers, then, and try to forget about him.'

Gina was alarmed at how snappish she sounded, but fortunately her words made Sam smile.

'OK, nanny, but only if you stop being cross with me.'

'Sam – don't . . .' Gina began to laugh at his mock little-boy expression.

She knew it was partly due to the fact that her emotions were raw – still too near the surface – but she was soon giggling helplessly. He pulled her into his arms and held her there until the laughs turned to hiccups and finally to gentle sobs.

'Hush, hush,' he murmured. And then, 'There's still so much that we ought to talk about – but you're in no fit state tonight. I think I ought to take you up to bed.'

Sam removed his arm from around her shoulders and Gina watched while he knelt by the hearth and damped down the fire, heaping it with ashes to make it burn more slowly. Then he pulled forward a clinder guard and put it in place.

His movements were spare, efficient and Gina realized what a practical man he could be. It was something she hadn't known until now. But then, there was so much that they didn't know about each other.

'Now then, Madam –' Sam rose and, reaching for her hands, he pulled her up in one swift movement. Then, without giving her time to react, he swept her up into his arms as if she were a small child.

As he carried her upstairs, she had a fleeting image of a scene in *Gone With The Wind*. It took place in a big old house, like this one, and Rhett Butler was carrying Scarlett up to their marriage bed . . .

'Oh, Rhett, you're so masterful,' Gina murmured softly.

Sam looked startled and then he grinned. 'Behave yourself. We all know how that scene ended.'

Gina felt herself flushing and she buried her head in his shoulder so that he couldn't see her face.

'Put me down here,' she whispered when they

reached the door of her room. 'We don't want to disturb Natalie.'

Sam set her down. 'Goodnight, Gina,' was all that he said, before he strode away along the upper landing.

Gina leaned back against her bedroom door and watched him until he was swallowed up by the shadows.

She was bone weary and yet she couldn't sleep. Remembering that night in South West France, when Sam had first said that he loved her had opened the floodgates of her memory.

She had been so happy working for David, especially as not long before that, she had thought that no respectable family would ever employ her again.

But even if her own family hadn't believed in her innocence there had been those who had, good friends, who were willing to provide references when the job came up in France.

When she had first arrived at the Villa Des Pines, the tragedy of Nadine's death hung over the household like a pall. She had been told only that, not long after the birth of her daughter, David's wife had been involved in a driving accident on a mountain road.

Only when David was dying had he told her that Nadine had been upset when she had rushed out and driven off that terrible night. He had felt guilty ever since . . . but he had not told her why . . . And as for Natalie, poor motherless mite, Gina adored her from the start. David's housekeeper, Florence Bernat, had taken to Gina immediately and fussed over both her and the baby like a mother hen.

And then Sam, Nadine's brother and Natalie's uncle, came to visit them . . .

Once more Gina found herself going over in her mind everything that had happened the night that Sam had first told her he loved her.

If only she had insisted that he listen to what she had to say. She would have told him why she had lost her job with the Harringtons and she could have told him what had really happened.

She had sensed, even then, how dangerous it would be if he ever heard the story first from anyone else.

CHAPTER 16

South West France

Marco stood in the small, windowless bathroom of the hotel. Using a hairdryer, he wafted hot air gently in the direction of a couple of strips of negative that were pegged to a traveller's washing line stretched from wall to wall.

The separate pieces of his developing tank were lying in the wash-basin and some plastic bottles of chemicals were on the floor. Hotel managers the world over never objected to his using their bathrooms as a darkroom, because they never found out.

Unlike some photographers, he was a clean worker. He never left any spillage – never left any evidence. That was a way of life to him.

Eventually, he switched off the hairdryer. He would leave the film hanging while he had an early breakfast. As he turned away, he caught sight of himself in the mirror on the tiled wall.

He paused and examined his reflection. He couldn't help himself. He grinned because he knew that he was vain but also because he was pleased with what he saw.

Even early in the morning with his dark blond hair tousled and with last night's stubble on his chin, he knew that he had more sex appeal than any of the rock stars, film stars, sportsmen and other assorted celebrities he had photographed during his successful career as a paparazzo.

More than one passing amour had told him that he ought to be in front of the camera rather than behind it.

He frowned suddenly and pulled his shoulders back, standing straighter. He examined himself more critically. He was wearing a black T-shirt and black jeans. Marco usually wore black because he kidded himself that it made him look taller. If there was one thing that bothered him it was that he was only just medium height.

Perhaps that was why he felt obliged to work so hard at any relationship, no matter how brief he intended it to be. He wanted the woman to think he was perfect. More than one of his past conquests had believed that he was in love with her when, if the truth were known, Marco could love only one person. Himself.

He followed the cable back to the wall socket in the bedroom, unplugged the hairdryer and stowed it into his travelling bag. Then he reached for the house phone that was next to the bed and persuaded the chef, who had only just come on duty, to send up breakfast.

He would take it in his room this morning. It wouldn't hurt to let anyone who was interested, think that he had left town with most of the others.

A little later Marco sat at the table by the bedroom window savouring his second cup of coffee. Then, pushing the cup aside, he turned his attention to the strips of colour negative he had brought in from the bathroom.

He held each up to the light in turn. From his vantage point on the mountainside, he had homed in on any open or half-open door or window of the villa. He'd had to use his longest lens but, nevertheless, each shot was sharp and clear with no trace of camera shake.

All that was revealed in shot after shot was a view into an empty room. Except for a series of three pictures that showed Madame Bernat, the housekeeper, hanging out the washing on a line strung between the trees in the orchard.

It looks like they've bolted, he thought. I suppose they could be hiding from view, but I was up there for hours taking shots at different times around the clock. They'd have had to crawl round on their hands and knees not to have come into view at some time or other. And how could they have controlled the child?

Marco began to slot the strips of film back into a negative envelope. He glanced out of the window. It was still very early and the sun-dappled town square was peaceful. In another hour or two, he guessed, any of the reporters and photographers who were still here would be leaving and the local people could go about their business without interference once more.

There were still a few tourists about but they were easy to spot with their point-and-shoot cameras and their expensive casual clothes.

Yes, Marco thought, I'll have the place to myself, but before I take anything for granted, I'd better spend one more day on the mountain.

A lone pigeon pecking between the cobbles near the fountain was the only sign of life when Marco left the hotel. It raised its head and cocked it to one side as if observing him.

In his black jeans, T-shirt and sunglasses he presented a slightly sinister figure as he paused in the doorway. When he had satisfied himself that he was unobserved – apart from the pigeon – he strode along the pavement and ducked into a narrow side street; it led to a strip of waste ground bordering on to the river. This was the car park used by the hotel guests.

Marco had hired a four wheel drive off-roader which had proved useful on the rough terrain. He took a back road out of town and crossed the old bridge that led directly to the mountain road. As he began to climb a little, the drop at the river side of the road became steeper.

The sound of water rushing through the narrow gorge was deafening. He decided to wait until he had taken the mountain track and put some distance between himself and the river before he would pull over and make his phone calls.

Emma didn't answer, but at least she'd remembered to leave the answering machine on this time. Marco imagined her out with the dogs in the pearly dawn light. He closed his eyes and he could see the lush greens of their own woodland walk and the sky of palest blue, fading to white where it touched the low hills.

He thought about Emma, striding through the wet grass, savouring the earthy smells of the damp ground, and he felt like crying at the shame of it all. Emma, so careless of the way she looked and yet so lovely.

He didn't leave a message. He found that he had nothing to say. How could he go on apologizing day after day, year after year for not loving her in the same way that she loved him?

The second call was one that he had been planning ever since he had arrived in France. The story of the nanny who'd inherited a fortune had been a good one – especially as there had been a younger lover and a disinherited child. But from the beginning Marco had been convinced there was something more.

The name 'Gina' had nudged at his memory. She was Gina Shaw now, but it wasn't hard to discover that her maiden name was Rowlands and the memory began to firm up in his mind. None of the other reporters on the story had seemed to know about it and Marco kept quiet.

If he was right, the additional information could kick-start the story into life all over again and he would be the only one on the spot. If he wanted to make the information public, that was. Marco had his own personal reason for wanting to unearth something unsavoury about Gina Shaw.

He made his second call.

'Marco! Darling! Is that really you?'

Marco knew how early it would be in London but Prue Harrington didn't complain. She was delighted – and very surprised – to hear from him.

'Yes, it's me. Did I wake you up?'

'Oh, that doesn't matter. But where are you calling from?'

Marco hated direct questions and he paused. Prue hurried on, 'Are you still in France?'

'Now, how did you know where I was?'

'Well, darling, no one but Marco Doyle could have snatched some of those shots of that dreadful girl and her lover.'

Marco smiled. It was going to be easy. 'So you've been following the story?'

'Of course, scandalous isn't it? But I'm not really surprised.'

'Really? Why not?' he murmured encouragingly.

'Well, leopards don't change their spots, do they?'

Get on with it, girl, Marco wanted to yell. He restrained himself because he didn't want to appear to be prompting her – as if he were seeking information.

But, infuriatingly, Prue Harrington seemed to think the topic had been dealt with and she asked, 'What's the weather like, over there?'

'Super, but Prue, listen –'

'Yes, oh, wait a moment, Marco . . .'

He waited whilst she gave orders to someone who

it seemed had just walked into the room at the home she shared with her divorced mother in London's Belgravia.

'That's right, Maria,' he heard her say, 'sorry to summon you so early, but I simply must have a cup of tea – oh, and seeing I'm awake, you can bring me some breakfast – toast and orange juice will do.'

Marco heard the respectful murmurings of the maid and then, 'Still there, darling?'

'Yes, Prue, I'm here.'

'Sorry about that. Now what were we talking about?'

Marco suddenly remembered why he had ended the affair with Prue Harrington even earlier than he usually did – in spite of the fact that she had a terrific body and was fantastic in bed. Every time they had stopped making love long enough to allow her to talk, she had infuriated him with her grasshopper chatter. It depressed him to think that he would have to see her at least once more – but it was in the line of duty.

He brought her back to the required track. 'You were telling me that you've been following the Gina Shaw story.'

'Was I? Oh, well yes, as I said, it's obvious, it's *her*, isn't it?'

Marco's feeling of satisfaction changed into one of excitement but he pretended to be puzzled. 'What do you mean, "it's her"? Do you know the girl?'

'Well, of course. She used to be Gina Rowlands, didn't she? Don't you remember what she did? I told you all about it!'

'Prue, I don't know what you're talking about,' he lied.

'Marco, precious, I thought as much at the time – you don't really listen to me, do you? I could see it in those fabulous, tawny-coloured eyes of yours. Whenever I started talking about something really interesting, you would just switch off!'

It was true, Marco thought. It was a self-defence mechanism with someone like Prue, otherwise you ran the risk of being bored to death. But he had never 'switched off' entirely – you never knew when you might overhear something useful.

So he had half-remembered Prue telling him some rigmarole about her stepmother dismissing her children's nanny for scandalous behaviour. And he thought the nanny's name had been Gina Rowlands.

'Look, I really am sorry, but you'll have to remind me,' he said.

Prue sighed ostentatiously, and Marco could imagine her settling herself amongst her pillows like a contented cat. 'Well, if you really don't remember; she was nanny to my two sweet little half-sisters until my stepmother dismissed her on the spot. She had to – she found her in bed with my father.'

'And it's the same girl? You're sure?'

'Marco – are you laughing at me? I know you don't believe half the things I tell you! Of course I'm sure. I met the girl more than once when I went over to visit my father and my little half-sisters.'

'Sorry I doubted you, now Prue –'

She couldn't be stopped, which was just what Marco had hoped for. 'And do you know, no one blamed my stepmother one little bit when she threw the girl out on the street!'

'Didn't they?'

'Of course not, poor Paula had been at the hospital all night with her mother when she came home and found them together. The girl deserved what she got!'

Marco would have liked to have asked what punishment Paula had meted out to Prue's father but he kept quiet and let her continue.

' – And yet, you know, I was quite shocked at the time . . .'

'Shocked? By the girl's behaviour, you mean?'

'Well, yes, but more because she didn't seem the type. She seemed so sweet and sensible and my little half-sisters absolutely adored her. They were broken-hearted when Paula kicked her out.'

'So she had you fooled, then?'

'Too right! All the time she was looking after the children and telling Paula not to worry and spend as much time as she liked at the hospital, she had designs on my poor unsuspecting father!'

Marco couldn't quite accept this concept of Jeremy Harrington as a completely innocent participant in whatever had happened, but none of that mattered.

'And love him as I do,' Prue continued, 'I have to say it wouldn't be because of his looks or his important position in life – poor daddy's probably one of the most insignificant men in London. No, it must have been because he's loaded. It was his money she was after.'

'If you say so.'

'Marco – am I boring you? I am, aren't I? You should have stopped me rattling the family skeletons like that. I'll put them all back in the cupboard. Now, why did you call me so early in the morning?'

'I just wanted to make sure that you're not going away in the next week or two.'

He heard her catch her breath. 'Why's that, Marco?'

'Well, I may be coming back to London soon, and . . .'

'You want to see me?'

'Don't sound so surprised, we're old friends, aren't we?'

'More than just friends, I hope.' She suddenly sounded coy – flirtatious.

'I like to keep in touch with old friends. I thought we might meet up for a drink – or I could take you out to dinner.'

'We-ell . . .' she sounded hesitant, vulnerable and Marco almost felt guilty at the way he was fooling her.

'What is it, Prue? Don't you want to see me?'

'Of course I do. But this is such a surprise – I mean you don't usually take up again with your old – er – friends – do you? That's not your style.'

The last comment was acerbic and Marco hurried

on, 'Maybe so, but I've been thinking about you and – and the great times we had together.'

'Have you? Have you really, Marco?' He could hear how much she wanted to believe him.

'Yes, so when I get back to town, I'd like to call you. Is that OK?'

'Yes . . . that's wonderful! What shall we do? Dining? Dancing? The theatre? I'll have to go shopping – buy some new outfits –'

'That's great, Prue, now I really must go. I'll call you as soon as I get back –'

'Wait a minute, Marco!'

'What is it?'

'Couldn't you sleep last night?'

'You've lost me.'

'I mean if you had to call me so early in the morning, I dread to think what your – er – state of mind must have been!'

Marco laughed flirtatiously because that's what was expected, but he ended the call as soon as possible after that.

He would look up Prue Harrington when he returned to London because he usually paid his debts – so long as it didn't conflict with his own interests. In his line of work it was useful to be able to call in favours.

As he climbed further away from the river, the road became little more than a track, deeply rutted, and rarely used since the road tunnel had been blasted through to the Spanish side of the ridge.

It wasn't Marco's way, like some of the cheekier

snappers, to march up to the front entrance of the villa or harass the couple close up. Instead he relied on his selection of tele-photo lenses to catch them when they were unawares.

From the start he had beaten any of the others, who had had the same idea, to the best vantage points for getting sneak shots of the Villa Des Pines and its inhabitants. But, of course, unknown to the others, Marco had been here before.

When he decided that he shouldn't risk driving any further, he pulled over and parked in the shade of an outcrop of rock. Not only would this keep the off-roader cool as the sun rose and grew hotter, but it would also provide camouflage – from a distance no one would be able to distinguish the greeny-brown vehicle from the rocks.

He got out and shouldered his camera bag. The track ahead of him grew more treacherous and soon he left it and followed a narrow footpath that struck horizontally along the side of the mountain.

The heat of the sun, the aromatic smell of the shrubby vegetation and the shrill chirping of the cicadas enclosed him, but Marco didn't falter until he reached his goal, an ancient shepherd's hut. This was his hideaway.

He set down his camera bag and stepped forward to look down on the red tiled roofs of the farm buildings scattered across the lower slopes on both sides of the valley.

On the mountainside opposite to where he was standing there was a small village. Just a little further up the mountain and probably just under a mile distant from his vantage point, was an impressive villa – David's villa.

He hunkered down and opened his camera bag, took out his camera and fitted a twelve-hundred-millimetre mirror lens. Then with the camera on a tripod, he made himself as comfortable and as steady as he could on the steep slope before looking through the viewfinder.

He brought the villa into focus and then swept over the living quarters, the terrace, the gardens, the studio and gallery in turn. He saw no sign of life until a sudden flash of light caught his attention and he focused on the swimming pool in the grounds.

The water sparkled and splashed again and Marco realized that someone was in the pool, driving powerfully through the water.

Even though it wasn't what he had expected – hadn't wanted – to find, there was some satisfaction for him that he had bothered to come back today to take more shots.

'So-oo,' he breathed softly and he pressed the shutter release. The camera's motor whirred as he took shot after shot.

The game isn't over yet, he thought. After days of keeping out of sight, lover boy has suddenly decided to go for a swim. Now does that mean that Gina and the child are still here in France, or are they trying to be clever – playing a game of some kind?

I'd better hang around and find out.

CHAPTER 17

Northumberland

Wind, she could hear wind hurling rain against the window and howling its way around the corners of the old house.

It sounds like a full-blown gale, Gina thought. Reluctantly, she opened her eyes and saw from the pallid light edging its way around the curtains that it must be morning.

She raised herself a little and peered at her travel clock on the bedside table. Not quite seven o'clock – too early to get up. She decided to snuggle down beneath the bedclothes and try to snatch another hour's sleep.

But, just as she was about to pull the bedclothes over her head, she heard a small whimper. She sat up again and, as her eyes became accustomed to the half light, she realized that Natalie was wide awake, too.

Her stepdaughter was half-sitting up in bed, propped up on her elbows. Gina got up and went over to her. The child's eyes were round with wonder.

'What's the matter, sweetheart?'

'I don't like that noise.'

'Neither do I. But it's only the wind – the wind and the rain. Come and see.'

They stood by the window and looked out. The wing of the house where Sam's study was, was in darkness – there were no lights in any of the windows. The stonework was wet and glistening.

The tops of the hills, which rose beyond the grounds of Northmoor Hall, had disappeared into the lowering rain clouds. In the fields on the lower slopes, hardy cheviot sheep huddled together, seeking shelter near the ancient, drystone walls.

'Look, Gina,' Natalie pointed towards them, 'look at the poor lambs.'

'Don't worry, sweetheart, I expect they're used to it.' Gina shuddered as the window rattled in its frame. She left the curtain fall and knelt down and hugged the little girl. 'But we're not and if we stand here very much longer we'll get cold.'

'I don't want to go back to bed. I'm wide awake.'

Gina realized that Natalie's internal clock was still adjusting itself and that it would be no use fighting it. 'OK, let's get ready and go down and have breakfast,' she said.

She had intended to make the breakfast for the two of them herself, but she found that Agnes was already sitting at the kitchen table drinking tea.

'Didn't you go home last night?'

Agnes was writing a list of some sort; she looked up and smiled. 'Of course I did. But I always get here early. Did the wind wake you up?'

'Mmm, and Natalie, too.'

'I thought it might. Don't worry it'll soon blow itself out and then we might have quite a nice day.'

'Is it OK if I make us some breakfast?'

'No it's not.' Agnes looked offended. 'I'll make your breakfast, that's what I'm here for. Now just sit down – pour yourself a cup of tea while you're waiting, if you like. I'll get some milk for Natalie.'

Gina was grateful to do as she was told. The kitchen was warm and clean, an oasis of comfort in a stormy world. She sipped a mug of tea appreciatively, whilst Natalie had a beaker of warm milk.

She wasn't as physically exhausted as she had been the day before, but she felt that she still had weeks and weeks of missed sleep to try to catch up on. She hadn't had a proper night's rest since David had gone into the last stage of his illness – and Juan had been right when he'd said that she hadn't been eating properly.

But this morning she had no choice. She was presented with a large glass of freshly squeezed orange juice, followed by scrambled egg with strips of bacon on top, then toast and marmalade. To her surprise, she did quite well.

'It's the air here,' Agnes said as she regarded Gina's empty plate approvingly. She pulled out a chair and sat at the end of the table, ready to chat. 'Sharp and bracing – it will soon bring back your appetite.'

'It's sharp and bracing, all right,' Gina agreed as she gazed out of the kitchen window. The sky was lighter now but the clouds were hurtling across the sky as if some giant was playing blow football with them.

'You'll soon get used to it,' Agnes said. 'But it's not always fretful like this you know. The summers can be pure heaven.'

'It's the uncertainty that would bother me,' Gina said. She drew her breath in through pursed lips and shook her head.

'What on earth are you talking about, lass?' Agnes frowned.

'Well, I notice you said that the Summers *can* be pure heaven. So that must imply that at other times they're pure hell.'

Agnes gave her a long, old-fashioned look and then did her best to suppress a smile. 'Well, I suggest the best thing that you can do is stay around and find out for yourself – Goodness gracious where's the child!'

'What . . .?' Gina put down her cup and gazed at Agnes in alarm.

They both looked towards the place where Natalie had been sitting. Her chair was empty – and more puzzling, her breakfast plate was missing, too. They stared at each other in consternation, then they rose as one.

'Did you notice her go?' Agnes asked.

'No . . .'

'I didn't hear the door open or close, did you?' Agnes whispered, her eyes sharp with worry.

'No – hush – what was that?'

'What?'

'A thumping sound . . . there it is again . . . it's under the table,' Gina said.

'I hear it – let me look . . .'

As they knelt down, one at each side of the table, Gina already knew what they would find, the giggling gave the game away.

'Well I never,' Agnes breathed. 'Just look at the young scamp.'

'Which young scamp do you mean?' Gina asked her. 'The scamp who's licking his lips and wagging his tail because he's just finished off the scrambled eggs? Or the scamp with a ribbon in her hair, who encouraged him?'

Agnes laughed. 'I'd forgotten the dog was there. It was too wild for his morning walk with Jock earlier, so I brought him here with me.'

'Are you cross, Gina?' Natalie had crawled out from under the table, closely followed by Rebel.

Gina had to try very hard not to laugh. There were two pairs of eyes staring up at her with mute appeal. It was almost as if the dog knew that he and the child had transgressed some grown-up rule.

'No, poppet, not really. But I think you ought to ask Mrs Robson if she's cross. After all she made your breakfast for you.'

Even before Natalie had turned towards her, the housekeeper was laughing and shaking her head. 'I don't mind this time Natalie, pet, but next time you want to feed him come and ask me for his own dinner dish.'

Natalie and the puppy settled themselves in the big old armchair by the Aga whilst Gina helped Agnes Robson clear the table.

Natalie was looking at one of Jock's seed catalogues and telling the dog all about the pictures of the flowers. Rebel cocked his head to one side and watched the child intently. He actually seems to be listening and trying to understand her, Gina thought.

'They'll be happy for a while,' Agnes murmured. 'Now, these dishes!'

As Agnes washed and Gina dried she asked the housekeeper, 'Was that a shopping list you were writing before?'

'Yes, if we're to have a houseful of guests, I thought I'd better stock up a little.'

Gina felt acutely embarrassed. 'Oh, Agnes, I'm sorry.'

'Whatever for?'

'Well, Natalie and I arriving here without warning must have been bad enough – '

'It's your house now, Mrs Shaw – '

'Yes, but then my parents turned up too. I never intended to cause so much bother.'

'It's no bother. I prefer to be busy – although . . .'

'What is it?' Gina was worried by how serious Agnes suddenly looked.

'Well, if you don't mind I'll get the cleaning woman to come in more often while your guests are here.'

'Cleaning woman? Do we have a cleaning woman?'

Gina realized for the first time that she would have to make it her business to find out more about the running of Northmoor Hall. She couldn't just leave it all to Agnes; although she suspected that Agnes would be perfectly happy if she did.

'Yes, Mrs Shaw.' Agnes had become all formal. 'While the house is empty, or while it's just Mr Redmond who's here, Mrs Sutton from the village comes in two days a week.

'She and I can manage – after all a lot of the rooms aren't being used. But if this is going to be a family home again –'

Family home, Gina remembered the housekeeper's speculative look when she had brought her a cup of tea in bed the day before. Did Agnes imagine that one of the reasons Gina had come to David's childhood home was because she was expecting his child . . .?

'Agnes,' she blurted out, 'I'm not pregnant you know.'

She had been right. She watched the woman fight her disappointment as a hope died. 'Well, never mind,' was all she said. 'You've done the best thing bringing David's daughter here.'

David's daughter . . . Gina thought. They loved David and now all they have is Natalie . . .

'Well, yes, I'm glad we came here but I don't really know how long we'll be staying . . . I mean Natalie and I might go back to France . . . I don't know when . . .'

'Might you?' Gina knew she wasn't just imagining

Agnes's disappointment this time. The small, spry woman emptied the dishwater down the sink and set about cleaning the bowl.

She didn't look at Gina when she said, 'Well, for however long you stay – and certainly for as long as your parents are here – I think Mrs Sutton should come in more often.'

'Oh, definitely. Please have her come as many days as you think necessary.'

At that moment the door to the courtyard opened and Jock came in with a blast of cold air.

'Shut the door and take your wellingtons off before you step off that doormat,' Agnes said, without even turning round.

Gina looked at him to see his reaction to his wife's imperious tone; he winked at her as he began to unbutton his waterproof coat. 'Now Agnes,' he said, 'what would you say if it was Arnold Schwarzenegger who'd just come in?'

'Exactly the same as I've said to you.'

'Even to Arnie?' Jock grinned and said in an aside to Gina, 'She's got a soft spot for big Arnie, you know. Drags me all the way into Berwick whenever one of his films is on at the Playhouse. It's a good job I'm not a jealous man.'

'Stop that, Jock Robson.' Agnes turned and faced him but she was smiling as much as he was. 'There's no need to give away my secrets. But, yes, even Arnold Schwarzenegger would have to respect my clean floor. Now get your boots off and have a cup of tea before you take Rebel for his

223

morning exercise – if he doesn't go soon, he'll start complaining.'

'Let me do that,' Gina said suddenly.

'Do what, dear?'

'Take the dog out – Natalie and I together, it would be fun for her.'

Agnes gazed speculatively through the large kitchen window at the sky, 'Well, the rain seems to have stopped . . .'

'And the wind's dying down,' her husband added.

Agnes turned and smiled. 'If you're sure you don't mind, that would mean Jock could drive into Brackenburn all the sooner and get these groceries.'

'Of course I don't mind – come and get ready, poppet.'

Natalie was at the door before her and they went upstairs to collect their outdoor clothes. She knew that she would have to talk to Sam sooner or later, and her parents would also be expecting to see her. But, for the moment, all she wanted to do was escape for a while.

Even though the sun had broken through the clouds, Gina dressed Natalie in warm trews and a padded anorak with the addition of a red woollen hat and mittens. She looked like a picture-book child.

For herself she'd settled for her jeans and a warm, cream-coloured sweater over a cinnamon-coloured polo top.

When they returned to the kitchen, Agnes was waiting with two pairs of wellington boots. 'Here you are, Jock brought them over from the cottage, they belong to my daughter and one of her little ones.'

'Thanks, Agnes.'

Gina put on her boots and helped Natalie with hers whilst Agnes attached the leader to Rebel's collar.

'Now,' she said as she straightened up, 'I'd better start preparing breakfast for the others. What's the matter?' Gina had paused by the door.

'You don't think I should stay, do you?'

'No, dear, I think you need to get out for a while. Mr Redmond is quite capable of looking after your parents.'

Gina suppressed a twinge of unease at the thought of her parents alone with Sam. It wasn't her father she was worried about, it was Sandra and what she might say. She could not rid herself of the idea that her stepmother had a hidden agenda.

Agnes came over and pushed her gently towards the kitchen door. 'Get away with you. Now if you go across the stable yard and down to the end there, you'll see a path that goes by our cottage. Go that way – the path climbs a small hill – not too difficult for the child and it won't be as wet and muddy as the way through the woods.'

Gina flushed as she remembered the state Rebel had got himself into the last time she took him out. She wondered if, in spite of Jock's promise, Agnes had found out. But, if she had, she didn't seem cross. She waved and smiled as Gina, Natalie and Rebel set out across the yard.

There were pools of water in the yard and Natalie had fun jumping over the smaller puddles, whereas

Rebel raced straight through them, pulling Gina along after him. They were all out of breath – even the puppy – by the time they reached the Robsons' cottage and began to walk up the hill path.

Rebel was content to slow down and Gina had time to take in the surroundings. The stony path wound its way between high grassy banks and the ridge above them was crowned with trees.

The storm had brought down a lot more leaves and the outlines of the trees were starkly beautiful against the horizon. Now that the wind and rain had stopped the sky was a bright, clear blue.

David had once told her that there was nothing so beautiful as an endless Northumbrian sky – and yet he had chosen to spend most of his adult life in another country.

Gina thought she knew why. The people here would not have understood him. If they had known the truth about him they would have been puzzled and hurt. They might even have rejected him. It had been easier for him to make a new life for himself with strangers.

Half way up the hill, Gina let Rebel off the leader and he began to run ahead, but not too far. Every now and then he stopped and waited for Natalie who had run the roses back into her cheeks.

Gina was content to dawdle along after them so the child and the dog reached the brow of the hill well before she did.

'Look, Gina, look!'

She looked up to see Natalie pointing ahead at

something she could not see. Her stepdaughter was almost jumping up and down with excitement and Rebel decided to race back and chivvy her along.

He barked and swerved almost as if he were rounding up a stray lamb and Gina was laughing at his antics by the time she reached the spot where Natalie was standing.

'What is it, poppet?' she asked when she had recovered her breath.

'The tower – I can see the tower!'

Gina looked in the direction that the child was pointing and on a distant hillside, at the other side of a small valley, with a road running through, she saw an old stone structure that looked like a small castle.

'It's lovely, Natalie. It's like – it's like something in a story book. Who do you think lives there? A fairy princess?'

'Don't be silly.' Natalie was giggling. 'It isn't a princess who lives there, it's Sam's friend, Miss Maxwell.'

'How – how do you know that, Natalie?'

'We went there, yesterday and, oh, Gina, she's so pretty! And she's so small – when she gave Sam a kiss she had to stand on tiptoes!'

Gina stared at her stepdaughter in consternation. She felt as though ice had started to trickle through her veins.

'Sally – this Sally – kissed Sam . . . ?'

'Oh!' Natalie gasped, 'I'm sorry, I forgot – I wasn't supposed to tell you!'

She looked so crestfallen that Gina kneeled down

and took hold of her shoulders. 'What weren't you supposed to tell me, sweetheart?'

'I wasn't supposed to tell you about going to the tower or meeting Sally – Sam said it was a secret.'

'I see.' She made the effort to pull her lips into a smile. 'Well, don't worry, I'll pretend I didn't hear you.'

Natalie was looking at her doubtfully so she pulled the child into her arms and hugged her. 'Cheer up, I promise you I won't say anything to your uncle – and you know I always keep my promises.'

Natalie pulled back and regarded her solemnly and then she grinned. 'Well, anyway, it'll be a nice surprise and Sam said he'd tell you all about Sally and the tower quite soon.'

'That's all right then,' Gina managed but she was feeling far from all right. Her stomach was churning up the ice cubes that had settled there.

Throughout this exchange the puppy had been waiting patiently, but now, sensing that the time had come to intrude he pushed in between them and tried to lick Natalie's face.

She started laughing as she turned away and began to run on ahead. 'Come on, Rebel,' she called, 'let's go down here.'

Gina suppressed the urge to call after her and question her further. It wouldn't be fair. Sam had extracted a promise from his niece and it would be wrong to strain her loyalty.

Damn the man, she thought, doesn't he know that

he shouldn't do that kind of thing to small children – turn them into accomplices . . .

She was clenching her fists so tight that it hurt and she was horrified to realize where her thoughts had been taking her.

Who was Sally Maxwell? she wondered. And what exactly did she mean to Sam? Why had he taken Natalie to see her?

Without warning she remembered that awful scene in the kitchen just after Juan had left to return to France. Sam's words echoed in her mind . . .

. . . let me make it quite clear, when you leave here, you leave alone. I won't allow you to take Natalie with you . . .

Why had she remembered that now?

Later, Sam had apologized for his harsh words – but he'd never actually retracted his threat. He'd said that he'd wanted to stay on and get to know his little niece. He'd admitted that Natalie seemed to love Gina and might be better off staying with her – but he'd also left Gina with the impression that she was on trial.

So what if she failed the test? What if Sam decided that she wasn't a fit guardian for his sister's child? Would he snatch Natalie, after all, and run off to Sally Maxwell's tower with her?

And then would they all start playing happy families, Gina thought viciously, Sam, Natalie and pretty Sally Maxwell!

Natalie and Rebel had reached the bottom of the hill and they had stopped where the path turned to run alongside a wall. They waited for Gina to catch up with them.

She smiled as she joined them but all her enjoyment of the walk had dissipated. She glanced up at the tower, now seeming to loom so high above her on the hill at the other side of the road.

A cloud passed over the sun and threw shadows across the hillside. The tower seemed dark and threatening – the perfect lair for the wicked witch, Gina thought grimly.

She acknowledged to herself how distressed she was – and, even though Sam would say she had no right to be – how angry.

Who the hell is Sally Maxwell, she thought, and exactly what does she mean to Sam? And, even more important, what's the big secret?

CHAPTER 18

Gina trudged down the path after Natalie and Rebel. For all his energy and high spirits, Rebel was still only a very young dog and he was tired after his run. He was now docile enough for her to allow Natalie to hold the leader on the way back.

The nearer they drew to Northmoor Hall, the more unhappy Gina became. Facing the press pack at the Villa Des Pines might be better than living on a knife's edge like this, she though.

I'll phone the villa later today . . . Juan ought to be back there by now. I'll ask him to let me know the moment he thinks it might be safe for us to return.

Agnes was at the open kitchen door, obviously looking out for her.

'Is something the matter? Has Sam – Mr Redmond been asking for me?'

Why had she said that? Gina felt herself flushing under Agnes's appraising glance.

'No, Mr Redmond's in the study working, he's very strict with himself about that.'

Good for Sam, Gina thought cynically. No matter

231

what else was going on in his life, Sam still had the discipline required to get into his study every day and work on his novel. She envied him his dedication.

'No, it's your parents. They both came looking for you while you were out. Separately, that is. First your father and then your mother –'

'Stepmother.'

'Stepmother, then. But anyway, I'm sure they want to talk to you about something.'

Gina thought it was significant that they hadn't come looking for her together. Did each of them want to talk to her about something different?

She imagined that Sandra's concerns would be something to do with her new status as a wealthy widow. But her father . . . what could he want to talk to her about?

She acknowledged sadly that her father had not sought a conversation with her for years. Probably not since before her mother's death. So why now? She couldn't believe that he had been swayed by her new wealth – he had never been greedy or unscrupulous, even when he was a successful businessman.

So what could he want to talk to her about? Did he have a problem? She found that, in spite of all his failings as a father, the thought that he might be troubled about something upset her.

'I suppose I'd better go and see what it's about. Would you look after Natalie for a while?'

'Of course I'll look after the child but I wouldn't go hurrying after them, if I were you.'

'Why ever not?'

232

'We-ell . . . but, don't just stand there, come in – I'll brew some coffee – and warm some milk for Natalie. Relax for a while and try to get your spirits up.'

'What do you mean, Agnes?'

'I watched you coming back down the path just now. You looked as if you were carrying all the troubles of the world on your shoulders.'

'Did I?'

'Now, you don't have to tell me what's bothering you –' she paused but when Gina didn't offer any explanation, she continued, 'but I think you should relax a little before you deal with your parents. Get your thoughts together, as they say.'

'You're right, Agnes.' Gina gave way meekly, glad of any excuse to delay things.

She knelt down to help Natalie take off her boots before dealing with her own. Agnes got to work drying Rebel's paws with an old towel and soon Natalie was giggling at his antics as he tried to shake himself free from Agnes's grip.

Gina sank gratefully on to a seat at the scrubbed table. She would have to try and free herself of all the worrying thoughts about Sam and the beautiful and mysterious Sally Maxwell.

So Sally had to stand on tiptoes when Sam had kissed her, had she!

She knew she would have to banish the disturbing image of Sam kissing someone else if she were going to have all her wits about her for her conversation with Sandra.

How dare he do that in front of Natalie!

'My goodness, the fresh air's brought the colour back to your cheeks!'

She looked up to see Agnes watching her.

'Really?'

'Yes,' Agnes smiled suddenly, 'I can't decide whether that's a healthy glow, a feverish flush or you're just darned angry about something!'

Gina laughed in spite of herself. 'Do you know, Agnes,' she said, 'you have a very clever way of asking questions without actually asking them.'

'I don't know what you're talking about.'

'Yes you do – and I'll have to keep all my wits about me.'

'Well drink up this coffee then. But if ever you do want to talk –' Agnes suddenly looked serious ' – I've brought up three daughters, I'm a very good listener.'

'And very wise, too, I think.'

Agnes flushed and concentrated on pouring the coffee, but after that the she left Gina in peace.

The aroma of fresh-brewed coffee was strong but somehow comforting and the warmth from the Aga seeped across the kitchen to enfold her. Gina was content just to enjoy the feeling of well-being it engendered.

She took her time over the coffee and tried to keep her mind blank. Agnes moved quietly around without disturbing her and the swish of water from the sink and rhythmic chopping as she prepared the vegetables produced a state in Gina that was almost trance-like.

'Just look at that.'

Gina blinked and looked up to see the housekeeper smiling in the direction of the old armchair. Natalie was asleep deep in its cushioned folds with the puppy beside her; lying half across her knee. They both looked comfortable and deeply contented.

'Just leave her there,' Agnes said, 'and go and freshen yourself up before lunch. It'll be ready soon and you'll be able to deal with your parents all the better when you've got a good meal inside you.'

'What about Natalie?'

'I don't think we should disturb her, do you? When she wakes up I'll give her a bowl of home-made broth, here in the kitchen.'

Gina didn't argue. Agnes was right, Natalie needed to sleep; but she guessed that the house-keeper was only too pleased to have an excuse to keep the little girl near her.'

Gina would have loved to have stayed in the kitchen too, but she knew she couldn't avoid her parents indefinitely.

She was piqued to discover that Sam would not be joining them in the dining-room. Apparently he usually lunched on sandwiches while he carried on working.

Agnes didn't approve of this practice – she thought it couldn't be very good for his digestion – but there was nothing she could do about it.

Sandra pretended to be disappointed that Natalie wasn't going to join them.

235

'She's happy in the kitchen with the Robsons and her new friend, Rebel,' Gina explained.

'Oh, how sweet,' Sandra cooed insincerely. 'And that's nice for you, too, isn't it?'

'Well, obviously I'm pleased that she's happy, but –'

'I mean it gives you a break,' her stepmother continued. 'After all, it must be tiring for you to have to be solely responsible for such a young child – and she isn't even your own daughter.'

'No, she isn't, is she? But, you know, it's funny, I don't mind that one little bit.'

The two women stared at each other across the table and their eyes expressed the animosity of years. Nothing has changed, Gina thought. Sandra wanted to marry my father because she was getting past her best as a model and he was a good catch. She must have been horrified to discover that a teenage daughter was part of the package.

But it was more than that, Gina realized. It wasn't just that I was an inconvenient nuisance. That's what I thought for years . . . but now I realize that she didn't even like me, right from the start. And that hasn't changed . . .

But why? I was prepared to like her . . . I didn't resent my father bringing her into our home . . . I was lonely . . . missing my mother . . . we could have been friends . . .

But we weren't, ever. And now, I'm supposed to believe that she's come hurrying here to offer her support . . .

And then, Gina knew with a terrible certainty that Sandra was her enemy. That she would have to find some way of making her go. But first of all, I must speak to my father, she thought.

'You haven't eaten much lunch, dear,' Sandra said as if nothing had passed between them, 'and that clever little woman has provided such a lovely meal. I could hardly believe that she'd made the quiche herself and as for the bowls of salad – they look good enough to eat!'

Gina choked quietly over her last mouthful and when she looked up to monitor Sandra's reaction, she met only her father's gaze. His eyes were twinkling with genuine amusement at Sandra's words.

Gina suddenly had an insight into her father and stepmother's relationship. He knows she's not too bright, she thought, and he doesn't care. In fact it amuses him – it makes him more fond of her, if anything.

This flash of intuitive understanding was immediately followed by the acknowledgement that her stepmother might not be socially everything she wanted to be, but she was by no means stupid.

She may lack education, Gina thought, but that doesn't mean she doesn't have a basic, street-wise kind of cleverness that would always enable her to work out what was best for Sandra!

Strangely, after that, Gina found that her appetite had returned. It was as if being able to laugh at Sandra, even though it was only in her mind, had reduced her stepmother's power over her a little.

I mustn't allow myself to be intimidated by her, she thought. After all, I'm a grown woman, now, not a lonely teenager.

When they had finished eating, Gina rose from the table and went over to one of the floor-to-ceiling windows. The red velvet curtains had been closed when they had dined here with Sam the night before. Now, they were draped and hooked back and the oak-panelled room was flooded with sunlight.

She looked out across the relatively cultivated parkland towards the woods and the wilder terrain of the hills rising beyond them.

'It's a marvellous view, isn't it?' She turned to her father and smiled. 'Come and see.'

He looked surprised 'Mmm? Oh, all right.'

Henry Rowlands put down his coffee cup and came over to stand beside her. He looked out of the window obediently.

She grasped his arm as if the idea had only just occurred to her. 'Would you like to come out with me, daddy? We could walk as far as the woods over there . . . just you and me . . .?'

Once again she could hear her own young voice echoing across the years . . . those years when her father had never wanted to spend any time alone with her . . . never wanted to go anywhere without Sandra . . .

'Well – er – the ground looks a little wet – perhaps a bit muddy . . .' He looked down at his expensive shoes doubtfully.

'Don't worry about your shoes. I expect Jock

could find you something more sturdy. Come on, the fresh air would do you good.'

'I should have thought you had enough fresh air this morning, Gina.' Sandra sounded acerbic. 'You went out so early and stayed out so long that we thought you were avoiding us, didn't we, Henry?'

Her father looked uncomfortable and Gina pinned on a smile. 'I'm sorry you thought that, Sandra. But, if you did, then perhaps I can make it up to my father now. If we go for a stroll in the grounds it's a perfect way of spending some time together, isn't it?'

She didn't add, 'without you', but she didn't have to. Sandra had got the message and she stared at Gina with barely veiled hostility.

Her father shifted his position uneasily, but surprised Gina by saying, 'Do you – er – mind, Sandra? I would rather like to have a talk with Gina.'

Sandra acknowledged defeat as gracefully as she could. 'Of course I don't mind, dear. I think it's an excellent idea. As a matter of fact, I'm going to take my second cup of coffee upstairs and lie down for a while. But, Gina?'

'Yes?'

'I think it's time that you and I had a little talk, also. Just you and me. Mother-and-daughter stuff. I'll see you when you get back.'

'It was good of Sandra to want to come and see if she could help you, wasn't it, Gina?'

Dressed in the waxed jacket and green wellingtons that Jock had produced for him from somewhere

239

called 'the boot room', her father looked rather like a country gentleman, Gina thought. He also looked anxious.

She was cautious when she answered his question. 'Was it entirely Sandra's idea?'

'Oh, yes. Sandra's been following your – the story right from the start – and I suppose she could see that I was worried about you –'

'Were you?'

'Of course.'

'Really?'

Henry flushed. 'I know I've neglected you over the years, Gina, and I'm not proud of my behaviour. I always wanted a quiet life – to take the least line of resistance – even when your mother was alive –'

'Yes, I know. But somehow it didn't matter, then. I think it was because my mother always tried to do whatever was best for us – *all* of us.'

'And I was happy to let her organize the domestic side of things,' Henry added uncomfortably. 'When I married Sandra, I genuinely thought that she would want to . . . to –'

'Take over where my mother left off? Surely you must have realized that she was a very different type of woman?'

They had reached the edge of the grassland and Gina paused before taking the path that would lead through the wood. She looked at her father incredulously. He looked embarrassed.

'Well . . . of course, I knew that. But Sandra was young and attractive and so full of life that I honestly believed she would get on with you – that she would be good for you. You had become very introverted you know.'

'I wasn't introverted, I was just unhappy! I was still grieving for my mother. And far from helping me, Sandra thwarted everything I wanted to do. In fact, you could almost say that she ruined my –'

'Gina, stop!' Her father reached out towards her and she was shocked to see his face ravaged with genuine emotion.

'I'm sorry, it's pointless bringing up the past, isn't it?'

They looked at each other and this time her father didn't look away or fidget uncomfortably. 'Gina,' he said at last. 'I'm sorry about so many things; that's why I want to talk to you now –'

Gina smiled uncertainly at him. 'You're right. I didn't drag you out here just to quarrel with you.'

'I – I'm not quite sure how to begin . . .'

'Don't worry,' she squeezed his arm. 'Let's walk through the woods a little. You can get your thoughts together, as my friend Agnes would say.'

The ground was muddy and rainwater still dripped from the trees, but the colours of autumn were washed clean and vivid, and the earth smelled fresh and sweet.

Gina led the way along the narrow paths, now heaped with fallen leaves; every now and than she glanced back at her father and he would give a brief smile. She was curious but she sensed it would be better to stay quiet until he was ready to speak.

At last, when they paused in the same little clearing that David had painted so beautifully in water colours – and where Rebel had disgraced himself – her father said, 'I wanted to give Sandra the benefit of the doubt . . .'

It was almost as though he was talking to himself and Gina didn't interrupt him. 'In many ways she's been a good wife to me – I'd like you to believe that.'

'I do. At least, I know you've been happy with her.'

'Yes, I have. She's attractive, lively, likes a good time and she's made sure that I've had a good time, too.'

Gina couldn't help reflecting that her father had been even happier, but in an entirely different way, with her mother. If Tricia Rowlands had still been alive, he would have been enjoying an equally agreeable retirement – and it would have been a good deal more tranquil. But she held her tongue.

'I realized a long time ago that a lot of what happened was my fault,' he said. 'I mean the way – this is very difficult for me – the way Sandra treated you. I shut my eyes to it – I pretended it wasn't really happening – that conflict was to be expected between a new stepmother and an adolescent girl –'

Her father was looking more and more distressed and suddenly, Gina reached out and put her arms around him, as if he were the child and she the parent. 'Look, whatever you're trying to say, please consider it said – I understand.'

'Do you, Gina?'

'Yes, I do.'

'And do you forgive me?'

She took a step back and looked at his face. His anguish was unmistakable.

'I do.' And Gina knew that she spoke the truth. She both understood her father and she forgave him. But she was thankful that he had not asked her if she could forget.

'I'm glad we've had this talk,' he said at last. 'We don't see each other very often and, perhaps – I mean, I wanted to clear the air between us.'

Is that all? Gina thought. Surely what her father had just said couldn't have caused him so much difficulty. There must be more to it.

'But, surely there was something else,' she prompted. 'You said something about giving Sandra the benefit of the doubt?'

'Oh, yes.' His eyes looked troubled again. 'I meant that when she said we must find you and offer our support I was overwhelmed – I agreed straight away. I wanted to believe that she was going to do the right thing, at long last.'

'But, wait a minute,' Gina couldn't help saying, 'didn't you think that her attack of conscience might have been brought on by my newly inherited wealth?'

'Yes, and I was prepared to accept that.'

'But, how could you? I mean that's so hypocritical!'

'You're right and I didn't care. But whatever her motives were for wanting to help you I wanted to judge for myself – give her a chance . . .'

Gina sensed that there was something that Henry was holding back – something that he wasn't telling her – and that it had more to do with Sandra and himself than with Sandra and his daughter.

'Did you ever consider that I might not want your – I mean Sandra's help?'

'Yes I did. But I still wanted to see how she would behave towards you – and, of course, coming here will enable *me* to do something useful – if I have to . . .'

'Will it?' She was puzzled by his choice of words.

Her father couldn't meet her eyes again and, once more she had the feeling that he was holding something back. But he seemed to want to bring the conversation to an end.

'Better late than never, eh? And, at least my motives are genuine. Do you believe me?'

He looked so eager for her acceptance that Gina smiled. 'Yes, I do.'

'And whatever happens in future, will you believe that I have your best interests at heart?'

'I'll try to – but –'

'Good – that's good.' Henry wouldn't allow her any doubts. 'Now shall we just enjoy our walk together?'

Gina was left both mystified and troubled by their conversation. And more than ever convinced that there was something she did not know about.

For a while they kept a companionable silence as they walked a little further into the woods. Eventually, Gina managed to find the way back to the beginning of the parkland by a different route.

Her father paused just as they were about to leave the shelter of the trees. Northmoor Hall, built of limestone, looked almost golden in the afternoon light.

'The house is magnificent, isn't it?' he said. 'Do you think you'll spend much time here?'

'I'm not sure.' She didn't tell him that she was already considering making the trek back to France. The reasons for her flight would only have worried him.

'And the setting amongst the hills is so peaceful – so secure. I can see why Sam likes to come here and shut himself away from the world every now and then. Will that arrangement continue, Gina? Now that the house is yours?'

'I – I don't know . . . I haven't decided.'

Gina was surprised by her answer. If her father had asked her that question on the night she had arrived here, the answer would have been an emphatic 'No!'

But life, which was already difficult, had become much more complicated since then. When she had been walking by the lake with Sam she had kidded herself that it was only Natalie she was thinking about when she had agreed, so readily, that he should stay for a while.

But, in her heart, she knew that she had welcomed the chance to keep him here . . .

CHAPTER 19

With Agnes's obsession about clean floors in mind, Gina led her father round to the back of the house to return the borrowed waterproofs and wellington boots to Jock.

'Mmm,' Henry sniffed the air appreciatively, 'something smells good!'

Agnes had been baking. Scones and cakes cooled on wire racks on the kitchen counter tops and Gina was disconcerted to see that Sam was sitting at the table with Natalie. They both had slices of chocolate cake and a glass of milk. Rebel sat on the floor between them resting his head on Sam's knee and gazing up at him adoringly – or was it hopefully?

Sam looked up and smiled at Gina, his intelligent features seeming to radiate boyish pleasure, and she was shaken to discover how happy that smile made her feel. How dear to her his face was – how much she wanted to respond to him. She knew that she would have to guard her feelings if she didn't want to have her heart broken all over again.

'I'm taking a break,' he said. 'Why don't you join us?'

'That's right,' Agnes said. 'Why don't you and your father sit down and have a little afternoon tea? There's cake, home-made shortbread . . . apple pie.'

Her father looked eager but hesitant. 'Mrs Rowlands is still resting upstairs, she won't know that you're back yet,' Agnes told him – and they both grinned.

'In that case, I'll accept your invitation,' Henry said.

Gina excused herself. 'Just pour me a cup of tea,' she said. 'If it's OK I'll take it with me while I – I'll take it with me.'

'I'll go if you want me too – if you want to stay here with Natalie.'

Sam's voice was serious, the smile had gone and his expression was guarded. Gina hated the anxiety that immediately clouded Natalie's face.

She's so sensitive, Gina thought, she picks it up immediately – if there's something wrong between us. She smiled as reassuringly as she could. 'No – of of course not. I don't want you to go. It's just that I have something to do . . . really.'

'Here, take this.'

Whether she had sensed the undercurrents or not, Agnes had taken a small tray from a cupboard and set it up. As well pouring her a cup of tea, the housekeeper had cut a large slice of chocolate cake and put it on a plate with a couple of the home-made biscuits.

Gina knew it was no use arguing.

In morning-room the fire burned brightly, shedding a warm glow on the apricot and pastel shades of the walls and the soft furnishings. Points of light glinted on the glass face of the clock and on the antique candlesticks. Vases of fresh flowers filled the room with a delicate perfume.

Gina sighed; it was only mid-afternoon but she'd done a lot of walking since she'd got up this morning. She was tempted to sit by the fire for a while and enjoy Agnes's home baking.

But she set down the tray on the table between the two sofas, took one mouth-watering bite of chocolate cake, a sip of her tea and then walked over to the phone. It was placed on a walnut writing desk set between the windows.

Juan was back at the villa and he was pleased to hear from her – but the news wasn't what she was hoping for.

'No, *querida*, you must not come back, not yet. They are still here – watching the villa.'

'Oh, no, I was hoping that they'd have moved on to some more headline-grabbing story by now.'

'I think most of them have. Florence and Gerard told me that when they went on one of their shopping trips they saw many of the reporters leaving. But they have not all gone away.'

'How do you know?'

'Today when I was in the pool – I saw sunlight reflecting on something on the mountain side – probably the lens of a camera –'

'*Him!*'

'What do you mean, *querida*?'

'The rat with the telephoto lens and the hide-out in the hills! It's probably the same guy who got those shots of the three of us in the pool – and of the funeral.'

'Maybe. But I gave him his money's worth – that's what you say, isn't it? I stayed in the pool for more than an hour.'

'So, do you think whoever it was will believe that we're all still at the villa? After all, he must only have got shots of you.'

'Florence Bernat is making a great show of going to the shops in town every day and buying in much food. She hangs out washing – Natalie's clothes and yours as well as household linen.

'We must hope that the reporters will believe you and Natalie are staying inside – that you do not want to expose the child to any more publicity – so, therefore it is pointless for them to hang around. And yet . . .'

'What is it, Juan?'

'I am puzzled . . . if the others have given up on the story and moved on, why do you think this one stays here?'

Gina sighed, 'I have no idea.'

'I am worried about this, Gina, I cannot tell you why, because I do not know myself. But I think you must remain where you are for a little while longer.'

'Oh, no . . . I was hoping –'

'Gina, I will phone you the moment I think that it is safe for you to return, do you believe me?'

'Yes, Juan. I believe you.'

After Gina had put down the receiver, she stood by the writing desk for a moment with her eyes closed. She sighed. How much longer? she wondered. Life would be so much easier if she could just set some kind of limit to her time here.

Perhaps she should not have come here at all. Perhaps she should just have 'gone to ground' staying inside the villa or even hiding out at the Bernats' farm. Both Florence and her son, Gerard, had told her that she could.

And yet, she had sensed that not all the Bernat family would have made her welcome. Gerard's young wife, Céline, had never liked her. Gina had never taken this personally, because it was common knowledge that Céline didn't like any female that came anywhere near Gerard.

She was jealous almost to the point of illness; she imagined that her husband was so irresistible that any woman, no matter what her age, would want to make love to him.

Staying at the farm with Céline watching her every movement and crashing the cooking pots about sulkily would have been unbearable. And she would never have felt secure; she suspected that the young French woman would have betrayed her presence to the press readily, if it meant getting rid of her.

So she had decided to come here. She had never had a clear idea of how long she would stay, but she could never have imagined that David's childhood home would not be the sanctuary that she so badly needed.

'Oh dear, was that not what you wanted to hear?'

Gina spun round. Sandra was sitting on one of the sofas near the fireplace. Gina hadn't heard her enter the room. How long had she been there? How much had she heard?

'What do you mean?' Gina asked.

'Your phone call. Was it to your boyfriend? Missing him, are you?'

'How many times do I have to tell you that Juan Sanchez is not my boyfriend!'

'Don't get over-excited, darling. Look, your tea must be getting cold. Shall I go and warm it up for you?'

'And why on earth would you do that? You've never ever wanted to do anything for me in the past.'

For a moment, Sandra lost her poise and her face twisted with fury. 'I disliked you from the moment I set eyes on you, you precious little snob!'

Gina gasped at the sheer venom of her step-mother's outburst but, a moment later, the mask had readjusted itself and Sandra was smiling again. 'But it doesn't do to dwell on the past, does it Gina? We must think of the future. Now sit down and let's talk.'

'I don't want to talk to you, Sandra.'

'Oh, but I think you should. Did you enjoy your chat with your father?'

The change in direction took Gina by surprise. 'Yes, I did. Not that it has anything to do with you.'

She knew she sounded offensive – rude even – like the rebellious teenager that she used to be, but Sandra simply smiled. 'Come here.'

She patted the place beside her with a graceful gesture. Gina ignored the invitation and sat down opposite her on the other sofa.

'So? What do you want to talk about?'

'Well, first of all, I think your father is drinking a little more than he should lately, don't you?'

'I – er – I don't know.' Gina remembered watching him at the dinner table the night before. She had come to the same conclusion but she didn't want to give Sandra any satisfaction by admitting it.

'That's not very observant of you, Gina. But you can take my word for it that he has been.'

'So?'

'It's happened before. Whenever he's worried about anything. Remember just after your mother died –'

'I think that was grief, not worry, Sandra!'

'Maybe, I've already said I don't want to quarrel with you, but you have to admit that I got him out of that – I was good for him wasn't I?'

'If you say so.'

Sandra's smile was both supercilious and condescending and Gina could have kicked herself for sounding just like the sulky teenager she had once been.

'Anyway,' Sandra continued, 'all this nasty gossip about David's will, and then your taking a young Spanish lover – no, don't interrupt – so soon after your husband's death – perhaps even before he died. Well, it's upset your father to have to read all that.'

'I know and I'm sorry, but it was hardly of my choosing.'

'It will be a mercy when the whole thing dies the death, won't it? When the newspapers forget about you and drop the story?'

'I have to agree with you, for once, Sandra. Furthermore, I don't think we'll have to wait much longer for that moment.'

'You're right. So it would be a pity if it suddenly started up again, wouldn't it?'

'Why would that happen?'

'If the reporters discovered some new slant – something that happened before you married David – something that throws more light on your character – not a very savoury light as it happens.'

'How – how would they find out about that?' Gina knew that Sandra could only be referring to the incident with the Harringtons and she also had a very good idea what the answer to her question would be.

'Well, I would tell them, of course.'

Gina stared at her. She hadn't been prepared for Sandra to admit it quite so openly. 'But why?' she whispered. 'Why would you do that?'

'I need the money.'

'Money? You've lost me.'

'They would have to pay me for the story, of course. "The truth about Gina, as told by her sorrowing stepmother" – that kind of thing.'

'No doubt you'd sell it to the highest bidder?'

'Of course.'

'But why, Sandra? Why do you need money so much?' Suddenly, a thought occurred to Gina and she paled. 'My father isn't bankrupt or anything, is he? If he's in trouble, I'll help. You must have realized that – all you had to do was ask me – you needn't have even contemplated such a vile scheme!'

Sandra smiled complacently. 'Very commendable, darling, and just what I suspected.'

'Suspected?'

'That you're soft enough – or should I say loyal enough – to want to help your father.'

'Of course I am.'

'But, you see, the problem is that it's not Henry who needs the money – it's me.'

'You want to leave him!'

'Very quick of you, darling. That's why I need money of my own. But of course I'd rather not go to the newspapers with your sordid little story – and you can stop me.'

'Don't tell me – you want me to pay you off – you're blackmailing me, aren't you?'

'I wouldn't put it quite like that.'

'Well I would. And if I refuse to pay?'

'You'll be back in the news again and your father might start drinking even more heavily – it's his way of dealing with stress. Now, at his age, that wouldn't be very good for him, would it?'

'I would see to it that he was forewarned – I would protect him –'

'Maybe you would, Gina, and maybe he would be OK. He's not so far gone that he couldn't pull himself together – with your help. And it would have to be *your* help because I'd be gone by then.'

'Have you considered that he might be well rid of you?'

Sandra laughed. 'So you've got claws after all, Gina. Maybe he would be "well rid of me" as you so delicately put it, but actually, he wouldn't thank you for exposing me. He loves me – or haven't you noticed?'

They stared at each other; the only sound in the room was the fire crackling in the hearth. It should have been a cosy sound – a cheerful sound, but Gina could find no comfort in it.

Sandra was right. Even if her father knew about her threats of blackmail, he wouldn't want to lose her. And if Sandra walked out on him? He would be utterly miserable. He might even come to resent Gina no matter that it wasn't her fault.

'After all . . .', Sandra said. Gina blinked and tried to concentrate. Had she missed something?

'. . . Henry has believed your version of the Harrington business all along.'

'And why shouldn't he?'

'But there's someone else who may not be quite so charitable,' Sandra continued as if she hadn't spoken. 'It was lucky for me finding him here – and what his wishes are, wasn't it?'

'Who . . . who do you mean?'

'Don't act stupid, Gina. Whatever else you are,

255

you're not stupid. I mean Sam, of course. You told me yourself that he wants his little niece to live with him. His case for guardianship of the child would be all the stronger if it appeared that your morals were even more questionable than they appear to be at present.'

Gina stared at Sandra in horror. She had suspected all along that her stepmother had an ulterior motive for coming here, and that it would be something to do with money. But she'd had no idea that it would be anything on this scale.

'How much do you want?'

Even as she asked the question she contemplated the horrors that lay ahead. Blackmailers were never satisfied with one payment, were they? Would she have to keep on paying blood money to Sandra for the rest of her life?

'Hush, darling!'

'What?' Gina was confused. Sandra's head had swivelled towards the door. It was ajar.

'I thought I heard something – no, my mistake. Now where were we?'

But before she could continue, the door was pushed open and her husband entered; he was smiling.

'There you are, girls,' he said. 'Do you know, after Sam went back to his study, Natalie and I had such an interesting time talking about a house she went to that looks like a castle in a story book.'

'D-did you?'

'Gina, you look pale,' he said. 'Would you like to

go and rest until dinner time? I could go and tell Agnes – I'm sure she'd be happy to keep Natalie with her for a while. She seems genuinely fond of her.'

'Yes, she is . . . I think I might . . .' She allowed her father to put his arm around her and lead her gently towards the door.

'Well, we'll see you at dinner then, shall we?' Sandra called after her. 'I suppose Mr Redmond will be dining with us again? He's such an interesting man – I do enjoy talking to him.'

At the bottom of the stairs her father leaned across and kissed her brow. 'I'll get Agnes to bring you up a glass of warm milk or something – no – I'll bring it myself.'

Gina could only nod. She knew that she would have to summon up enough strength to decide what she was going to do and she wanted to be alone.

By the time her father brought the milk she had taken off her top layer of clothes and slipped into bed.

'Now you're not to worry about Natalie,' he said as he placed the milk on the bedside table. 'Agnes is going to take the child across to the cottage to sleep tonight –'

'Oh, but, no –'

'Oh, but, yes! Natalie is very keen to sleep in the cottage with Rebel – well not literally in the dog basket, of course! And Jock will baby-sit when Agnes comes back to see to the dinner. Now, I'll go and leave you to rest – and Gina?'

'Yes, daddy?'

'Don't worry.'

When he had gone Gina turned her face into her pillow and sobbed great, dry sobs that left her eyes burning with unshed tears and her throat aching. She lay for a long while wondering how on earth she was going to face everybody at dinner . . .

Sandra, with her dirty little schemes of blackmail; how far would she go? Would she start dropping overt hints over the dinner table?

Sam, who would probably be only too pleased to learn anything bad about her that Sandra could tell him . . .

And her father, who was trying so hard to make up for the years of neglect but couldn't have any idea how bad things might become for her.

CHAPTER 20

'Come upstairs, I want to speak to you.'

Sandra looked up in surprise as Henry walked in.
He sounded – different. His voice was level but there
was an undertone of – what? She felt a twinge of
unease.

She'd been sitting here in the morning-room ever
since he'd felt it was his duty to run around after Gina
– fussing about getting hot milk as if she were a child.
Let him get on with it, Sandra had thought, it keeps
him out of my way for a while.

She'd rung the bell for the housekeeper and got her
to bring a tray of tea and dainty, little sandwiches.
While she enjoyed them, she slipped off her shoes
and curled up on the sofa, dreaming of Miguel and
what they would do when she had some money of her
own.

But now, her exciting little fantasy vanished
abruptly. There was no denying it, underneath his
customary veneer of good manners, Henry looked
grim.

'What is it?' she asked uneasily.

'Come to our room and I'll tell you.'

'Oh dear, is Gina ill? Is that it?'

She didn't for one moment think that was the answer and her heart and her hopes began to plummet. The stupid girl has told her father about our conversation, she thought. But, then she realized that even if she had, it didn't really spoil things.

It might make things more difficult – Henry knowing what she was up to until she and Miguel were established could be awkward – but it didn't alter the fact that the custody of the child was the issue here. Gina still wouldn't want Sam to know about her past.

She decided to tough it out; to act ignorant for as long as she could. 'Why can't we sit here, Henry, darling? This is such a pleasant room – and I can ring for Mrs Robson and get her to bring you a tray. What would you like?'

'I would like you to come to our room – now. I want to talk to you and I don't want to run the risk of anyone overhearing our conversation.'

He opened the door wider and held it for her as he spoke. Sandra felt the muscles of her stomach knot together – Gina hadn't told her father about her threat to blackmail her – she hadn't needed to!

She remembered the moment earlier when she had been talking to Gina and she had suddenly heard a noise behind them. She had looked round, seen nothing, and then a moment later, Henry had entered smiling. At the time, she'd thought that what she'd heard must have been Henry crossing the hall.

Now she knew that she'd been wrong – he must have been standing outside the door and listening – goodness knows for how long. And it was her own fault. She, herself, had left the door ajar when she had sneaked in on Gina. Now, as she took in his expression of disgust her face drained of colour.

'Yes, I heard how you threatened my daughter,' he said.

'So?' She tilted her chin and stared at him. 'What are you going to do about it?'

'I'm going to stop you.'

She was so unaccustomed to Henry being masterful that she made the mistake of laughing at him. His eyes widened with pain, but only for an instant. The next moment he came striding across the room towards her. She cowered back against the cushions of the sofa.

'Don't worry, Sandra. I'm not going to hurt you; I've never struck a woman in my life. But if you don't come upstairs immediately, I shall make sure that everybody in this house can hear what I've got to say to you. And I promise you that you won't like that one little bit.'

She believed him. There was no way of knowing exactly what he meant, but the glint in his eyes was dangerous. She watched him warily, as she reached down on to the floor and felt around until she found her shoes.

Without bothering to put them on, she rose unsteadily and, clutching her shoes to her body, she made an inelegant scramble for the door. As she

hurried up the stairs she was aware of Henry following her purposefully.

When he closed the bedroom door after himself
she moaned with fright. But he simply picked up
their suitcases and travelling bag and tossed them on
to the bed.

'Start packing.'

'What?'

'I said start packing. We're leaving, now.'

'But what about dinner? We're supposed to be
having dinner with Mr Redmond and G-Gina . . .'

As soon as she'd said Gina's name, she regretted it,
but Henry merely flashed her a warning glance. 'I've
already told Sam that we have to leave earlier than we
planned –'

'But that's not true! We don't have to go – I *won't*
go!'

Henry carried on as if she hadn't spoken, 'And I've
left a letter for Gina telling her not to worry – that –
that no harm will come to her if I can help it.'

Sandra began to rally. She was mad with herself
for reacting the way she had. She'd allowed herself to
be frightened just because Henry had acted so much
out of character. He'd ordered her upstairs and she'd
obeyed him meekly, because his words had implied
some kind of threat.

But what could he do to her? It was unfortunate
that he'd heard her conversation with Gina, but he
had, so the damage was done. Now, more than ever,
she would have to get away from him.

'Look, Henry, you can go if you like, but I'm

staying until I've finished my – finished my business here.'

For an answer Henry opened the wardrobe and the chest of drawers and began tossing things into the cases.

'Stop that! You're spoiling my clothes!'

Sandra made a frantic grab for a silk blouse he was holding and was mortified when she heard the seams rip. 'Now look what you've done!' she yelled.

'Keep your voice down.' He threw the blouse into the case and faced her across the jumble of belongings on the bed. He said quite calmly, 'Do you remember how we met, Sandra?'

She stared at him in astonishment. Had he taken leave of his senses?

'Well, do you?' he demanded.

'Yes . . . it was at the airport . . . Manchester Airport. There was a crowd of young ruffians . . . you helped me get my luggage.' That's it, he's flipped, she decided. Packing the cases has brought it back and it's all too much for him.

But Henry went on patiently, 'But do you remember why you were there?'

'Of course. I'd just been on a shoot – Milan – a fashion collection.'

'No, not Milan, the young football supporters had been to Milan. You had just returned from North Africa, you'd been working in Tangier.'

'Oh yes, Tangier, but what does it matter?'

'It matters a lot, because it wasn't a fashion shoot at all, was it, Sandra?'

263

'I – yes – I don't know what you're getting at . . .'

'Do you remember that I took you to dinner at my hotel that night?'

'Of course, I do – and I remember a lot more!'

Henry sighed. 'Yes, I took you to bed. But before that, we talked and laughed and I thought you were very beautiful and utterly charming . . .'

'So?' Sandra was uneasy. 'Where is this little trip down memory lane leading us?'

Henry smiled wearily. 'It's leading us to the point where you showed me your portfolio – all your beautiful photographs. I was so impressed. But I was also a little puzzled. You'd been careful to add dates and places but there were no recent photographs.'

'I told you why.' Sandra sensed what was coming and her voice dropped to a whisper. 'I told you – jobs are shot months in advance and . . .'

'And photographers let you down about sending on prints. Yes, I know that's true, but you weren't such a good liar then, Sandra, and I sensed that you were – equivocating.'

'No . . . no . . . I wasn't . . .'

'Much as I loved you, I made it my business to find out what it was that you were hiding.'

Sandra sank down on to the bed and began to shake her head. 'So you knew . . . all this time you knew . . .'

'Yes, my dear, I knew. I discovered that for some time the only kind of job you could get was posing for pornographic magazines – there was even a movie. In fact that was why you had been to Tangier.'

264

'So why did you marry me?'

'Because I loved you.'

'How could you – if you knew all this – how could you?'

'I don't know. But the sad truth is that I did – and I still do.'

'What?' She looked up at him incredulously.

'So, you are not going to blackmail my daughter and you are not going to leave me. If you do either of those things, your glamorous friends such as Barbara Samuels and, more importantly, Miguel –'

'Miguel, wha –?'

'Oh, yes I know about your tender feelings for the little hairdresser – your girlfriends are not as discreet as they should be. But, as I was saying, Barbara and Miguel would suddenly find some very interesting photographs in their morning mail.'

'You've got photographs? No, that's impossible!'

'Why should it be impossible? The magazines were on sale in the usual outlets – so was the video film. Your agent thought I was a prospective client – she was only too pleased to tell me where I could buy them.'

'All right, I can understand why you wanted to find out the truth about me,' she said sullenly, 'but I can't understand why you would keep the evidence all these years.'

'Perhaps, somehow, I knew from the start that I would need to. And, by the way, Sandra, the "evidence" as you call it, is with my solicitor. If you outlive me, as you probably will seeing you're so much younger than I am, he'll hang on to it to ensure your good behaviour.

'And, furthermore, if anything should happen to me unexpectedly, he knows what to do.'

'I wouldn't – you don't think –' Sandra was genuinely shocked.

'I hope not my dear. But you'd better be good to me.' With a faint smile, he leaned over and kissed her on the brown.

Then he drew himself up and the smile drained away. 'Now be a good girl and pack this lot up properly. We're going to leave here with dignity, while Gina is sleeping. We'll drive to the airport, if we can't get a flight tonight, then there's a perfectly good hotel.'

'I don't understand you, Henry. Why do you want me to come back to Marbella with you?'

'You don't have to understand, Sandra. Just come home, try to pretend that you're happy to be with me and I promise you that life won't be so bad. Oh, but you'll have to change your hairdresser.'

Gina awoke with a sense of dread. The room was flooded with moonlight and the house was silent. Something was wrong. She clicked on the bedside light and looked at the clock.

Midnight!

Dinner would be long over . . .

She leapt out of bed and grabbed her robe then, heart racing, she opened the door and ran to the head of the stairs.

At that point she realized the folly of her actions but the impetus provided by her panic forced her on, down the stairs, across the hall to the door of the dining-room. She wrenched it open.

The room was in darkness.

Gina stumbled forward until she found one of the chairs. She pulled it out and sat down, resting her arms on the table.

What had been said in here earlier?, she wondered. How far would Sandra go when I wasn't here to defend myself?

No . . . she won't have said anything, yet, she wants money from me and she'll be willing to wait a little longer . . .

Gina groaned and, spreading her arms out across the table, palms down, she dropped her face on to the cool, polished surface.

I wish I'd never come here, she thought. I wish I'd stayed in France. Oh, David, I'm trying to keep my promise to you that I should be Natalie's guardian, but neither of us guessed just how difficult it would be.

And what of my promise to Sam? I've agreed to stay here long enough for him get to know his niece – but if I stay and Sandra carries out her threat, Sam might take Natalie and then what would become of my promise to David?

Gina groaned, she was aware that her mind was running around like a rat in a laboratory maze trying to find a solution to her problems.

Suddenly there seemed to be only one way out –

I'll have to leave here, she thought. I'll get up very early before anyone else is awake . . . I can pack everything, put it all in the Range Rover and then go to the cottage and collect Natalie.

I'll go back to France, take Natalie to the only home she's known until now and then, surely it would be more difficult for Sam to take her away from me . . .

CHAPTER 21

South West France

Marco Doyle could think himself into his victim's situation. Get under the unfortunate man or woman's skin – try to live inside their heads and make his own mind work in the same way.

Or, if he had succeeded in panicking them to act irrationally, he would try to actually experience their emotions and imagine where this would lead them – what they would do next.

That was why he was so successful. Newspaper editors never questioned the fact that his would be the best available pictures of people in the news. They would take anything he offered them, often without asking to look at the shots before buying them.

If any of them could have seen him now, they might have wondered why one of the world's most successful paparazzi was staying on in a small town on the French side of the Pyrenees when every other reporter and photographer had moved on to the next story.

Marco Doyle was used to hunting much bigger game than a nanny on the make . . .

It was early morning and, as usual, he was the first person to order breakfast at the Hotel Lion d'Or. The sun was already warm but *la terrace* was still in shadow under the striped awning; Marco had chosen a table well to the back.

Before leaving his room, he had examined the shots he had taken the day before – the good-looking young Spaniard, Juan Sanchez, in the pool at the villa, Juan Sanchez sunbathing in the grounds, Madame Bernat hanging out yet more washing on the line strung between the trees in the orchard, her son, Gerard working in the grounds in a desultory manner.

He also had shot after shot of seemingly empty rooms, half-glimpsed through open windows; but neither Gina nor the child appeared in any one of them.

So-o, are they there but keeping out of sight, he mused, or did Juan take them somewhere and then come back to show himself and put anyone who might still be interested off the scent?

Marco poured himself a second cup of coffee and grinned. That's what I would do, if I were in that situation. But if that's the case, where are they? At the Bernats' farm? It might be worth nosing around up there.

Whatever the plan was, it was obvious that the Bernat family was heavily involved. Why? Was Gina buying their loyalty? She could certainly afford to. Or do they actually like her? he wondered, and frowned. It wouldn't suit his purposes at all if he discovered that people liked the girl . . . people who might speak up for her.

Suddenly Marco eased his chair back further into the shadows. He had spotted the farm pick-up truck turning into the square and it looked as if the entire Bernat family was inside: Gerard, his mother Florence, and his wife Céline.

A couple of tourists took their places at a nearby table and Marco dropped his napkin to the ground as if by accident. As he bent to retrieve it he kept his face close to the table and his eyes on Gerard's truck. It rolled past and drew to a stop outside the supermarket as on previous days.

So, another ostentatious shopping trip to make believe that the villa is fully occupied, he thought. But there's always the chance that Florence is stocking up because Gina and the child are coming home – they could be – especially if they believe that the coast is clear.

Wherever she's hiding out, Gina must surely be waiting for Juan to tell her that it's safe to return – that will be it – so from now on, I'd better keep a very low profile.

Northumberland

Sandra waited miserably in the concourse at Newcastle International Airport while her husband endeavoured to book them a flight to Marbella.

They had no luck the evening before and had spent probably the most miserable night of their married life in the airport hotel. However, the hotel had at least been comfortable and, this morning, Sandra would have preferred to have waited for Henry there. But he wasn't prepared to let her out of his sight.

After a snatched breakfast, with the young waitresses still half-asleep and bleary-eyed, they had arrived at the airport as soon as the airline desks opened for business. Now, it seemed that Henry was prepared to try every airline and wait in queues all day, if necessary, until he got what he wanted.

Every so often he would appear at her side, as if checking up on her. Not that she could go anywhere – he had made sure that he had the passports, the credit cards and all the spare cash.

Normally, Sandra would have been interested in observing the crush of people, speculating about their lives and where they might be going. But, this morning, she was too damn miserable to care.

She just couldn't believe that her plans had come to an end so abruptly and in such a humiliating way. Who would have thought that Henry could be so devious? She had misjudged him badly all these years.

After his shocking revelations she'd had no option but to pack up meekly and leave Northmoor Hall. That stuck-up little brat Gina would be left with all that money and, by the looks of it, a choice between her Spanish boyfriend and the intriguingly attractive Sam Redmond.

Sandra hadn't missed the way that Sam had looked at Gina so hungrily, even if the stupid girl herself had been totally unaware of the effect she seemed to have on him.

He wouldn't think she was so wonderful if he knew why she lost her first nannying job, Sandra thought viciously. And how I would have loved to have been the one to break the news.

She glanced up and saw Henry walking towards her, smiling broadly. He was holding up a couple of tickets. She sighed.

They would be home before the day was ended and it seemed that Henry was determined to act as if nothing out of the way had happened. Sandra dredged up the ghost of a smile and started walking towards him.

She would just have to make the best of it.

Gina opened her eyes. Unlike the morning before, when the storm had been raging, the sun was shining. The curtains were open. Why?

And what am I wearing? she wondered. My robe over my underclothes . . .? She frowned as she tried to sort things out in her mind.

She pushed herself up from the warm cocoon of her bedclothes, blinking in the slanting light. The other bed was empty – not just empty, it was neatly made. Where was Natalie?

And then she remembered that her father had told her Natalie was going to spend the night in the Robsons' cottage. She also remembered that the

273

curtains were open because she had never closed them the night before. She had come upstairs in the late afternoon, intending to rest until dinnertime, but instead, she had slept until midnight.

Midnight!

Oh, no, I decided to leave here . . . I was going to get up early and go before Sandra could do any damage!

She looked at her travel clock. Nearly eleven o'clock! Gina groaned and rested her head in her hands, cursing herself for not even having had enough sense to set the alarm. But no wonder I forgot to do it, she thought – I was so panicky and confused and too miserable to even think straight.

When I came back up to bed I must have just crawled under the bedclothes, dressed as I was, too weary to care.

She sighed and got out of bed. She would shower and go down to find Natalie. It was too late to make her escape from the house when everyone would be up and about. So, sooner or later, she would have to face Sandra and her demands for 'hush' money. But she still didn't know what she was going to do about it.

Then she noticed the white envelope lying flat on the bedside table next to the clock. She picked it up and saw her own name, 'Gina', in her father's handwriting. She sat down on the edge of the bed again, and frowned as she opened it. Why would her father write to her?

My Dear Gina,
You're sleeping now and perhaps that is just as
well because this is easier for me to write in a
letter. I'm sorry we won't see you at dinner,
tonight, but I have decided that it is better if we
go back to Spain, immediately.

Gina stared at her father's words hardly daring to
believe that what she saw was true. She was not the
only one to have missed dinner last night. Her father
had decided to go back to Spain.

Inconsequentially, an image sprang to mind of
Sam sitting in solitary splendour in the dining-
room. She blinked to banish the disturbing picture
and continued to read.

I'm so pleased that we were able to talk alone
together, at last, and I want you to know that I
have always believed in you and that, whatever
happens in the future, I am on your side. In fact,
I always have been and I am ashamed that I did
not support you more robustly in the past.
But, at least I am able to do this for you,
now. You see, I overheard Sandra's attempts
at blackmail and I am in a position to do
something about it. You can rest assured that
she will not carry out her threats.

The sense of relief was overwhelming. She had no
idea how her father was going to achieve this miracle
but, somehow, she had the utmost faith in him.

She scanned the rest of the letter. There was not much more, her father simply assured her of his love and expressed the hope that it would not be too long before they met again.

I'll go to him, she thought. As soon as my life is sorted out, I'll go and try to establish some kind of rapport, build some kind of relationship. I'm older and wiser now, not just a grief-stricken teenager, I can accept that he loves Sandra but I won't let her come between us, ever again.

The needle-sharp water of the shower shocked her into life and she dressed for comfort in jeans and a long, loose sweater.

Agnes was alone in the kitchen. 'Where's Natalie?' Gina asked.

'Out with Jock and the dog, don't worry.' She was placing food from various dishes into foil freezer containers. She smiled, ruefully. 'Last night's dinner.'

'Oh, Agnes, I'm sorry.'

'There's no need to be. The freezer is a marvellous invention. But your parents missed a grand meal, I can tell you.'

'And so did I.'

'You needed the sleep, obviously. Sometimes your body just takes over and forces you to take the rest you need.'

Or your mind takes charge, Gina thought. I wonder if my sleeping like that was simply an escape route from my problems? And while I was asleep my father solved at least one of those problems for me.

'Why so pensive?' Agnes asked – and didn't wait for an answer. 'Sit down, lass, and I'll make you some breakfast.'

'Oh, no, I'm not hungry.'

'You'll take tea and toast then?' It was more of an order than a question and Gina sat down obediently.

Agnes sliced bread for the toaster and poured boiling water over the tea in the pot. 'Mr Redmond didn't eat much dinner last night,' she said. 'It's funny, he's used to eating alone – but last night he looked like a lost soul.'

Gina tested out the image. Sam Redmond, lost soul. Strangely, it matched the picture that had come to mind earlier of Sam, dressed in black, and sitting alone at the head of the mahogany dining-table, brooding darkly. Like a character in a classic, romantic novel, she mused.

But which one? Heathcliff? No, Sam could never be deliberately cruel to anyone. Mr Rochester? Sam would never lock a poor, mad wife away in an attic! Mr Darcy, then? Gina giggled weakly. Fitzwilliam Darcy, handsome and proud, had had all his character defects sorted out when he fell in love with a right-thinking young woman. Yes, Darcy would do . . .

'What's funny?' Agnes was smiling at her as she placed toast, butter and marmalade on the table. She poured them both a cup of tea.

Gina looked at her speculatively. 'I was just thinking, could you see Sam as Mr Darcy?'

Agnes raised her eyebrows but she sat down and gave the question serious consideration. 'Mmm, perhaps I could. He's the right type. Tall and dark and handsome. But as you know, I prefer a different-looking kind of hero –'

'I know, Arnold Schwarzenegger. We all have our dreams, Agnes, we all have our dreams.'

When Natalie came back, she wanted to tell Gina all about sleeping in the cottage and her walk with Rebel.

'Why don't you two go upstairs to the old play-room?' Agnes said.

'Playroom?'

'Yes. Generations of Shaw children used to play there and, do you know, there are still some of Master David's books and toys in the cupboard. And there are some drawing books and crayons.'

'I'd like to go to that room,' Natalie said, imme-diately. 'But can Rebel come with us?'

'Of course,' Agnes said. But she saw that Gina was uncertain. 'Go on, it's nice and cosy and I've given it a good clean.'

'No, it's not that – it's just that I may have a phone call . . . Juan – my friend, Juan Sanchez, he may phone and tell me what's happening at the Villa Des Pines . . .'

Gina stumbled over her words. She was aware of Agnes's appraising glance and she was annoyed with herself for being embarrassed. But Agnes seemed to understand.

'You'll want to know if the press have gone – that's natural. But if they have, does that mean you'll be leaving us?'

Agnes sounded sad but Gina couldn't lie to her. 'It might.'

The housekeeper sighed. 'Well, I suppose the child will want to get back to her own home – that's understandable. Now get along to the playroom – if there's a phone call for you I'll come and get you straight away.'

Gina hesitated. 'What is it?' Agnes asked.

'The phone . . . will you be answering it? I mean . . .'

'Mr Redmond has unplugged the phone in the study. He doesn't like being interrupted when he's working. Is that what you wanted to hear?'

'Yes, Agnes. Thanks for understanding.'

'I've told you before – I've raised three daughters – and if you ever want to talk about –'

'OK, Agnes.' Gina grinned and, taking Natalie's hand, she set off to find the playroom.

As they crossed the hall Gina glanced towards the study door. Sam was in there, getting on with his novel and, no doubt, oblivious to anything happening in his immediate vicinity.

Gina envied Sam his dedication – and, once more, she couldn't help feeling guilty. Had her coming here made it more difficult for Sam to concentrate on his writing?

And then she smiled at the very idea of it. She had

no doubt that Sam had very clear goals in life, and that he wouldn't allow anything or anyone to get in his way.

Sam emerged from his study eventually, but it wasn't until Natalie was having her supper at the kitchen table. He sat and chatted to her while Gina watched surreptitiously from the old armchair by the Aga.

Natalie and Sam are like old friends, she thought. He's not used to children and yet he doesn't condescend or patronize as some adults might. In fact they're talking to one another like equals. She also couldn't help noticing that everybody else in the room was excluded.

Agnes and Jock, at the other end of the table, talked quietly to each other over his seed catalogue, and even Rebel had deserted his new friend and had come to stretch out in front of the Aga. The scene was so deceptively peaceful – so domesticated – that no stranger observing them could possibly have guessed at the undercurrents of emotion – and fear.

The fear was Gina's, of course, and it was centred on Natalie. It wouldn't matter if I didn't love her so much, she thought. But the very idea of losing her is too much to bear.

She remembered how incredulous she had been when David had eventually told her the truth about the night that Nadine had died. I suppose I can understand any woman who is so unhappy that she has to leave her husband, Gina mused. But I'll never understand how she could have run off and left her baby daughter.

Unexpectedly, tears came to her eyes and she blinked and then closed them. The old armchair was comfortable and, for a while, she simply rested her head back against the cushions and decided to suspend all worries. She gave herself up to the warmth radiating out from the stove.

The voices receded into the background and she allowed herself to drift into that half-awake, unfocused state that is neither sleeping nor waking. It was so peaceful here . . .

'Tired, Gina?'

'Mmm? No, not now, I feel deliciously rested.' She stretched luxuriously as she opened her eyes. She had answered without thinking and now, she looked up to see that Sam was standing over her. He was smiling.

'That's good. I was afraid I would have to postpone my plans for tonight.'

She frowned. 'You'd better explain.'

'I want – I'd like to take you out to dinner.'

'Oh, but no, there's Natalie.'

'Agnes is baby-sitting.'

'But –' Gina sat up straight and looked round wildly. The others had gone, she realized, even Rebel. She was alone with Sam. She thought she had closed her eyes just for a moment, but she must have fallen asleep.

'We didn't like to disturb you,' Sam explained when he saw her puzzled expression. 'The Robsons have taken Natalie to the cottage again. Don't worry – we didn't have to force her to go!'

'No, I'm sure you didn't,' Gina smiled. 'But why do we have to go out? If it's Agnes's night off, I can make us something here.'

Sam hunkered down beside her. 'Gina,' he said, 'it isn't Agnes's night off, I don't want you to make us something here, I simply want to take you out to dinner.'

'But why?'

'For goodness' sake, woman,' a look of amused exasperation crossed his face, 'stop asking questions.' He reached for her hand and, without realizing it, he had found the most effective way of silencing her.

She tried not to look at her hand resting in his and, to her utter confusion, found herself looking into his eyes instead.

Annoyingly, all her thought processes began to scramble. 'But, Sam . . . we . . . I can't . . .' she managed.

He smiled, patiently. 'What can't you do?'

Suddenly Gina understood what was meant by drowning in someone's eyes. Sam's eyes, so dark, so deep, so unfathomable – she forced herself to close her own while she remembered what it was that she couldn't do.

'I can't go out with you,' she said, and hurried on in case he should misunderstand. 'I mean we can't go anywhere where I might be seen – might be recognized –'

'I know.'

'You know? Then why? How . . . ?'

'Don't worry. You have my word that you'll be safe from the media. Trust me?'

And for some reason she did. She found herself nodding, silently.

'Good. Now why don't you go upstairs –'

'Upstairs?' She hated herself for the way her voice became a comical squeak. Her heart began to pound.

'Yes. Do your face, do your hair, do whatever you have to do, and then put that lovely red dress on. I've booked a table, the car's waiting and I'm taking you out to dinner.'

CHAPTER 22

The country road was shadowed and mysterious where it passed under the trees. Twilight makes driving more difficult, distorts perspective; Sam concentrated on the way ahead. Gina cast a covert glance at his strong profile.

It was strange to be in such an everyday and yet, at the same time, intimate environment with him. She had never been in a car with Sam before. For the few short weeks that they had known each other in South West France, they had walked everywhere.

Whenever they'd had the chance to be alone, usually after Natalie was asleep at night, they had simply strolled in the grounds of the villa, in the orchard, or down the winding mountain road to the tiny village.

There, they would sit at one of the tables outside the little café in the cobbled square, sip a glass of the local wine and talk about nothing in particular. Sometimes they would simply sit in silence, holding hands and smiling foolishly, enjoying the new-found feeling of warmth and love.

But they had never had very long. Gina had not liked to impose upon Florence Bernat, although the housekeeper had been only too willing to stay late and take charge of the beloved baby.

Also, David had grown strangely silent; his usual easy-going kindliness uncomfortably absent once he noticed the swiftly developing relationship between his brother-in-law and his child's nanny.

Gina thought it was because he was worried that he was going to lose her, and what that would mean to Natalie. She had to admit that she'd been worried herself – already beginning to wonder what she would do if Sam had asked her to go with him when he left.

But, when it came to it, her feelings and her loyalty had never been put to the test. Sam had simply gone without even telling her.

She looked at his hands gripping the steering wheel. Is he remembering too, she wondered, or is he going over in his mind what he's going to say to me? Perhaps what he wants to say is so serious that he feels he has to wine me and dine me first, from a sense of compassion. The condemned woman enjoyed a last meal of . . .

They had left the road to the village about a mile back and now they were climbing up through a wooded area. Every now and then, Gina glimpsed a stretch of water down through the trees. It looked like the lake – was it the same one that she had visited with Sam or another?

She realized that she knew very little about the

countryside outside the immediate grounds of Northmoor Hall.

'Sam, where on earth are we going?' she asked at last. 'I imagined we were going to a quiet little restaurant and yet we seem to be driving out into the country.'

He glanced at her briefly and smiled. 'Worried, Gina?'

'Why should I be?'

'I could be taking you deep into the forest, or up on to the moors to have my wicked way with you and then abandon you for ever.'

'No, you wouldn't do that.'

Suddenly, he stopped the car and switched off the engine. 'Wouldn't do what? Have my wicked way with you, or abandon you on the moors?'

'Neither, I hope!'

'Oh, I don't know . . .' he turned and smiled at her as he unloosened his seat belt.

Instinctively, she fumbled to unloosen her own and, at the same time, she shrank back against the passenger door. 'Why – er, why have we stopped?'

'Because we've arrived. And I agree, I would never harm you, Gina. I'm only going to lock you up in a tower!'

As he spoke, he got out of the car and came round to open her door. She allowed him to help her out and she looked up in bewilderment. They had drawn up outside a tall building with a castellated top silhouetted against the darkening sky.

The light was poor but Gina could make out that

parts of the building were covered in ivy and that there were lights here and there, twinkling behind tall, mullioned windows.

'What is this place?' she asked. 'It – it looks like a castle, but, perhaps not quite . . .'

'You're right, it's not quite a castle; it's a pele tower,' Sam explained. 'In the days of the Border Reivers, many a local chieftain built himself a primitive stone tower for his family and friends – and his cattle, too.

'When the Scots came raiding over the border everybody retreated into the tower until the danger was over.'

'But this is more than just a primitive tower . . .'

By now Gina had taken in the two-storied addition at one side and the graceful sweep of the drive where one or two other cars were parked.

'Right again. As some of the families prospered – probably from their own cattle raids into Scotland – they added more gracious dwellings to the original tower. Perhaps the lady of the house got sick of having to share her quarters with the livestock!'

'So, why have you brought me here?' But Gina thought she knew and she was dreading the answer. She had remembered who lived in a tower. Sally Maxwell who, according to Natalie's innocent eyes, seemed to be on very good terms – on kissing terms – with Sam.

Did he want her to meet Sally? Want them all to have dinner together so that he could demonstrate to Gina what an ideal couple Sally and he would be?

And how they would be capable of looking after Natalie?

'I'd love to lock you up in a tower, of course,' Sam said and he laughed softly. 'So long as I was the only one to have a key! But, I'm afraid I've only brought you here to enjoy a very good meal.'

Great, Gina thought. So Sally's a wonderful cook as well as being good-looking and charming – and probably very rich. Although she had to admit that Sam wasn't the type to be impressed by mere money.

She felt like getting back into the car, but Sam had already locked it and had taken her elbow to steer her towards the entrance. She tried to pull away but he held on.

'Careful,' he warned. 'This gravel is a hazard if you're wearing high heels. I've told Sally that she'll probably have to have a new drive laid.'

'So that none of your high-society, lady guests will break an ankle – or worse?' Gina quipped.

'*My* guests?' Sam sounded puzzled.

'Yours and Sally's then?'

'Oh, I just give friendly advice. I have nothing to do with the running of The Tower, no financial interest.'

Gina tried to digest this piece of information but it was too complex. What on earth did he mean by, 'running of the place' or 'financial interest'?

But, by then, they had climbed a shallow flight of wide, stone steps and paused outside a massive oak door. Sam pushed it open, and as they stepped into the light and warmth, it all became clear – or almost.

She looked round at the portraits and the fearsome, old weaponry hung on the walls, the suit of armour standing guard at the turn in the oak staircase. And then at the huge vases of fresh flowers – flowers that had been exquisitely, and probably professionally, arranged.

Most of all she looked at the discreet reception desk in one corner of the panelled hall, where another newly arrived couple were talking to a smartly dressed young woman.

'Sam, please explain – is this Sally's home, or is it a hotel?'

'Both – or nearly both. It's Sally's family home and it's a high-class restaurant – although there are a few bedrooms for guests who have travelled some distance and who don't want to spoil the occasion by restricting their intake of fine wines.'

Gina's gaze returned to the couple by the desk. The woman was fashionably dressed – they both were – and the man, tall and attractively craggy, was vaguely familiar.

'Recognize him?' Sam whispered.

'Should I?'

'What kind of music do you like?'

'Oh! It's – it's . . .' Gina's eyes widened as she looked at Sam for confirmation.

'You've got it. A genuine rock millionaire. One of the many North Country boys made good in the music business and who now has a magnificient mansion in the Scottish Borders – as well as a few other luxury homes dotted around the world.'

Gina couldn't stop herself from watching as the couple were led through a curtained archway, presumably into the dining-room. She knew she was behaving like a star-struck fan; she heard Sam chuckle softly. 'Gina, look at me.'

'Mmm?'

When he had her attention, he murmured, 'The trick is to either pretend that you haven't recognized him or that bumping into him is an everyday occurrence.

'And don't be surprised at who else you might see here tonight. There are a couple of famous actors living within driving distance and a well-known television personality – not to mention a multi-millionaire business entrepreneur and an oil magnate.

'The Tower is a very exclusive watering place – and famed for its discretion. If any of the guests ever found themselves in the gossip columns, Sally's reputation – and her business – would be ruined.'

'So that's why you said I'd be safe coming out with you tonight?'

'Partly. But I really don't think anyone would be expecting you to turn up here. There've been no reporters sniffing around the vicinity of Northmoor Hall – I think you've got away with it.'

For a moment Gina thought she saw a flash of the old hostility in Sam's eyes but he recovered himself quickly. Her own mood hardened.

'Are all the guests who come here famous, then?' Gina's tone was sardonic and Sam grinned.

'No, not necessarily. Just very rich – or a close friend of the proprietor as I am.'

And that brings us back to Sally, Gina thought, and wondered all over again exactly how 'close' Sam's friendship with her was.

Just then, a fresh-faced young woman in a long, green plaid skirt and a white blouse came forward to take Gina's coat. 'Thank you, Amanda,' Sam said. It was obvious that he felt at home.

And he looked at home too, Gina mused. He had dressed formally in a dark grey suit and he looked distinguished, at ease – and so damn handsome!

Then Sally Maxwell appeared to greet them. She was also wearing a long skirt but it was of dark green velvet, her high-collared blouse was white silk with a jabot of fine lace. A silver brooch set with amber stones pinned the lace at her neck and she wore matching earrings.

She looks good in this setting, very romantic, Gina acknowledged grudgingly. Sally was small and somehow ethereal-looking, her magnificent, dark red hair hung long and lustrously around her small, exquisite face. No wonder Natalie had been taken with her, Gina thought, and she fought to swallow the bitter taste of rancour.

Sally welcomed them as though they were cherished guests. 'Gina, how lovely to meet you at last. Sam has told me so much about you.'

'Has he? – Oh, er, I didn't know . . .'

Gina felt herself flushing and she knew that she sounded startled, gauche. But it made her feel very uncomfortable to learn that Sam had talked about her to this beautiful, doll-like woman. Especially as he had told her nothing about Sally Maxwell.

Sally was charming. She adopted a rueful expression and said, 'Oh dear, I can see that Gina is a little taken aback. I suspect that in your usually super-casual fashion you have told her nothing whatsoever about me.'

She laughed and reached up straighten Sam's tie. It didn't need straightening and, in that instant, Gina hated Sam for the way he just stood there like an overgrown schoolboy and allowed the woman to manipulate him.

'Don't look so cross, Gina.' Sally had finished fussing with Sam and turned to smile at her. 'Sam's the original strong, silent male, never gives any more away than he has to. He likes to play things close to his chest. Luckily some women still prefer their men that way.'

I am *not* looking cross, Gina thought, but anyone would forgive me if I were! She was glad when Amanda reappeared and told them that their table was ready.

'Oh well, enjoy your meal,' Sally said. She glided across the hall to greet another couple who had just arrived.

'What was all that about?' Gina muttered to Sam as they followed the young waitress into the dining-room.

He laughed. 'Sally loves to dramatize everything. That's part of her charm.'

Is it indeed, Gina thought viciously. But she held her tongue.

Sam continued, 'I simply came along here to book a table for us. I told Sally that I wanted the meal to be special –' He fell silent because Amanda had stopped and turned towards them, smilingly.

They had reached their table which was in an alcove near a window. The young waitress settled them in their places. 'You don't need a menu, do you, Mr Redmond?'

'That's right. I've already ordered.'

As the girl hurried away, Gina asked, 'When? When did you order?'

'I arranged everything when I came here with Natalie. I told Sally that I wasn't sure when we would be able to come but that I would phone to give good warning. And then, I would trust her to serve us the best she has to offer.'

'You obviously have great faith in her.' Gina knew she sounded waspish.

'Oh, Sally knows what I like – what my tastes are.'

Gina wished she hadn't said anything.

'And Natalie was in on the secret,' Sam added. 'When I brought her here she was very excited. She thought it was a castle from a story book –'

'And no doubt that Sally was a fairy princess.'

Sam could hardly miss the acid tone and he raised his eyebrows and smiled with faint surprise. But he was completely unruffled as he continued, 'So I had to swear Natalie to secrecy. I told her that I wanted to bring you here and that I wanted it to be a lovely surprise.'

So it was as simple as that, Gina thought. Sam plans a night out and he asks Natalie to keep the secret. Well, of course, she accepted that – the Natalie part of it, anyway. But why here? Why did he want to bring her to The Tower, Sally Maxwell's domain?

And why did he want to bring her out to dinner, at all? She couldn't accept that it was simply for the pleasure of her company.

'Gina, if you could see your face . . .'

'Mmm?'

Sam reached over the table and, taking her chin in his long-fingered hand, he turned her face towards the window where she could see her reflection.

'Look – look at that scowl,' he said.

The reflection looked affronted, scowled even more deeply and then, of course, it had to laugh at itself.

'That's better,' Sam said. 'Ah, here comes the wine.'

After that, the meal went smoothly enough. To Gina's surprise, the food was not pretentious. They started with baked field mushrooms and then went on to chicken pie and buttered vegetable marrow with a selection of fresh vegetables.

Sam kept her wineglass topped up as they made their way through the different courses, but he stopped drinking after one glass and had only mineral water.

'Oh, I'm sorry, Sam,' Gina said. 'If I had thought about it, I could have stuck to water and driven us home.'

'There is a way that we could both enjoy this vintage wine, you know?' He looked at her keenly.

'And that is?'

'If we stayed here, tonight.'

'No,' Gina looked down at her plate. 'No, I don't think so.'

'Very well, but if you change your mind . . .'

Gina made no response and, for a while, she concentrated on her meal. Every now and then she glanced surreptitiously at the other diners. Some of their meals looked much more sophisticated than Sam's and hers, so she decided that Sally was indeed a very skilful hostess. She had obviously seen to it that Sam got the kind of meal that he would enjoy.

To finish with Sam indulged himself with the cheese board – he explained that some of the cheeses were produced locally – and Gina couldn't resist a mound of fresh, juicy blackberries topped with a sinful amount of cream.

By the time they were sipping their coffee, Gina felt contented and relaxed enough to talk casually about music, books, and their mutual interest in travelling to far-away places.

'Sometimes when I'm on an assignment abroad,' Sam told her, 'I promise myself that I'll return when the crisis is over – when there'll be more time to explore, meet the people, study the culture.'

'It must be frustrating to have to leave, sometimes, just when you're getting interested on a personal level,' Gina sympathized.

'It's my job to tell people what's happening. But I've promised myself that life won't always be so hectic. Or so lonely . . .'

Gina caught her breath. What did he mean? Was he just about to warn her that he was planning a future with Sally? Is that why he'd brought her here? Was her prediction about to come true?

'Gina –'

'Yes?'

She was so convinced that Sam was about to tell her that he planned to marry Sally, that she was completely thrown by what he actually did say.

'I did leave you a letter, you know.'

CHAPTER 23

'Do you believe me?'

Gina knew that he was referring to the time that he had left her – to report back to duty as she now knew. She remembered how puzzled and hurt she had been. How the ensuing days had merged into a haze of misery; only her love for Natalie and David's steadfast friendship had made her life bearable.

David . . . she had been so grateful to him. His kindness, his steadfastness, his generosity and his support. She knew now that he must have been already clearing the way for his proposal of marriage . . .

But, of course, he had needed her even more than she needed him . . . and it seemed that he had been prepared to play dirty.

Sam was staring at her over the table, waiting for her answer. 'I believe you,' she told him, 'but do you believe me when I tell you that I never received your letter?'

'Yes, Gina, I think I do.'

'Sam . . . this is difficult, but I've guessed what happened –'

'So have I. I got the phone call from my producer very late one night. David and I had been sitting on the terrace talking about – about times gone by.

'Anyway, I had to go. Everything was arranged, my plane tickets were waiting at the airport; I was booked on the first flight out in the morning. I had to pack and leave immediately.'

'Why didn't you awaken me? Why didn't you tell me?'

'I couldn't have borne that. To see you – to hold you – and then to have to leave you. I wrote you a letter instead. That was one of the worst decisions of my life.'

'Sam . . . what did the letter say?'

'Can't you guess? I told you how much I loved you. How I wanted you to wait for me. How I hoped that, before very long, we would have a life together. I gave you the name of a contact at the television studios who would forward letters to me. Of course none ever came.'

'You gave the letter to David, didn't you?'

'Yes, I trusted him. But now I realize that he must have already been in love with you.'

'No, it wasn't quite –'

'But it's obvious, isn't it? Take your pick of the old sayings, "Love is lawless" . . . "Love and war are all one" . . . "All's fair in love and war" . . . It's been the same since time began.

'David was my friend, but more than that, he was a

man like any other man. He was jealous so he must have destroyed the letter.'

Gina knew that she had flushed; she turned her head away. Sam hadn't quite got it right, but she didn't think that she would ever be able to tell him the truth. It would shock him. And not just that . . . there was more, so much more . . .'

She found herself gazing out into the night. The Tower was high on the hillside and she could see out across the valley. The moon had risen, leaving a silver trail across the lake. Beyond the water she saw moving lights which must have belonged to cars making their way along a distant road.

'Gina?' Sam reached for her hand across the table and, reluctantly, she turned back to face him. 'At the time I thought that you had decided that you didn't love me.'

'Sam . . . oh, Sam . . .' Gina felt a lump of misery in her throat. Scalding tears pricked at the back of her eyes.

'My pride was hurt, I suppose, but I wasn't man enough to come and try to – try to convince you that we were right for each other.'

'If only you had!'

'It seems David knew me only too well – there was another time in my life when I gave in too easily . . . he remembered that.'

'When – when was that?' But she thought that she knew.

'Oh, a long time ago, when we were all at college together.'

299

'I see.'

Gina looked down at her hand lying in his. She remembered what Sam had told her about his first love, and how Marco Doyle had stolen her away from him. She wondered if there were still moments when he regretted that long-ago lost love.

She heard him sigh and looked up to find him smiling sadly. 'Anyway, eventually I realized that you were more important to me than hurt pride. I decided to come to France and find out for myself.'

'You did? But when – ?'

'I'd left it too late. It was then that I received a letter from David. He told me that you had chosen not to answer my letter –'

'How could he! I can hardly believe that of David!'

'Can't you? Then you obviously don't know what men – even the best of men – will do when they're driven by powerful emotions . . . by love –'

'No! You don't understand!'

'I think it's you who don't understand, Gina. David told me that he planned to ask you to marry him and that he was confident you would accept.'

That's right, Gina thought, David told me that he'd had it all planned for some time. But he never told me that he'd written to Sam – and I never thought that he could have been so deceitful. But then, he probably already knew that he didn't have very long to live, that the hereditary disease had taken hold. His urge to protect Natalie was already overpowering – perhaps he wasn't quite sane . . .

Sam hadn't noticed her distress and he continued, 'So I kept away. I shut my mind to the pair of you – and that's why I didn't even know that David was ill, that he was dying.'

Sam's expression was sombre. Gina knew that there was nothing she could say that would ease his pain.

He sighed and then he continued, 'Did you fall in love with David, Gina? It hurts me to admit it, but if you were never given my letter, if you thought that I had abandoned you, I suppose it's understandable . . .'

'Stop it Sam. Please don't go on!'

She looked at him in distress. What could she tell him? Should she invent some easy lies? Pretend that he had guessed correctly and that she had been grateful to David for being there for her, that gratitude had turned to love?

Well, that was partly true, but she had never loved David, not in the way Sam meant. And she could never lie to Sam – he deserved the truth. But the truth – the whole story – would wound him, wound him deeply.

'Sam, Gina, have you enjoyed your meal?' Sally had come over to their table and she was looking at them curiously.

Self-consciously, Gina withdrew her hand from Sam's and she noticed that he made no attempt to stop her.

After a slight pause, Sam answered, 'Yes, it was marvellous, as usual.'

'Then why the long faces?'

'Oh, Gina's tired, I think we both are. In fact it's time we were leaving.'

'Oh, no! I was hoping that you might stay on a little – come up to my private sitting-room and have another coffee. I haven't had a chance to talk to Gina.'

Sally looked genuinely disappointed but Gina wasn't altogether convinced that it was because she was leaving. More likely she wants another chance to make it clear how close she is to Sam, Gina thought, and hated herself for being so suspicious and mean-minded.

Sam guided her past the other tables into the reception hall. She was glad that she didn't have to speak; Sally and he kept the conversation going and, while they waited for Amanda to bring Gina's coat, they moved aside slightly.

She watched as Sam bent his head down to listen and Sally smiled up at him fondly. Gina suddenly realized that everything Sam had implied about her and David could equally apply to himself and Sally.

She had no idea how long they had known each other but, what if Sally had been there for Sam? There to console him when he had returned from his assignment to find that his best friend was planning to marry the woman he loved . . .

Then later, when he learned that his friend had died . . . and worse, the woman he'd loved was now consoling herself with a handsome young Spanish artist. Had he believed all those stories? Had Sally offered him understanding and sympathy?

To Gina's mind there was no doubt that Sally loved Sam, but did he return that love? Or were his feelings for her based on gratitude and friendship?

They barely talked on the way home. It had begun to rain. At first just gently, but before they were half way there, it was almost as heavy as the night Gina had arrived.

Sam left the gates open. 'Jock will close them in the morning,' he said. 'And now I think I'll just pull up at the front door and leave the car here for the night.'

They ran up the steps together and, as soon as Sam opened the door, Gina could hear the phone ringing.

'Oh, which . . . where . . . ?'

'My study's the nearest.' Sam hurried across, opened the door and picked up the phone before Gina had even crossed the hall. She heard him answering, and by the time she entered the room, he was talking quietly.'

Gina paused in the doorway. She felt uneasy. On hearing the phone her first thought had been that it must be Juan. Something had happened at the villa – perhaps he wanted to tell her it was safe to come home. He would feel awkward that Sam had answered . . .

But Sam went on talking quietly – just one word answers that meant nothing to her. When she looked at Sam's face she realized that it couldn't be Juan. He looked mystified, concerned but not angry. She began to back away. The call couldn't be for her; but when he saw her, Sam held up his other hand, 'Wait, Gina . . . this is for you.'

'Is it . . . is it Juan?'

A spasm of displeasure crossed his face then he said, 'No, it's not Juan.' Then into the phone, 'Yes, she's here now . . . of course. Thank you for telling me . . . of course, whatever you say . . . I had no idea, believe me.'

Sam's part of the conversation seemed to have come to an end and he held the receiver out towards her. Gina walked forward hesitantly. 'Who – ?'

'It's Robert Hargreaves. Apparently he's been waiting for you to get in touch with him. He's only just found out that you're here.'

Mr Hargreaves!

Gina remembered stuffing his letter back into her handbag the morning after she had arrived here. She had completely forgotten that she was supposed to contact him.

'I'll leave you to talk, then,' Sam said and Gina watched as he left the room and closed the door after him.

She couldn't understand why he looked so serious, sounded so subdued. She sank down on to the chair beside the desk.

'Hullo, Mr Hargreaves.'

'Gina, I'm sorry to phone so late – I did call earlier but your Mrs Robson said that you had gone out to dinner. That is after I'd got her to admit that you were there at all!'

Gina heard Mr Hargreaves chuckle and then he went on, 'She was almost as fierce as Madame Bernat – I had the devil of a job convincing Florence that I was who I said I was. She only believed me when I gave details of the marvellous meals she'd cooked last time I was at the Villa Des Pines.'

The smile left his voice, no doubt he was remembering why he had been to the villa – and that it was the last time he had seen David.

'Anyway, when you didn't contact me, and when I realized what a bad time you were having with the press, I realized that it was up to me.'

'I'm so sorry – I should have phoned –'

'You don't have to apologize, Gina. I know what a harrowing time you've had. But there's something you ought to know so, eventually, I phoned the villa. Madame Bernat pretended she couldn't understand English, so I switched to French – that confounded her – so, then she just simply refused to let me speak to you – she was evasive as to your whereabouts.'

Gina laughed. 'I'm sorry if she gave you a hard time.'

'That's what solicitors are for – to do battle on behalf of their clients. The trouble was in persuading her that we were on the same side!'

Gina had begun to relax. Whatever Mr Hargreaves had wanted to talk to her about couldn't be too serious or he wouldn't be taking it so humorously.

'I thought she was just being protective,' he continued. 'I never imagined that you'd actually taken flight – although I should have done – it must have been like being under siege living at the villa. And it never crossed my mind that you would go to

Northmoor Hall.'

'Oh dear,' Gina detected the change in Mr Hargreaves's tone, suddenly he wasn't quite so relaxed as he had been. 'You'd better tell me why that's a problem,' she said. 'It is a problem, isn't it?'

For the next two or three minutes Gina didn't say anything. She allowed Robert Hargreaves to explain what he had discovered about David's will and when he had finished she felt sick with shock.

'Are you still there, Gina?'

'Yes, I'm sorry. And you say that he didn't know about this?'

'No, we wrote to him, of course, but we have only his London address. Apparently he hasn't been there to pick up his mail for some time.'

'Yes . . . that's true . . .'

'You know you might be able to challenge it. After all, David was very ill; you could say that he wasn't in his right mind.'

'I would never do that!'

'No, I didn't think you would. And, after all, it's not so bad, is it? I mean you will still be able to take very good care of Natalie – and that was what David wanted, wasn't it?'

'Yes, that was what David wanted.'

'Gina, now that I know that you're in England, it would simplify things if you called in to the office – or I could come up to Northmoor Hall, I suppose – ?'

'No, you know that wouldn't do.'

'I suppose not. So, when – ?'

306

'Mr Hargreaves. I've got to think things out, but don't worry, I'll contact you soon – I really will this time.'

'All right then, but Gina, whatever you decide, you know I'll do my best for you, don't you?'

'Of course.'

After Gina put the phone down she sat for a moment, gathering her strength, and then she left the room and walked into the hall. Sam was sitting near the old fireplace. He stood up as soon as he saw her.

'Gina –'

'Don't say anything.'

'But, we'll have to talk –'

'Not now.'

She hurried upstairs leaving him standing in the middle of the hall. Her face was grim and she knew he had sensed that she wanted to be left alone.

How could you, David? she fumed as she stormed into her bedroom and slammed the door shut behind her. She became aware that she was shaking and she stood for a moment leaning weakly back against the door, then she stumbled over to her bed and collapsed, weeping with shock.

Why, David, why? Why didn't you tell me that the codicil to your will wasn't just to safeguard Juan's position at the gallery? What on earth was going on in your mind?

Why on earth couldn't you have told me that you suddenly decided to leave Northmoor Hall to Sam Redmond!

CHAPTER 24

Sam watched in consternation as Gina ran upstairs. 'Gina!' he called, but she wouldn't listen, wouldn't wait.

He wanted to take her in his arms – tell her that he was as stunned by the news as she was – tell her that they could sort things out together. He raced after her, calling out, trying to explain, but she wouldn't listen. Perhaps she wasn't even aware that he was following her.

He wasn't quick enough. She slammed the door of her bedroom in his face and he heard the key turn in the lock.

Sam stared at the door in despair. She was past reasoning with. He stood there for a long time, listening to the sounds of her distress and, only when her sobbing had subsided, did he turn away and go to his own room.

He lay awake for hours, wanting to be with her, close – and tormented by the knowledge that they were alone in the house together and yet so far apart.

* * *

It was still dark when he went downstairs the next morning. Dressed in jeans and an old Aran sweater, for comfort, he went to the kitchen and made himself a cup of coffee. Agnes had not yet arrived and he was tempted to linger by the Aga in the quiet warmth.

However, his ingrained habit of self-discipline led him to his study and work. His first task was to go over the text he had written the day before and, soon, he began to lose himself in he world he had created.

When he had finished reading he laid the papers aside on his desk and sighed. He was pleased, no, more than just pleased, he was elated that his novel was going so well, but he was also deeply worried. He was beginning to wonder if he had a major character flaw. How could he continue to write like this when his private life was such an awful mess?

But perhaps the writing was an escape route? Whenever he came into this room he closed the door on the world around him, not just literally, but metaphorically too. When he switched on his computer, he entered another world, a world of imagination which was, nevertheless, fuelled by his own life experience.

There was a soft knock and he was on his feet in an instant. Could it be Gina? Was she ready to talk now? Sam strode across the room and opened the door to find Agnes standing there.

'Would you like your breakfast now, Mr Redmond? I'm sorry I'm a little late, this morning.' The housekeeper looked flustered.

'Late? I hadn't noticed. But anyway, I'm not really hungry.'

'Now then, that isn't good enough. When will I get a chance to clean the hearth and see to the fire if you won't leave the room for five minutes? And anyway, your breakfast is all ready for you.'

Sam surrendered to her determined onslaught and allowed himself to be chivvied along to the kitchen. He tried to do justice to the man-sized plateful of bacon, egg, mushrooms and tomatoes that Agnes put in front of him but, when she went to see to the fire in the study, he found an ally in Rebel.

'Don't say a word,' he told the grateful puppy as he sneaked at least half of his breakfast on to the dog's dish in the corner. 'And for goodness' sake eat that up before Agnes comes back!'

The warning was timely, Agnes was back in no time, but by then, Rebel was lying innocently stretched out on the rug in front of the stove.

'Sit down, Agnes, share this pot of tea with me.'

'Thanks, I will.'

Sam watched as she settled herself at the end of the table and poured herself a cup of tea. He wondered if he ought to broach the subject of the ownership of Northmoor Hall. Jock and Agnes would have to be told that David had left the house to him but he hadn't decided yet what he was going to do about his unexpected inheritance. No . . . perhaps he had better wait a while . . .

And looking at Agnes now, he decided that it was just as well he wasn't going to give her anything else to worry about. She seemed strangely distracted, he thought, definitely not her usual sensible self. She had barely had time to enjoy the tea, when she was up again and hurrying about the kitchen.

She bustled about with unnecessary vigour, making a lot of noise as she opened and closed the kitchen drawers and cupboards. Every now and then, Rebel would raise his head and direct a reproachful glance at her.

I know how you feel, old chum, Sam thought, but Agnes is a law unto herself and it's best to leave her to get on with whatever she thinks she's doing.

Then, 'Where's Jock?' he asked. 'Doesn't he usually come in for a cup of tea round about now?'

Agnes dropped a pan and it hit the floor with a clatter. The puppy jumped up and barked with fright.

'Whoops, clumsy of me. Jock – er – Jock's washing your car. You left it out in the rain last night and it's all streaked and muddy,' she added accusingly.

'I'm sorry about that.'

'Oh, it's all right. He's washing the Range Rover, too – and I told him to make a good job of it and finish off by washing our own little Fiesta.'

Poor Jock, Sam thought. Agnes is in one of those moods. He didn't have a clear view into the courtyard from where he was sitting at the kitchen table, but he could hear Jock moving the cars around.

He wondered if he ought to go and help but, by the time he'd eaten the mountain of toast that Agnes suddenly slapped before him, her long-suffering husband appeared in the doorway.

A strange thing happened. Agnes forgot to give him the usual command to remove his boots before he took a step further. Instead, she looked towards him expectantly and said, 'OK?'

'Aye, lass, it's OK,'

Then she seemed to remember her priorities. 'Good, take your boots off and sit down. I'll do you a bacon sandwich.'

'Trouble with one of the cars, Jock?' Sam asked.

'No, Mr Redmond, why should there be?' He looked mystified.

'Well, Agnes asked you if everything was OK, so I thought –'

'It's our own car,' Agnes said as she turned the rashers of bacon on the grill pan. 'Trouble with the – what was it, Jock?'

'Oh, yes, the starter,' her husband said. 'But I fixed it. Now, I'll have my bacon sandwich and, after that, I'll take that dog for a run through the woods.'

Rebel leapt up and wagged his tail; he came to rest his head on Jock's knee. 'I didn't mean right away, you daft pup,' Jock said as he surreptitiously slipped him a bit of crispy bacon rind, 'now, just be patient.'

Sam realized that he was no longer a priority in Agnes's kitchen; he got up to go back to his study. He paused in the doorway, tempted to ask if Gina had been down for breakfast yet.

He supposed she must have been, for there was no sign of Natalie either, and if the child was not with the Robsons then she must be with Gina. They must be in the playroom again, he thought, and wondered if he should go and find them.

He remembered the scene last night and how she'd been so determined not to speak to him. Perhaps I should wait until she's ready to talk about it . . . I'll see how she feels at lunch time . . . 'Did you want something else, Mr Redmond?' Agnes had noticed him waiting there.

'Yes – or rather not yet. I mean, don't bring my sandwiches to the study today. I'd like to have lunch with – with you all in the kitchen.'

'Oh –' Agnes looked surprised and he grinned.

'Well you're always telling me that I should have a proper lunch, aren't you, Agnes?'

'Yes – er – well, I'll call you when it's ready.'

She didn't look pleased and Sam went back to his study more than ever convinced that Agnes was having an 'off-day'.

He closed the door after himself and, collecting a large notepad from the desk, went to sit by the fire. He had reached a stage in the writing of his novel where he wanted to stop and think about how he was going to develop the next part of the story. He made himself comfortable and tried to clear his mind.

At first, all went well, but gradually real-life people began to jostle with the fictional characters for Sam's attention.

His younger sister had been as beautiful as any character in a romantic novel, he reminisced, and she had had a tragically short life . . .

She had never been very far from Sam's thoughts since she had died. For so much of his young adult life, after he left university, he had had to be both mother and father to her. And then she had married David Shaw.

Sam had been stunned. There had never been any romance between his sister and his friend as far as he knew. Whenever they had met in the past, David had seemed to regard her simply as Sam's kid sister.

Nadine had been pregnant, of course, and at first Sam had been angry, but on reflection, they seemed to be the perfect couple. David was a distinguished artist and Nadine was a promising beginner. He was sure that they would be happy.

And so they would have been if Nadine hadn't died in that dreadful accident when Natalie was still a tiny baby.

And, now David was dead and Natalie had been deprived of two loving and talented parents. David had made Gina her guardian. He must have trusted her – and, of course, he had loved her. But, for the life of him, Sam could not understand why Natalie had been left out of her father's will.

Sam forced himself to push any distressing speculation out of his mind and get back to work. By the time Agnes brought him a cup of coffee at eleven o'clock, he had made all the notes he needed and was back at his computer. He looked up and smiled his thanks for the coffee and discovered that the housekeeper was hovering, nervously.

'What is it, Agnes? Did you want to tell me something?'

'Er – yes. I mean no – er, that is, lunch will be a little late, today.'

'That's all right.'

'Er – I'll come and tell you when it's ready, then . . .'

'That's fine, really, don't worry.' Sam wondered if Agnes was heading for a nervous breakdown. Perhaps he should suggest that Jock take her away for a holiday?

But he didn't worry about it for too long, for the work was going well. So well, that a couple of hours flew by. The next time he looked at his watch, he was surprised that the housekeeper had still not come to inform him that lunch was ready.

He was ready for a break but did not want to harass Agnes, so he decided to go for a stroll. He didn't want to go too far, in case she called him, so he confined himself to the gardens at the front of the house and, eventually, he went round to the courtyard.

I'll go and see what Jock is up to, he thought. Perhaps he might tell me what it is that's bothering his wife.

But Jock was nowhere in sight. Sam decided to try the old stables. Many years ago now, part of the stable block had been converted into a large garage and a workshop. Sam knew that Jock spent a lot of time there.

But there was no sign of him. Sam looked at the cars. The Audi and the Fiesta were washed and polished until they gleamed. But where was the Range Rover?

Sam stood stock still in the garage as everything began to fall into place. Then he swivelled round and strode across the courtyard.

Agnes and Jock were sitting at one end of the table drinking tea. They looked up in alarm when Sam burst into the kitchen.

'Oh – er – Mr R-Redmond . . .' Agnes stuttered.

'Is my lunch ready, Agnes?'

'Oh, yes, of course.' She stood up and waved feebly towards the pans steaming on the stove. 'Jock was just going to set the table for me, weren't you, Jock?'

'Yes, straight away.' Her husband jumped up and opened the knife drawer.

'How many places are you going to set, Jock?' Sam asked; his voice was deceptively quiet. 'Agnes, tell me, how many of us are eating lunch today?'

Neither of them answered him. They simply stared at him in dismay.

'She's gone, hasn't she?' Sam asked at last. 'That was what all that rigmarole was about this morning, wasn't it?'

'Rigmarole? I don't know what you mean.'

'Oh, yes you do, Agnes Robson. You kept me busy with that enormous breakfast in the kitchen while Jock somehow helped Gina to leave without my noticing.'

Agnes pursed her lips and Jock coughed nervously.

'So how long were you going to keep me waiting for my lunch, then? Were you delaying it as long as

316

you could, putting off the moment when you'd have to tell me?'

'I – she – Mrs Shaw came over to the cottage very early this morning,' Agnes said. 'She asked us to help her. She said that she'd discovered the house now belonged to you and it would be better if she went back to France. She said that she didn't want any unpleasantness.'

'For goodness' sake, Agnes, who does she think I am? Bluebeard? Did she think I would keep her prisoner here if she really wanted to go?'

'No, of course not. It's not her, it's Natalie . . . she thought you might want . . . thought you might . . . she wanted to get away as far as possible before you found out . . . oh, Mr Redmond, I'm so sorry!'

Sam looked at their stricken faces and was filled with remorse. 'Look, it's me who should be apologizing. None of this is your concern. You should never have been drawn into it. I wouldn't blame you if you decide to give notice.'

'No, Mr Redmond.' It was Jock who spoke. 'We don't want to leave you. We're just hoping that, one way or another, you'll be able to sort this sorry business out.'

317

CHAPTER 25

'Gina! Where are you?' Jill Taylor managed to sound surprised, pleased and excited all at the same time.

'I'm at a service station just north of York.'

'York? Then you're in England!'

'Yes,' Gina smiled at the enthusiasm in her friend's voice. At least someone was glad to hear from her. 'I'm on my way to London, as a matter of fact.'

'On your way to London? And you're north of York? Then where on earth have you *been*?' Without giving Gina a chance to reply, Jill hurried on, 'Elaine and I have been wondering what had happened to you. We guessed that you must have fled the villa but which way did you come to England – via Norway?'

Gina smiled. Geography had never been one of Jill's strong points but she was more or less right. If Gina and Natalie had been heading for London straight from one of the channel ferry ports, she shouldn't have been phoning from somewhere in Yorkshire.

'It's a long story, Jill, I'll explain as much as I can, I promise, but at the moment I have to go and visit David's solicitor at his office in London and then –'

Jill didn't wait for her to finish the sentence. 'You've got to stay in London – no problem. There's a bed for you, right here, and for Natalie too; it goes without saying.'

'Won't Elaine mind?'

'Of course not. She knows what a good nanny I am to her three little monsters and she likes to indulge me.'

Gina knew that Jill was joking, but she also realized that her friend's employer wouldn't be a problem. Elaine Spencer had offered help once before – when she had most needed it.

When Mrs Harrington threw her out and Sandra had refused to let her go Marbella, she'd had no one else to turn to except Jill, the friend she had made at college. Jill was also working in London and they had managed to keep the friendship going.

Gina had met Elaine when she'd visited Jill. She'd been overwhelmed when she'd insisted that she should stay with them until she could sort her life out.

'Gina? Are you still there?'

'Yes – sorry – I'd better get going, but I'll see you later. I'm not sure how long it will take – about three and a half hours, perhaps, but I've got to stop now and then, for Natalie's sake. She's very good but she's only a child.'

After saying goodbye, Gina put the phone down.

Her stepdaughter was with her in the phone box and she had looked up at her when she heard her name.

'Am I a good girl, Gina?'

'Of course you are, sweetheart.'

Natalie had taken it well when Gina had explained that it was time to go home to France. Her trust in her stepmother was complete – and paradoxically, that made Gina feel even more guilty for causing such upheaval in her young life.

'I didn't like leaving Rebel behind, you know.'

Gina sighed, 'I know, but we couldn't bring him with us, could we? He belongs to Mr and Mrs Robson.'

'I know.' The child sounded resigned. 'And Mrs Robson would cry if she lost her puppy, wouldn't she?'

They had reached the car park and Gina knelt down and gathered her little stepdaughter into her arms for a fierce hug. 'Yes she would. Would you like a puppy of your own – when we get home?'

'No.'

'No?' Gina drew back, astonished. She had thought that the answer would be an enthusiastic yes.

'I'd rather have one of the kittens from Madame Bernat's farm. Céline said I could have one. She's nice.'

'Céline said that?'

Gina was astounded. Natalie thought that Gerard Bernat's sulky young wife was *nice*? 'When did she tell you that you could have a kitten?'

'When we were playing that game – you and Juan

320

and me hiding at the farm. Céline showed me the kittens, they were in a basket in the wash house. She said that when we came back I could have one because she knew I'd look after it.'

'My goodness – that was – kind of her.' Gina could hardly believe what she was hearing. Céline obviously had hidden talents; she had known how to be kind and understanding to a child who was in a puzzling and difficult situation.

'I've chosen one,' Natalie continued, 'she's keeping it for me. I'm going to call her Claude after the kitten in my story book.'

'That's – that's great.'

As Gina strapped Natalie into the child safety seat in the back of the car she reflected that Florence's daughter-in-law must have a totally unexpected softer side, a side she'd never revealed before. She was grateful to her. Céline couldn't have known it at the time, but she was making the return to France much easier.

Going to the Robsons' cottage at first light and telling Natalie they were setting off on a journey again had been the most difficult part of today's enterprise.

Natalie hadn't complained. The awful part had been parting from Rebel – especially when he had jumped in the car and settled himself as if he were coming too. Agnes, Gina and even Jock had been close to tears.

'Don't worry, Natalie,' Agnes had said as she hauled the disappointed puppy out of the car.

'You'll be coming here again – and Rebel will remember you.' She'd turned to Gina, 'Now I'd better go in and see to Mr Redmond's breakfast. Jock will help you load all your things and get away. Come with me, Rebel.'

There had been no mistaking the misery in the housekeeper's voice and, a little later, as Gina headed south, she had tried to stop herself feeling like a traitor.

However, the incident with Rebel had prevented Natalie from asking more awkward questions, Gina thought as she pulled out of the car park and eased into the slow lane of the A1. But she wasn't to be spared much longer.

'Gina?' Natalie spoke up from behind her.

'Yes, poppet.'

'I'm sorry we didn't say goodbye to Sam.'

'Er – yes – but, I told you – it was very early – and – er, he was fast asleep. . .' Gina faltered. She hated lying to the child.

'Will he come to see us?'

'Yes, I'm sure he will.'

And that was the truth, Gina thought. She was convinced that Sam would follow them sooner or later and she couldn't prevent him from seeing his sister's child; she didn't even want to. But, if she was to safeguard her own position as Natalie's guardian, she would have to be prepared.

When Gina reached the Spencers' house in Holland Park she pulled on to the paved area that had once been a garden but now served in lieu of a garage.

The door opened before Gina had lifted Natalie out of the car and Jill hurried out of the house and down the short flight of steps towards them surrounded by three excited small boys. Their mother smiled her welcome from the doorway.

Gina and Natalie were swept along by the excitement of it all and it wasn't until much later, when all the children were in bed, that the three women were able to relax in the kitchen for a while.

Gina sat at the kitchen table and watched as Jill made the coffee. Jill was small, blonde and pretty. She was extremely capable – and she had an outrageous sense of humour. She was also an only child and she and Gina had been drawn to each other from the first day on their training course at college.

Jill had chosen the course because she wanted to work with children until she fell in love – she was confident that that would happen – got married and produced a houseful of her own.

Gina also loved children but she was good at languages and she had really wanted to teach – until Sandra had vetoed the idea of her going to university . . .

Jill's employer, Elaine Spencer, tall and glamorous, opened the door that led to the back garden and looked for all the world like a guilty schoolgirl as she lit up an illicit cigarette. 'My last chance before Peter gets home – promise you won't tell!'

'You know I won't,' Jill said. 'But why don't you just give it up? It's a filthy habit and I'm not sure if you're not corrupting me by making me lie to your husband.'

'You don't have to lie – just don't say *anything* to him – or to the boys either!'

'Elaine – I'm teasing. But I still wish you'd stop smoking.'

'Stop nagging. I don't know why I put up with you!'

'You know why you do – no one else would look after your ghastly children.'

'You love them really.'

'Of course I do.'

Gina smiled as she listened to the easy banter. Momentarily, she wondered how different her life would have been if she had found a job with a family like the Spencers rather than the Harringtons.

Perhaps shamed by Jill's disapproval, Elaine soon stubbed out her cigarette and hid it in the depths of the rubbish bin. She joined Jill and Gina at the table but, before she sat down, she swept up their coffee mugs and dumped them in the sink.

'Hey!' Jill protested, 'I hadn't finished that – neither had Gina.'

'I know,' Elaine grinned at them over her shoulder as she reached below one of the kitchen counters into the fitted wine rack. 'But I think the occasion calls for something stronger than coffee.'

Elaine poured three generous glasses of red wine and, at first, they gossiped almost inconsequentially about the children, Peter's hopes for promotion and

Elaine's dreams of being able to afford a holiday home.

'I'd like somewhere warm and miles away from traffic and city bustle!' she said.

'You can always come and stay at the Villa Des Pines, once life gets back to normal – although I don't know when that will be.'

Gina stared broodily into her glass and Jill reached across the table and squeezed her hand. 'Do you want to talk about things? You know you can trust Elaine and me.'

It was surprisingly easy to talk. Gina didn't know whether it was the wine, the cosy warmth of the kitchen or the genuine sympathy of her two companions. It was probably a combination of all three, plus her deep-seated need to confide and share her worries, she thought.

She spoke quietly and it didn't take long. When she was finished there was a small silence. Jill looked close to tears, too full to say anything in fact, so it was left to Elaine to be the first to speak.

'So you had no idea that David was going to add a codicil to his will?'

'Well, yes, I did, but he told me it was to make Juan's position more secure.'

'Oh, yes, the gallery and the paintings. But he didn't tell you that he was going to leave his property in the UK to his old friend Sam Redmond?'

'No – otherwise I shouldn't have gone there. I thought Northmoor Hall belonged to me now.'

'Along with everything else.'

Elaine's tone was dry and Gina flushed.

'What are you suggesting, Elaine?' Jill had caught the undercurrent too, and leapt in, in defence of her friend.

'Oh, don't worry,' Elaine assured her. 'I'm not criticizing Gina. I'm sure that David Shaw must have had a very good reason for marrying his child's nanny –'

'Of course he did – he loved her!'

'Be quiet, Jill,' Gina said softly. 'Let Elaine speak.'

Elaine smiled at Gina and continued, 'As I started saying, David must have had a very good reason for marrying Gina and for not mentioning his own daughter in the will –'

'That's not quite right,' Jill said. 'He made Gina Natalie's guardian.'

'That's right. So he trusted her, but it still doesn't explain everything, does it Gina?'

'No.'

'And, for some reason, you can't tell us why he did this?'

'No, I'd be breaking a promise. A promise I made to David when he was dying.'

'And that's the crux of it, isn't it, my dear? Now you find yourself the object of outrage, anger, scorn, all the facile emotions stirred up by people anxious only to sell their newspapers or make their television reports more scandalous.'

'Yes.'

'And you won't defend yourself?'

'I can't.'

'Oh, Gina,' Jill looked worried. 'What are you going to do?'

'Keep a low profile until it's all over. That's the only course open to me.'

'Don't worry, Jill,' Elaine said. 'The media interest won't last. Gina probably did the right thing when she left the villa. I'm sure most of the reporters have packed up and gone away. That's right, Gina, isn't it? I mean you are keeping in touch with Juan?'

'Ye-es . . .

'What is it? A problem?'

'Juan thinks that one of them, at least, is still there – and I think I know who it is. It's the one who took the shots of the funeral – and the one by the swimming pool. Marco Doyle.'

'I see.'

Elaine frowned and Jill looked puzzled. 'Is that bad?'

'Could be. Marco Doyle is a rat of the first order. He may be a very good photographer but he's also a supreme egotist; if he has a moral code at all, it would be based on what was best for Marco Doyle.'

Gina remembered uneasily that that was more or less what Sam thought. 'Do you know him?' she asked Elaine.

'Only by reputation. Remember, I used to have a career in public relations before I sank into blissful, domestic obscurity!'

'But why would he still be hanging around?' Jill asked. 'Surely the story's been done to death by now?'

'I think the real question is, why is a paparazzo in Marco Doyle's league interested in Gina in the first place?'

Elaine sounded subdued and Gina glanced at her worriedly. That was exactly what had puzzled Sam. 'The only thing I can think of,' she said, eventually, 'is that he hopes to squeeze some more scandal out of my situation – revive the story – by – by –'

'By revealing your lurid past,' Elaine finished for her.

'Oh, no,' Jill breathed. 'How could he know about that?'

'We-ell,' Elaine said, 'Marco mixes with a pretty flighty bunch of society people. I suppose he could have heard a rumour about what happened at the Harringtons'.'

'But that's awful!' Jill exclaimed. 'Gina was completely innocent!'

'We know that – but Marco doesn't have to prove anything – I'll bet he's a dab hand at steering clear of being sued. No, there's a way of presenting things – rumour and innuendo have ruined many perfectly innocent people.'

'I could kill that Jeremy Harrington,' Jill suddenly exploded, 'trying to force his way into your bed, while his wife was sitting with her mother in hospital, and then letting you take the rap for it when she came home unexpectedly!'

'The pity of it is,' Elaine interjected, 'Paula Harrington's set may have had their suspicions – they must all have a pretty good idea what Jeremy's

328

like – but they would never openly say that they believed your version of events.'

'You know, at the time I thought my life was ruined,' Gina said. 'I certainly didn't think I would ever get another job as a nanny. No references and a dodgy reputation!'

'Well, we soon sorted that out, didn't we?' Jill smiled at her.

'Yes, you did – both of you and Peter, too.' Gina remembered how Elaine and Jill had encouraged her to look for another job and how, when the time came, the Spencers had been prepared to give her a glowing reference. 'Even though you had to perjure yourselves!'

'If you mean the reference,' Elaine said, 'Peter and I didn't tell any lies. We were able to base our judgement on the time you spent living with us – on the way you helped Jill with our children. And, remember, the principal of your former college was emphatic – she said she would never accept that you would behave in such a despicable manner.'

'We-ell,' Gina sighed. 'One of the best things you did was to persuade me to tell Mr Hargreaves everything – luckily he believed me.'

It was David's solicitor who had placed the advertisement for a nanny for Natalie. David had asked for his help when Nadine had been killed in the motor accident on the mountain roads near his villa.

The successful applicant would have to be good at languages, especially French and Spanish, and that was what had prompted Gina to apply, although she didn't hold out much hope for herself.

Robert Hargreaves had conducted the interviews in London. Gina and he had got along from the start and she would always be grateful to him for choosing her – no matter what had happened since. She had adored Natalie from the start . . .

She became aware that Elaine was watching her. 'So Gina, no regrets, I take it?'

'No, no regrets.'

'And what are you going to do now – and can we help?' Jill asked.

'You've already helped by just being here. And right now I'm going to help you make a meal in time for Peter coming home.'

Gina grinned as Elaine glanced up at the kitchen clock and exclaimed in mock panic. But Jill was still frowning.

'Seriously, Gina,' she said, 'what's the plan?'

'I'm going to see Mr Hargreaves tomorrow, he's expecting me, and I'd be grateful if Natalie could stay here –'

'Of course!' Elaine and Jill chorused in unison.

'And then we'll head back to the villa.'

'Even if Marco Doyle is still hanging around?'

'Yes, Jill.'

'But aren't you afraid of what he might do?'

'I'm worried, naturally, but whatever he's up to will have to be faced sooner or later. I can't let him keep Natalie and me away from our home indefinitely.'

CHAPTER 26

'So there's nothing for you to worry about, Gina. The will is watertight. You are your husband's principal heir and you are Natalie's guardian – that's what David wanted.'

Robert Hargreaves smiled encouragingly across the wide expanse of his desk. Dust motes danced in the afternoon sunlight filtering in through tall windows; Gina could hear the muted sounds of the London traffic. She was tired and she had to force herself to concentrate.

David's solicitor had insisted on taking her for lunch at his club before they discussed business; she had felt that she couldn't refuse. She suspected that his motives were to establish a relaxed and friendly atmosphere – and to assure her that, whatever happened, he still considered himself to be a family friend.

'But if anybody should challenge the will,' Gina said, 'I mean challenge my right to be Natalie's guardian?'

'And who would do that?'

'Sam . . . Sam Redmond.'

'Has he intimated that he might?'

'Well, yes, I suppose so . . . I mean he's her uncle and . . .' Gina trailed off, uncertainly. She was unwilling to tell this kind man exactly why Sam thought that she was unsuitable. Even though Robert Hargreaves knew the truth of the situation, it still hurt to admit that anyone should suspect her of acting dishonourably.

'But why?' Robert Hargreaves looked perplexed. 'Surely he understands that Natalie has known and loved you all her young life? Sam Redmond may be Nadine's brother but his work means that he's constantly on the move. What kind of stable background could he provide?'

Gina shifted in her chair uncomfortably. 'He – he may think that I'm not suitable,' she admitted.

'I see.' Mr Hargreaves leaned back in his chair and frowned. Then he sighed. 'Gina, listen to me,' he said. 'If he should try to take things to court, I would act for you – defend your position. You know that, don't you?'

'Yes . . . I suppose so.'

She knew that she ought to feel reassured, but she didn't. Once a case of this kind went to law, there was no knowing what the outcome would be.

'Now,' the solicitor smiled and continued as if that was settled, 'have you got your cheque book and credit cards with you?'

'Yes.' Gina was surprised by the question, she wondered what was coming next.

'Then you have no immediate problems. Remember David had already opened a joint account with you when he had to give up running the gallery.

'You are free to draw on it and I can assure you that the balance is very healthy – very healthy indeed. Natalie and you must have anything you need – you can take a holiday, go anywhere you think best, until the present situation resolves itself.'

'I've already decided where I'm going.'

'Good, where's that?'

'Back to the Villa Des Pines – I'm going home'

Mr Hargreaves looked grave for a moment and then he nodded. 'That's probably the right decision. You, and particularly Natalie, probably need to be in familiar surroundings.'

'Perhaps I shouldn't have left in the first place.' Gina sighed. 'I certainly wouldn't have gone to Northmoor Hall if I'd known what David had done.'

'I don't blame you for wanting to get away from that media circus. And, as for Northmoor Hall, are you sure you don't want to challenge that?'

'I'm sure.'

Gina didn't say why she was so sure and Robert Hargreaves didn't press the point. But, if he had asked, she wouldn't have known how to account for her decision. How to explain why she didn't feel that she had any right to the house . . . and how Sam seemed to belong there . . .

The children had already had their tea when she got back to Holland Park and they were watching a video.

'It's *Jungle Book*,' Jill told her. 'The boys never tire of it and Natalie says she's never seen it before – you've got to let her stay and see it to the end.'

'I wouldn't dream of spoiling her fun,' Gina replied. 'And besides, I don't want to set off for Dover until the rush hour is over.'

Jill laughed. 'You might be here a while, in that case. The rush hour in London is elastic – it goes on for longer than you think!'

'Also Peter wants to check over your car and fill up the tank for you before you go,' Elaine added. 'And I want to make sure you have a good meal and a rest.'

'Well, I have to admit that I'm tired after the long drive yesterday.'

'Look, why don't you stay one more night and set out in the morning?' Jill asked.

'No, I'd like to catch an early ferry – before it gets too busy. I thought I might drive down this evening and find a hotel. That way I can avoid the crowds.'

'Good thinking,' Elaine said. 'Once the roads are less busy it should only take you about a couple of hours from here. So you've time to sit back and take it easy for a while. I'll put the kettle on.'

Why on earth didn't I think of phoning ahead!

Gina hunched over the steering wheel and glanced despairingly at the 'No Vacancy' signs in the windows of the row of guest houses and small hotels near the ferryport.

The only alternative to finding somewhere to spend the night was to embark on one of the night ferries and she didn't think that would be wise. This time, she didn't have Juan to share the driving and with Natalie's safety in mind she knew she ought to have a proper night's sleep.

She pulled up for a moment, and glanced round at her stepdaughter guiltily. The poor child hadn't made a fuss when she'd had to say goodbye to her new friends and she'd been as good as gold during the journey from London to Dover.

There've been so many changes in her young life, of late, Gina thought. Thank goodness she trusts me.

Her stepdaughter was staring out of the car window curiously. Gina turned her attention back to the road and continued to drive.

'What are you looking for, Gina?'

'Somewhere to stay for the night.'

'And somewhere to eat, too?'

'Yes, love. Are you hungry?'

'Mmm. Why don't we go to that place there?'

Gina realized that Natalie must mean the large, floodlit, hotel ahead of them. She started to say, 'Oh, no, it'll be too expens –' Then she stopped in mid-word.

Of course it isn't too expensive, she thought. Mr Hargreaves has just assured me that I have no financial worries whatsoever. Then, acknowledging to herself the fact that it might take her a while to get used to her new status, Gina turned into the drive that led to the hotel car park.

'Clever girl, Natalie,' she said. 'This looks like the very place for us.'

After the formalities of checking in, she looked round the twin-bedded room and bathroom with pleasure. It was quite an adventure for Natalie to be in a hotel and the little girl experimented with the television and the radio before settling for the joys of a bubble bath.

Gina had not wanted to risk going to the dining-room for supper. I'm probably being paranoid, she thought, but there's still a chance that someone could recognize me.

She settled for room service and Natalie was delighted with the novelty of having her meal brought up to her. She had ordered fish fingers and beans from the children's menu. Gina had the slightly more sophisticated pâté, toast and salad.

While her stepdaughter finished off her milky drink in bed, Gina sat on her own bed and made a phone call.

Juan answered straight away. When she told him that they were on the way home, he sounded troubled.

'That man is still here, Gina.'

'It can't be helped. I couldn't stay at Northmoor Hall any longer. It's too complicated to explain right now, but I'll tell you everything when I see you.'

'Well, please phone me at regular intervals as you drive through France. Keep me informed of your progress. And when you arrive, it may be better to go to the Bernats' farm rather than straight to the villa.'

'Juan, that . . . that man . . .' Gina kept her voice low because she didn't want to disturb Natalie who had settled down and was almost asleep. 'He surely can't still think that we're a front-page story, can he?'

'No, *querida*, I don't think that he does. I think it is something else.'

'But what on earth could it be?'

'I don't know, but Céline recognized him.'

'Céline? But how . . .? Where . . . ?'

Juan laughed, softly. 'Well, you know how Gerard's young wife will not let her handsome farmer out of her sight?'

Gina laughed in acknowledgement.

'And you know that Gerard has been taking his mother into town each day to go to the supermarket?'

'Yes, you told me that Florence was laying a false trail, trying to pretend that we're all still at the villa.'

'Well, this morning, while Gerard went into the supermarket with his mother, Céline saw this man coming out of his hotel.'

'But you still haven't explained how she could possibly know him.'

'She recognized him because he has been here before. She pointed him out to Gerard and Florence and they agreed that she was right. They told me that this man knew David, and that the last time he was here was round about the time of Nadine's accident.'

'I see.'

'Gina . . . are you still there?'

'Yes, Juan. Listen, I don't suppose the Bernats knew his name, did they?'

'They did. It's Marco Doyle.'

And that's no surprise, Gina thought. None of it.

337

She remembered Sam had told her that David had known him too. But he had said that their friendship with Marco had ended years ago, after Marco had made Emma pregnant and David had persuaded him to marry her.

She was sure that Sam did not know Marco had been to the Villa Des Pines in more recent years.

'Gina? Are you still there?'

'Sorry, Juan, I promise I'll keep in touch with you while I'm on the way. And I'll do whatever you think is necessary.'

'Take care, *querida*.'

Gina decided to ease away her travel-weariness in the bath. The hot water and the scented toiletries provided by the hotel soon soothed away any physical stress but her mind could not be easy.

Before turning out the bedside light, she punched in the code on the telephone for a morning call. The hotel started serving breakfast very early because most of the guests were travelling. But, in any case, room service was available for twenty-four hours.

The bed was very comfortable and in spite of her state of mind, Gina had no difficulty in getting off to sleep. But there was nothing she could do about her dreams.

She found herself in that strange state where she knew she was dreaming and yet she couldn't make herself wake up. She tried to shut out the images that appeared in her mind but they wouldn't go away.

So she tried to take control of her dream – to direct

what was happening – but it was useless. Something more powerful took over and she had no choice but to give in . . .

No matter how hard she tried, she could not turn back.

She was walking down the mountain road in the moonlight and, this time, she knew what kind of heartache was waiting at the café in the little square.

There were two Ginas. Her dream self was happy – was hurrying towards the café where she thought Sam would be waiting – and her other self, her real self, could not warn the poor phantom girl that he would not be there.

The girl who looked like Gina, who was wearing Gina's clothes, raced ahead of her, her feet barely touching the ground beneath her.

The real Gina hurried after her, calling out that she must turn back, but the girl did not hear her – *could* not hear her for the calls were soundless.

And then they reached the square together. The girl turned for one brief moment to glance at Gina. She was smiling radiantly. 'Look,' she said.

And Gina looked beyond her to see that Sam was indeed there. He was sitting at the table. He saw them and he rose and began walking towards them. The people at the other tables were watching, smiling, making soft noises of encouragement.

Suddenly, the real Gina knew that she must reach him before the other girl did.

The phantom girl sped ahead of her. Gina forgot

that this was only a dream and ran as she had never run before.

Just as Sam was going to take the other girl in his arms, Gina caught up with her, merged with her, the two girls became one and Gina forgot about the other girl's existence . . . she gave herself up to Sam's embrace.

He bent his head to kiss her and, as their lips touched, the people outside the café wavered and vanished, the tables vanished, the buildings and the very streets shimmered luminescently, dwindled and then faded away into the blue shadows.

She was kissing him, holding him, whirling with him through space and then sinking down with him into some timeless place that only lovers know.

His kisses became more passionate, his caresses more demanding, more arousing. Gina felt the age-old pulse of life begin to throb within her. They began to move together with a rhythm that could not be denied.

She opened up to him and, when he entered her, they clung to each other and cried out together, soundlessly, wordlessly, at the ecstasy of their union.

'Sam . . . Sam . . . I love you,' Gina whispered as the dream faded and left her to sleep deeply and undisturbed until morning.

CHAPTER 27

The English Channel

'Excuse me, would you take our photograph?'

They were in the cafeteria on the cross-channel ferry and girl smiled at Gina across the table; the boy held out his camera.

'Yes, of course.'

'It's all set up – just press the shutter release,' he said. 'Wait a minute –' he put his arm round the girl and they smiled self-consciously. 'OK – shoot.'

The camera flashed and Gina was about to hand it back to them, when Natalie said, 'I'd like my picture taken.'

'OK,' the young woman said, 'come and sit on my knee – but I don't know how we're going to explain you to my mum when she sees the pictures!'

Gina smiled. 'You're on your honeymoon, aren't you?'

'Is it that obvious?'

'I'm afraid so – but don't worry, even in these

341

cynical times, I think most people are still sentimental enough to be pleased for you.'

Natalie had her picture taken with the young couple. They explained that they had been married the day before in Cambridge, driven to Dover where they'd spent the night in a small hotel, and were planning to get to Paris by that evening.

'You should do it easily,' Gina said, 'you'll be able to stop somewhere for lunch on the way.'

'Oh, but we would have no idea where to go – and if I left the motorway to find somewhere –'

'He would get us hopelessly lost!'

'You wouldn't have to leave the road. Once the toll road begins at St Omer there are service stations every fifteen to twenty miles. The cafés and restaurants are usually very good.'

'Do you know France, then?' the girl asked.

'Er, yes, quite well.'

Gina left the cafeteria as soon as she could after that. She was relieved that it had not occurred to the young couple to ask for her address so that they could send a copy of the photograph.

Natalie wouldn't mind. To her, as to many small children, the posing and the actual taking of the photograph were more important than the resulting picture.

They spent the rest of the time on board in the children's play area. Gina was relieved to see how easy it was for Natalie to make friends with other children and to enjoy herself – in spite of all the upheavals she had been through recently.

Once she had driven off the ferry, it was a little easier to put Sam and the time at Northmoor Hall out of her mind. France was a different country after all; although she acknowledged that, now, a different set of problems was waiting to be dealt with.

But if she could overcome them, then she and Natalie could have a good life here. David had wanted his studio and gallery to go on as if he was still there and he had asked Juan to stay and run them for him.

Juan would have to be paid, of course, but David had talked over that side of things with both of them before his final illness made practical discussion impossible.

He had also told Gina that he trusted her to take care of Juan, although he realized that the young man might find someone else one day. In fact David had hoped that he would.

As usual, the traffic leaving Calais was heavy for the first few miles but Gina wasn't concerned. There was no need to hurry and, in any case, it took her a while to adjust to driving on the right hand side of the road with David's Range Rover which had been designed for roads in the UK.

She had decided not to try and get back to the villa that day. She would take it easy and they would stop for the night somewhere. It would make sense to travel well beyond Paris, beyond Orléans, even. Maybe she would stop at Montlucon, or just a little further, say at Clermont-Ferrand where she would have to leave the toll road and head for Toulouse.

As well as restaurants, some of the service stations provided excellent overnight accommodation, so she would leave it all to Natalie. If the child looked weary, she would stop.

When she made her first telephone call to Juan as she had promised, he agreed that that was a good idea. Then he added, 'And Gina, whatever the problems are, I am glad that you are coming home – we all are, even the fierce little Céline.'

'My goodness, Céline waiting to welcome me? I can hardly credit it!'

'Ah, she has changed – she has discovered that she is with child at last. Gerard is overjoyed, he can barely bring himself to leave her side. Céline is deliriously happy.'

'Let's hope the mood lasts!'

'Ah, *querida*, you are laughing. That is good. We will see each other soon and together we will solve all the problems, yes?'

'Yes, Juan.'

But Gina knew that there were certain problems that might never be solved.

County Waterford

Sam stood by the windows in the drawing-room of Emma's house and looked out towards the hills where the clouds were beginning to settle like a shroud.

The landscape was drenched with rain and the

windows were misted with a fine drizzle. The scene should have been melancholy but, on the glass, Sam could also see comfortable reflections from inside the room behind him. The gleam of the log fire burning in the huge old fireplace and the luminous glow from several lamps.

He looked at his insubstantial other self – a ghost self trapped by the window glass and framed by the room. He was startled to acknowledge how well he fitted in to such an environment – how much he would like a home like this. There should be someone else standing next to him – but not Emma, not now.

And not Sally Maxwell, either, even though he admitted, uncomfortably, to himself, that he had been guilty of – not exactly leading her on – but certainly of not making it clear enough that his heart had been given elsewhere some time ago.

He had phoned Sally this morning before he had left to come to Ireland and, as gently as possible, had let her know what his intentions were. She'd made it easier for him when she'd told him that she'd already guessed.

Suddenly he was not alone. Another reflection came and stood next to his in the window. Emma had joined him; she was carrying a tray of tea and sandwiches, a slab of rich, dark fruit cake and a bottle of whisky. She stood very still and he knew that she was seeing what he had only imagined fleetingly, a moment before – the two of them together in this room.

He turned and looked down at her at the same

moment as she looked up at him and caught the glitter of tears in her eyes. She sighed softly and then smiled. 'Shall we draw the curtains and make it cosier in here?'

'OK, but let me take that tray.'

'No, I can manage. You close the curtains; it's never really got light today and now the night's drawing in fast.'

While Sam complied, she moved away from him towards the warmth of the fireplace. He turned and watched her. The dogs were stretched out on the hearthrug, books and magazines littered the top of a low table and an open folder of notes and designs took up the seat of one of the armchairs.

But instead of looking untidy, the drawing-room looked peaceful, lived in. Emma had created a haven. He wondered if Marco appreciated it.

She had sunk down, still balancing the tray, to kneel by the table. She nudged the dogs aside with one knee and then, using the tray, she pushed everything off the table on to the floor.

Sam began to pick up the books and magazines as Emma began to pour two cups of tea. He grinned. 'Still tidy to a fault, I see.'

She smiled at him. 'I used to drive you crazy, didn't I? You were always scolding me – telling me that I would make life much easier for myself if I kept my little student's room tidy.'

'I didn't scold.'

'Yes you did. Oh, Sam, you were so pompous.'

'Pompous? Me? Never! I simply pointed out

the obvious – if you knew where you'd put your books and papers every night, you wouldn't waste so much time the next morning looking for something important.'

'I always knew where to find anything important!' Her cheeks were pink and her voice echoed the indignant protests she used to make all those years ago. 'And anyway,' she continued, 'being untidy is not the same as being a sloven. This old mansion might be crumbling but it's cleaner than it's been for years.'

'I'm sure it is.' His tone was conciliatory.

She glanced at him swiftly, just to make sure that she wasn't being patronized, then smiled a little ruefully. 'Just shove those things under the table for now, will you.'

Sam pushed the books and magazines under the table as he was told and sat back against one of the armchairs. He stretched his long legs out in front of him, to the disgust of the dogs who grumbled and made room begrudgingly. Emma handed him a cup of tea.

'Add your own milk and sugar. I've forgotten how you take it.'

He was surprised at how brusque she suddenly sounded. She was staring down into her own cup as she stirred two spoons of sugar into it and Sam guessed that she hadn't forgotten at all. She wanted to distance herself from him, he guessed. The atmosphere between them had become dangerously intimate – too reminiscent of old times.

For a while they sat and enjoyed their meal. Sam sensed that he should let Emma lead the conversation until her equilibrium returned. So he listened as she told him about the house. How she had seen it when they had been on holiday and how she had fallen in love with it.

'Marco went straight along and bought it for me – even although it wasn't up for sale.'

She saw Sam's startled glance and she went on, defensively. 'Don't worry – he didn't act the bully boy. He found out that the old lady who was living here was in terrible financial trouble. She was hanging on – living in one room – this one actually – and gradually selling off all the family heirlooms to pay her debts. She was just about starving, poor old thing.'

'But why hadn't she sold the house long before?'

'She was the only daughter. Her brother was killed in the last war, so was her fiancé. She looked after her old parents for years – she didn't want to move them out of the ancestral home, and by the time they died the debts had mounted and death duties added to the nightmare.

'She was worried that after selling the house she would still be in debt and would have nowhere to live. She thought Marco was an answer to her prayers.'

'What did he do?'

'He paid well over the odds for the property and bamboozled the old dear into believing that, as the new owner, he was responsible for paying her tax debts.'

'Marco did that?'

'He can be very generous you know.'

Sam restrained himself from saying that Marco was generous only when it suited him. In helping the old lady, he was also salving his conscience. Emma should have whatever she wanted, anything that was in Marco's power to give her . . . anything to assuage his guilt . . .

'So now, you're restoring the house?' he asked.

'Yes – and Marco says I can have anything I need. I try very hard not to be extravagant. The structural repairs were horrendously expensive, so now I'm doing my best to restore and redecorate without costing him another small fortune.

'I go to auctions, second-hand shops, and even junk shops. You'd be amazed at the kind of things people just throw away!'

She had warmed to her subject. Her passion for the house had obviously become a big part of her life. It was almost an obsession, Sam thought. He wondered if that pleased Marco. It probably did.

Marco travelled all over the world and Sam guessed that he hadn't changed. There must have been plenty of women over the years. And his wife was safe at home in a draughty mansion in County Waterford, with her dogs and her beautiful old house to keep her happy.

Sam watched Emma as she poured a generous slug of whisky into each of the two tumblers. Perhaps it was time to ask her about Marco. But Emma forestalled him.

'I'm sorry I called you pompous, just now.'

'I wasn't offended.'

'You were such a serious young man, you know. So orderly – so practical – and yet so kind, so very, very kind. I didn't really mind when you tried to organize my life for me.'

'Didn't you? As I remember it, you used to get pretty heated.'

'I was young. But I had the sense to realize why you behaved as you did.'

'Really?' Sam's tone was half-ironic. He hadn't realized that his behaviour had been analyzed all those years ago.

'Yes, it was because your father had died when you were so young, wasn't it? You had to help your mother and your sister . . .'

Emma sipped her whisky and closed her eyes for a moment then she said, 'When I read about her death – that dreadful accident, in the newspapers, I knew how terrible it must have been for you. I mean, after your mother died, you and Nadine only had each other, didn't you?'

'I was working as a television reporter for the BBC when I suddenly found myself responsible for an unhappy adolescent – she was still at school. Luckily I was earning enough to pay a housekeeper to make life easier for both of us.'

'But you did a good job of bringing her up, didn't you? I mean she did very well at school and went on to art school?'

'Yes, and I think she was happy. She was leading a

more or less normal student existence and there was no way she wanted to live at home with her big brother any longer. I breathed a metaphorical sigh of relief, I suppose, and began to get on with my own career, as a freelance.'

'So what went wrong?'

'What do you mean?'

'Something went wrong – I can sense it. Remember, you never were able to hide things from me.'

'That's true.' Sam stared at Emma across the low table. Her beautiful face was filled with compassion. He wondered, as he'd wondered so many times over the years, how anyone who appeared to be so wise could have given her heart to Marco.

'What happened before Nadine married David?'

Sam was stung by Emma's perception. He remembered that time of anxiety . . . how frantic he'd been.

'I – I'm not really sure . . . I was working abroad – Beirut – I phoned my sister regularly, I always had done even though it used to annoy her. She thought I was keeping tabs on her and, of course, I was.

'Well, anyway, suddenly I couldn't trace her. I phoned all her friends and anyone that we both knew, but no one had any idea what had become of her. It was as if she'd vanished from the face of the earth.'

'How dreadful!'

'By the time I got back to London I was frantic with worry. There was a letter waiting for me – Nadine was in France – she'd married David.'

'Were you surprised?'

'Pole-axed. There'd never been any romance

between them as far as I knew. Whenever they'd met David seemed to regard Nadine simply as my kid sister, nothing more.'

'Did she tell you why – or how it had happened?'

'No; the letter only gave the barest details. I flew to France immediately and found –'

'And found?'

'And found that she was pregnant – and, further-more, she must have been already pregnant when they married.'

'Oh.'

'I should have been furious with David, I suppose. I mean he was so much older – he must have taken advantage of her.'

'That's an old-fashioned thing to say.' Emma smiled softly.

'Is it? I suppose it is. Am I sounding pompous again?'

'Just a little – but you're forgiven.'

'Well, she was my kid sister, after all. But, anyway, the two of them seemed to be so happy – David could hardly wait for the child to be born – I just accepted the situation gracefully.'

'And why not?' Emma asked. 'After all, they must have been a perfect couple – both of them so artistic. They could have had a wonderful life together if . . . if . . .'

'If only her life hadn't been cut short so tragically.' Sam stared into the flames.

'Do you know how it happened?'

'Not exactly. When I arrived in France David was

withdrawn and uncommunicative. His grief was so raw that I didn't feel I could press him for information. You know, Emma, I still don't know why Nadine was driving alone down that mountain road that night . . .'

Neither of them spoke for a while; the only sounds in the elegant old room were the crackling of the logs in the hearth and the quiet snuffling of the dogs. One of them suddenly moaned and twitched in its sleep. Emma stretched out a hand and fondled its soft coat. 'Chasing rabbits in her dreams, no doubt,' she said.

As she bent, smiling indulgently, towards the dog, the firelight illuminated Emma's features. She looks happy, Sam thought, and yet, how can she be?

Suddenly she turned her head and looked straight at him. 'What is it that you want to know?' she asked.

'I – I'm not sure what you mean . . .'

'Yes you are. We haven't seen each other for years. So why visit me now?'

'To find out how you are?'

'Sam, don't insult my intelligence. You must have gone to a great deal of trouble to find out where I was living.'

'We-ell –'

'Then, when you get here, you let me talk about my life – probably to lull me into a sense of false security –'

'No, that's not fair.'

'Then you told me how troubled you were – and probably still are – by your sister's untimely death, but that's not it. There's something else worrying you, isn't there? And I suspect, since you've taken great care to hardly mention him, that it's something to do with Marco. Am I right?'

'Yes, you're right.'

'Is – is it something to do with what happened between us all years ago? Because if it is, I warn you I might ask you to leave right now.'

'No, it's nothing to do with the past. It's something that's happening right now.'

'I see.' Sam had expected her to look surprised, but she didn't. It was almost as if she had been waiting for this moment.

'Emma, how much do you know about Marco's work?'

'Are you going to criticize him? Because if you are, I won't listen.'

'No, I'm not going to criticize him. I need to know if you follow what he's doing – does he tell you anything about his – his latest projects?'

'His victims, you mean. You were going to say his victims, weren't you?' She stared at him belligerently for a moment and her features softened and she shrugged.

'I know how he makes his money,' she said, 'and I know he's good at it. But I don't – I don't care to know too much about the consequences. I suppose I began to shut my eyes to it all a long time ago.'

'So you don't follow the stories he's covering?'

'Not if I can help it. I know I'm being a hypocrite – but there's nothing I can do about it. I love him.'

'So – that means you don't know where he is now?'

'Yes, I do. I'm sorry, Sam, but I guessed that was it. Marco phones home regularly and I couldn't help catching the news on television when it all started – I couldn't help making the connection. You're worried about your little niece, aren't you?'

'Yes, I am.'

'Well I'm sure that girl – that nanny – isn't as bad as she's being painted. Marco will have been exploiting the situation for his own purposes – and the other reporters, too. I knew David too, remember, if he loved the girl I'm sure she's trustworthy.'

'Emma – I'm sorry – that's not quite the full story. I mean Marco is staying on there – the other reporters have given up on the story – he may be planning something further – I've got to know –'

Emma looked grave. 'He never tells me any details – he knows how I feel about his work. I'm not sure if I can help you.'

Sam was beginning to think that his journey had been in vain. Perhaps he should have gone straight to France. But he'd had a hunch that Emma might know something, something that would give him the advantage when he faced Marco.'

'You say that he phones home regularly?'

'Nearly every day.'

'Well, perhaps you could remember what he's told you – any little thing – it might help . . .' He knew that he was grasping at straws.

Emma looked at him consideringly. 'Tell me the truth, Sam. It's not just Natalie that you're concerned about, is it?'

'No.'

'I see.'

'Do you?'

'Yes, I think I do. So go ahead, ask whatever you need to ask and I'll help you if I can. But first I think I'd better pour us each another glass of whisky.'

CHAPTER 28

South West France

Gina lay with her eyes closed and stretched, lazily, on the padded lounger. It was good to be back in a land where summer lasted longer. In fact, if this little scene had not all been an act, she could even have begun to enjoy herself.

She heard a faint splash as Juan hauled himself out of the pool and she opened her eyes and sat up.

'You OK, *querida*?'

'I'm fine, Juan, but you'll wrinkle up like a prune if you stay in the water much longer.'

'I'm coming out now.'

He stripped off and dried himself on a large, brightly coloured towel before pulling on his underpants, jeans and a cotton sweatshirt. Then, slinging his swimming trunks and the towel over his shoulder, he began to walk towards the steps which led up on to the terrace.

'Where are you going?'

'Into the house, to get us some cool drinks.'

'Don't you think we could go in now?'

'No, not yet. If we are going to play this game, let's play it properly.'

Gina shaded her eyes and looked out beyond the grounds of the villa and up towards the lower slopes of the mountains at the other side of the valley.

Was he watching them? Had he observed the elaborate charade that she and Juan had been acting out for the last two days? But if he was there, on the mountainside, he was not taking any photographs. There had been no glint of reflected light to betray the presence of his lens.

Of course, Gina no longer believed that taking more photographs of them was really the purpose of Marco Doyle's protracted stay here.

She sighed and stood up to slip on a pale primrose, button-through dress and a long-line white, ribbed cardigan. Then she adjusted both loungers so that they were in a sitting position. When Juan came back they would drink and talk for a while, but not because they couldn't think of better things to do.

The whole purpose of their stratagem had been, firstly, to establish that Gina was here at the villa and, secondly, to force Marco Doyle into the open. Gina was convinced that he wanted to talk to her.

'Here you are,' Juan appeared with a tray bearing a tall, frosted jug of Florence Bernat's home-made lemonade and two tumblers. He hooked one sandalled foot around the leg of a small table and pulled it into place between them. He set down the tray and then he sat down and poured them each a drink.

'Thanks, Juan.' Gina raised her glass in a friendly salute and he grinned at her.

'Florence has made us a huge bowl of salad and she's left plenty of bread, cold slices, cheese, olives and fruit. But now, she is going to take Natalie back to the farm; it will soon be her bedtime.'

'Oh, Juan, I hate sending her away at nights!'

'I know. But we decided that was the best thing to do until we have sorted things out with this Marco person – until we know exactly what he's doing here, didn't we? You told me that you think he will come to see you?'

'Yes I do.'

'And, if he does, I think he will try to take us by surprise one night. So-o, it is best if Natalie is not here, isn't it?'

'I suppose so.'

'You know that you need not worry about her; Céline is only too happy to look after her.'

'I know,' Gina laughed. 'The young madam is demonstrating to Gerard what a perfect little mother she's going to be!'

'Poor Natalie.' Juan suddenly looked sombre.

'What do you mean? Don't you think that Céline is a suitable person to look after her?'

'I don't mean that at all. No, I was looking to the future. One day you will have so much to tell her and it may cause her sorrow.'

'Let's hope by then that she is quite secure in the fact that she has been loved – and still is.'

'She is lucky to have you to care for her, Gina.'

'And David – if he had not cared, I dread to think what would have become of her.'

'Yes, David was a good father, even though Natalie was not his child.'

'He loved her.'

'Yes, I am sure that he did.'

A cloud moved across the sun and they stared at each other solemnly. Gina shivered. 'Let's go in, Juan. I want to say goodnight to Natalie before she goes to the farm.'

'OK, but then will you come with me to the gallery? You haven't been in there since before David died, have you?'

'If you like.' She reached under the lounger for her sandals and slipped them on.

A little later, as they strolled through the extensive gardens, they heard the sound of Gerard Bernat's pick-up truck pulling away up the mountain road towards the farm.

'The Bernats have left the gates open, as you asked them,' Juan said. 'Perhaps that man has been waiting until Florence goes before he comes to see you.'

'He could have come yesterday. We didn't lock up until we went to bed.'

'Well, perhaps he is making up his mind. We must be patient.'

Juan took the key from his pocket, unlocked the door to David's gallery and they went inside. 'I wanted you to see that I have kept everything as David wished.'

'You don't have to prove anything to me, Juan.

You know that David trusted you to carry on with his work of trying to encourage young artists.'

'In the gallery, I can do that but I am not so sure about work in the studio. I do not have enough experience to be a teacher.'

'Don't worry, David was confident that other talents would be attracted here. Who knows, we may find someone who could take his role.'

'But, as I said, here in the gallery I know what to do – which artists to exhibit. I know what will sell – although I don't know if you will wish to sell any of David's own work. You know he allowed some paintings to go now and then in order to bring in more money to help his students.'

They walked through the gallery together. It was almost more than Gina could bear to see David's paintings exhibited with the others – knowing that there would never be any more. Juan was right, she did not know if she would be able to bring herself to part with any of them – and she knew that Juan felt that way, too.

She looked at his sensitive young face, his eyes huge as he tried to control his emotion. 'I understood about David, you know,' she said.

'Did you?'

'Oh, not at first. How could I? When I first came to work for him, he was still in shock after Nadine's death. I could only think of him as a truly a bereaved husband – which, of course, he was.'

'I arrived here not long after you came, remem-

361

ber,' Juan said. 'It was you who persuaded David to return to work. We were all grateful to you for that.'

Gina smiled at him. 'At first I was pleased that David had found a student who fired his enthusiasm. I wasn't surprised that he wanted to spend more and more time with you.

'And then I was puzzled, I wasn't quite sure if what I suspected was true but, when at last I realized that it was, and that he loved you – not as a friend but as a partner –'

'And I loved him the same way.'

'I know – and I wasn't shocked or offended.'

'Gina,' Juan suddenly took her hand, 'I have to confess that I told him he must not marry you.'

Gina withdrew her hand and looked at Juan, sharply.

'It was not because I was jealous. David had told me that it would not be a proper marriage. He knew that he was a sick man, the family illness, the "curse of the Shaws", he called it, had caught up with him at last.

'He explained that the marriage was for Natalie's sake – but I thought it was not fair to you.'

'David didn't deceive me, Juan. He told me everything he thought I ought to know –'

Gina broke off. She had realized within the last few days that David had withheld one vital piece of information. He had planned everything so carefully, and yet he had not warned her about Marco.

Perhaps he had thought that the actual name was not important. Or perhaps, until the end, he had hoped against hope that his fears would not be realized, who could say . . .

'What is it, Gina? You look troubled.'

'I was thinking about poor Nadine.'

'You can say that after the way she was prepared to abandon her daughter?'

'We don't know if she was. No one can know what was in her mind when she ran out and got into the car that night. But, I was wondering what she expected from her marriage?'

'A father for the child she was expecting? Someone to look after her? For much of her life she had had her brother to shield her from the world, hadn't she? I understand that when she was abandoned by the man who made her pregnant she just about fell apart. She should have been eternally grateful to David!'

'Perhaps what David was offering didn't prove to be enough.'

'Don't feel sorry for her, Gina, she doesn't deserve it!'

But she did feel sorry for David's first wife. She knew more about Nadine now, and knowledge always brings understanding.

'Well, anyway, when David asked me to marry him, he was completely honest with me. He told me that although Natalie wasn't his daughter, he loved her just as much as if she were.

'He told me what he intended to do about his will – and why. And he told me the whole truth about his relationship with you – although, of course, I had already guessed.'

'And yet you still agreed to marry him.'

'I loved David too, you know. Oh, it wasn't romantic love – it was based on gratitude. I'd had a pretty rough time in one way and another. Anyway, he persuaded me that it was the best thing to do.' Gina looked at Juan helplessly.

'David could be very persuasive.' Juan grinned and the mood lightened. Suddenly, he took her hand. 'Come with me.'

He led her to the door that connected with the studio and they walked through. 'Do you remember that portrait that David started? The portrait of you?'

'I do. He was working well but then the sessions got too tiring for him.'

'He asked me to finish it.'

'I didn't know that.'

Juan led her to the far end of the studio and it was like a moment in an old romantic movie when he walked up to a shrouded canvas on an easel and uncovered it with a flourish.

Gina caught her breath. The picture showed her sitting on the stone balustrade of the terrace at night. The dress she was wearing was bleached white by the moon. Her short, dark curls framed her face in such a way that her delicate bone structure was accentuated.

The shadows of the gardens behind her were in shades of blue, and so were the distant mountains. It was like a dreamscape.

'Do you like it, Gina?'

She was too full of emotion to answer. She reached forward and Juan took her in his arms. They were

364

standing clinging on to each other when they heard a sound behind them. They sprang apart and looked towards the door.

Sam had just walked into the studio.

Sam stared at them in despair. Ever since Gina had left Northmoor Hall – no, even before that – he had been telling himself that she would never have had an affair with one of her husband's students while the poor man lay dying.

She had almost convinced him that it was all lies and innuendo and yet, what was he to think now? He had found them in each other's arms and, when they sprang apart, had that look she shot him simply been fright? Or had it been guilt?

Nobody spoke. Sam's eyes were drawn to the portrait behind them. He was stunned. It was beautiful – romantic – very few artists painted anything like that today.

Was it Juan's work? If it was it was no grubby little affair they were engaged in. The man must be in love with her, deeply in love. What chance do I stand? Sam thought, and his very resignation made him relax a little.

'Gina, Juan, I'm sorry if I startled you.'

'That's all right.' She was making every effort to compose herself but he noticed that her voice was unsteady. 'Shall we go back to the villa?'

'I'll stay and lock up,' Juan told them.

The light was fading. As they walked along the garden paths, Gina's skirt brushed the tops of aromatic shrubs, releasing delicate perfumes into the air.

'Forgive me for just barging in,' Sam said. 'I found the gates open –'

'I know, that's all right.'

'I couldn't find you or Natalie –'

'She's at the Bernats' farm. She goes there each night. We – er – I think it's safer at the moment.'

'Safer?'

'We think Marco Doyle's still hanging around.'

'Yes.' Sam didn't tell her that that was one of the reasons he had come here.

'Anyway, you weren't in the villa or in the garden so I came looking for you.' And I wish I hadn't, he thought to himself.

'How did you get here?' Sam knew that she was asking about his journey to Les Haute Pyrenees, rather than his search through the grounds of the villa.

'I flew. From Newcastle to D- er – a business trip – and then on to London, Paris and, finally, to Toulouse where I hired a car.'

'All that must have cost you a fortune.' Gina smiled faintly. 'So why go to all that expense?' She looked tense again.

What could he say? Could he tell her that he had come because he loved her? That he didn't want to live another moment without her? After the scene he had just witnessed in David's studio, that would be the last thing that she wanted to hear.

'I wasn't happy about the way we parted. You

must believe me when I say that I had no idea David was going to leave me Northmoor Hall –'

'I do.'

'But you wouldn't talk to me – you just ran away. I wanted to tell you that I'm not even sure I want to accept the bequest.'

'Why ever not?'

They had reached the pool. Gina bent down to retrieve the drinking glasses and the jug of lemonade. She put them on the tray and began to walk towards the terrace.

'Because I don't think I have any right to it.'

'Why not? You were David's best friend.'

'But Natalie is his daughter – and – and he didn't leave her anything else, did he? I could – I could sign it over to her.'

Gina stopped and turned to look up at him. Her eyes were full of pain. 'Sam –'

'Gina, I'm sorry. I didn't say that to hurt you. David must have had his reasons for doing what he did and you don't have to tell me if you don't want to.'

Juan appeared behind them. 'Give me that tray, Gina. Why don't you sit here on the terrace and I will bring out the food that Florence prepared for us. There is quite sufficient for three.'

'If that's an offer of a meal, I'll accept it,' Sam said. 'Airline food is tasty but fairly insubstantial.'

'What, no comfort stops in a hotel on the way?' Gina teased.

'Nope, I hung about in airports waiting for cancellations.'

'Poor man. Sit down. I'll help Juan bring everything out; you'll eat all the sooner if I do.'

Sam was content to wait on the terrace. He did not particularly want to be inside the villa with them. He did not want to witness any further scenes of their intimacy or even domesticity if he went with them to the kitchen.

And he wanted to get his thoughts sorted out. What had he expected? That Gina would be so surprised to see him that the very shock of it would propel her to fall into his arms – where she would confess that she still loved him?

He smiled bitterly. Yes, he really had been thinking along those lines and, instead, he had walked in on a scene which could leave him in no doubt. Gina would never be his.

So how did he feel now? Did he still want to protect her from whatever it was he was convinced Marco had planned?

Restlessly, he left the terrace and strolled down through the grounds to the boundary wall. He looked down into the valley. The last rays of sunlight glinted on the roofs of the village not quite halfway between the villa and the little town. He had driven first to the town and booked in at a hotel before coming up here.

Just as well, he thought now. He couldn't have borne to spend a night in the villa with Gina and Juan.

He leaned on the wall and looked down, remembering how Gina and he used to walk down the twisting mountain road to the village. They would sit outside a café in the cobbled square and hold hands as they drank the local wine.

One day they had discovered that there was an old path leading straight down the terraced slopes. The road looped its way down the mountainside to the village and then on to the town but the path cut straight down through the vegetation.

If you were fit enough to stand the rough terrain you could get to either the village or the town in less that half the time it would take to drive.

Sam headed back through the shadowed gardens when Gina called him and told him that the meal was ready.

Juan was lighting scented candles. He placed the holders along the balustrade and one in the centre of the table. Sam stared at it in mute misery.

He remembered the nights he had sat here with David and Gina – long before Juan had come on the scene. He had fallen in love with Gina then and he had never stopped loving her. He looked up to see that she was staring at the candle, too.

Suddenly, Juan slammed his glass down so clumsily, that the wine slopped over on to the tabletop.

'What is it?' Gina was instantly alert.

'Did you hear that? Out there . . . somewhere in the grounds . . .'

'No –' she began but then they all heard it.

Juan rose to his feet and so did Sam. Gina remained sitting; Sam noticed that she had gone very still. She was staring into the darkness in the direction of the steps at the far end of the terrace – the steps that led down on to the orchard path.

And then a figure came up those steps. It was hard to make out because the figure was dressed all in black. But as it moved forward into the range of the flickering candles, Sam saw that it was the figure of a man.

Marco Doyle.

CHAPTER 29

Gina knew who it was immediately. Who else would bother to scramble over the wall into the orchard at this time of night, and then just stroll on to the terrace as if he had been invited?

'Would you like to sit down?' she asked. She had read somewhere that you could put your enemy at a psychological disadvantage by not allowing him to dominate the situation. She had to establish the fact that she was in control.

Was Marco Doyle an enemy? She glanced at Juan and Sam, they obviously thought so, although she didn't think that either of them could even begin to know how much more harm this man could do.

She nodded towards Juan and he pulled two of the chairs away from the table and indicated that their unexpected visitor should be seated. Marco shrugged and smiled as he complied; Juan took the other chair.

Sam remained standing by the balustrade. Gina noticed how tense he was. She caught his eye and signalled to him that she was all right. He sank down slowly, until he was sitting on the stone coping. The nearest candle lit his face from below, adding mysterious shadows.

We look like characters in a play, Gina thought. The terrace is a stage and the players have assembled for the final act – the *denouement*. The mystery will be solved and then the audience can go home. But so far the characters seem unwilling to speak. It seems they've forgotten their lines. They'll have to be prompted.

'What do you want, Marco?'

He raised his eyebrows. 'So direct, she is, and we haven't even been introduced.'

'Cut the blarney!' That came from Sam. Gina shot him a warning glance. *Please let me handle this*, was the message in her eyes.

'What makes you so sure that I want something?'

'Why else would you come here?'

'Because I once was a friend of David's?'

The question in his voice revealed that he knew that no one was going to accept that explanation. So when Gina shook her head he shrugged.

'OK, you've guessed the answer, anyway. I can see it in your eyes. I want my daughter.'

Gina shot a look at Sam. He was frowning, but she didn't have time to explain. She turned her attention back to Marco. 'That's out of the question.'

'Why should she stay with you?'

'Because I'm her stepmother.'

'Not really. David wasn't Natalie's real father.'

Sam had pushed forward from his seat on the

coping. Gina hurried on, 'David was more of a father to her than you ever were.'

'I came for her once before.'

'I know that,' Juan said with a sudden burst of anger. 'How is it that you dare come back here!'

Suddenly Sam exploded. 'What the hell is going on?'

Gina looked at him and was riven with pity. If only she'd had time to explain everything to him – and yet she hadn't wanted to. She hadn't wanted him ever to find out these things which could only bring him pain.

Juan rose swiftly, fluidly, and placed one hand on Sam's arm in order to restrain him if necessary.

Marco looked at the man who once used to be his friend. The man he had betrayed when they were so much younger. 'So David never told you? He never wanted you to know? I wonder what kind of twisted pleasure it gave him, to have you believing that he had fathered your sister's child?'

And now Sam did spring forward but Juan held on to him. 'No, Mr Redmond, no.' he said. 'Violence will not help us to discover the truth.'

Sam gave an anguished groan but he remained where he was.

'David's motives weren't twisted,' Gina said. 'He acted out of love. He wanted to help his friend's sister when she was desperate. It seems the man who had made her pregnant had abandoned her.' She was gratified to see that Marco could not meet her eyes.

But he recovered immediately and said, 'And

where was big brother? Where was the man who was supposed to be responsible for Nadine? He was off following his own career while the poor girl got involved with people who introduced her to all kinds of dangerous habits –'

From the corner of her eye, Gina saw that Juan was now having to restrain Sam forcibly. She prayed that he would be strong enough.

'The person who did her the worst service was whoever introduced her to you,' she said.

'I don't deny it. But I did want my daughter.'

'You'd better explain,' she said.

'I came here not long after Natalie was born. I spoke to David, I told him that there was no need for him to rear another man's child, that I would tell Emma –' he hesitated. He looked at Sam and, for the first time, Marco displayed a hint of unease.

Gina prompted, 'You told your wife?'

'No – there was no point in upsetting her until it was all settled.'

'Upsetting her?' Sam's voice was dangerously quiet.

'We-ell, you know, I'd have had to tell her that I'd had an affair with Nadine.'

Gina heard Sam give a strangled cry. Marco hurried on, 'But I knew that she would agree to have Natalie. She *wanted* a child so much and this baby was my own daughter – I knew that she would love her – bring her up as her own.'

'But David sent you packing,' Gina said.

'Of course.' Marco sighed. 'I should have known that he would. Oh, it wasn't just that he was acting honourably – like an old-fashioned gentleman – he genuinely wanted to help Nadine because of Sam.'

'Explain.' Sam allowed himself one word.

'Don't you realize that David would have done anything for you? He had principles. He believed in helping his true friends. But he wasn't being a complete saint, you know; it didn't hurt his image at all to have a beautiful young wife and a child. It gave him a respectable cover.'

'I don't understand . . .' Sam said. Gina looked at him anxiously.

'No, I don't suppose you do,' Marco agreed. 'But, whatever the reason, David wouldn't give the baby up. He was rich – even richer than I am – he was powerful, with the kind of life I led, I knew I would never stand a chance in the courts.'

'So you left.' Gina said. 'But what about Nadine?' Marco looked at her and frowned. 'Nadine?'

'Yes, Nadine. She was the mother, after all. Didn't you ask her if she wanted to give up her baby?'

'I – I didn't even see Nadine. She was with Natalie when I arrived. David didn't send for her – he sent me away as I told you. But – but she saw me leaving . . .'

Marco was staring into the darkness. Suddenly Sam moved forward, brushing off Juan's attempt at restraint. Marco saw him coming and rose to meet him.

'No!' Gina cried, rising to her feet.

Sam backed off a little. 'I just want to know what happened next,' he said. 'For God's sake tell me.'

'I'm not really sure. I was driving back down the mountain road when I became aware of another vehicle behind me. I thought the driver was drunk. Whoever it was, was swerving from side to side and driving far too fast.

'I was approaching a bend in the road – you know how steeply the ground drops away – I was frightened I would be pushed over the edge.

'So I pulled in to let the maniac overtake – but he – she – went straight over the verge and down into the valley. I found out later that it was Nadine.'

No one spoke for a while. They all just stared at Marco in horror. Eventually Gina asked, 'Did you know why she came after you?'

'I know.' It was Juan. 'After David and I became – became close – he told me something of what had happened. He did not tell me the name of her lover but he said that, on that night, Nadine thought he had come for her.

'She was angry with David for sending him away. She got into her car and set off after him –'

'But why?' Sam asked. 'When she was married to a man like David, why would she want to go off with Marco!'

Gina and Juan looked at him in consternation. It was Marco who answered and his voice was surprisingly gentle. 'Perhaps the kind of marriage David was offering wasn't enough for her. Do you know she was so naïve – so innocent in an odd kind of way – that

376

I sometimes wonder if she really knew what she was getting into.

'Perhaps, in spite of David's goodness, she had just about decided that she wanted more than simply being looked after. She had probably realized that her marriage wasn't going to work.'

'What are you saying?' Sam asked.

'I think you know.'

Sam shook his head as if he was trying to deny a growing comprehension. Then he asked, 'But the baby? How could Nadine go off and leave her baby?'

'I don't think she had any intention of leaving her,' Gina interrupted quickly. 'I've thought and thought about it and I've decided that Nadine was only trying to catch up with Marco – talk to him – ask him to take her away – we'll never know what she would have said. But I'm sure she would have come back for Natalie!'

'Ah, Natalie,' Marco said, 'which brings us back to why I came here tonight.'

'You're not taking her,' Sam said.

'I'm her father.'

'I'm her uncle – her mother's brother.'

'But the child isn't living with you, she's with her former nanny. Oh, I know David married the girl – another beautiful young wife, incidentally – and he left her all his money.

'Poor David – he must have suspected that he was going to die for a long time. Even when we were all at college together he used to brood about it sometimes. Perhaps, when it came, he was not completely sane –'

'Don't –' Juan made a soft sound of distress.

But Marco continued, 'David must have thought that if Natalie were penniless I wouldn't want her. What a crazy idea – it isn't the money. I want my daughter. Emma will want her too –'

'Stop this.' Gina said. 'Natalie is my stepdaughter –'

'Not really –' Marco began.

'Yes! I was married to her father. Her *father*, do you hear?' Natalie will always regard David as her father. Furthermore, I'm her official guardian – it's in the will.'

'Some guardian,' Marco challenged. 'What about the child's moral welfare?'

'If you mean all the stories about Juan and me – all that filth that you helped to spread –'

'Of course I don't.' He laughed. 'Oh, I took the pictures and sold them. Why not? And they'd be good evidence in a custody case, as a matter of fact. But I think I know what part Juan Sanchez played in this household.'

'Then what – ?'

'Why did you lose your last job, Gina? Your first job as a matter of fact? Was it because once you'd tucked up your little charges for the night, you couldn't resist tucking their father up to?'

'No!'

'Remind me of the facts. Paula Harrington found you in bed with her husband and threw you out – isn't that right?'

'No – not quite –'

'That's the gossip that circulated amongst the fast set at the time – and you can always find someone malicious enough to repeat it if necessary.'

Gina felt the blood rushing to her head. She staggered backwards and Juan leapt to her side to support her.

'And before anybody reminds me,' Marco continued, 'I know that I'm much more of a sinner than Gina has ever been, but I'm the child's *natural* father and my wife –' Suddenly his voice cracked. 'Emma is beyond reproach – anyone will tell you. She's – she's *good*, she's . . .'

'That's what this is all about, isn't it?' Sam had recovered his composure. 'Emma is childless because of something you did to her a long time ago. She's desperate for a child. That's it, isn't it?'

'Yes – no –'

'You feel guilty. Whatever else you've done, you've never abandoned Emma. You're right. She's a good woman. The only mistake she ever made was loving you. You want to make it up to her. That's why you want Natalie.'

Marco stared at him. 'Don't take your revenge on me now, Sam. I don't know if you've ever forgiven me for stealing Emma away from you, but if you deny me my daughter, it's Emma you'd be hurting more than me.'

'And what about Natalie? Have you not considered that you'd be breaking her heart if you took her away from the people she loves?'

'She's just a baby – she'd – she'd –'

'Get over it? No she wouldn't. She's an intelligent, loving little girl and I doubt if she would ever get over the hurt of being parted from Gina.'

'And I would rather give up all hope of ever having a child if it meant causing so much pain.'

A new voice spoke out clearly from the darkness of the garden. Everyone spun round in time to see the small figure climbing the stone steps and begin to walk along the terrace towards them.

'Emma,' Sam exclaimed, 'I thought you were going to wait at the hotel.'

'I was. But first I went to one of the little cafés for a night-cap. I saw Marco coming out of a restaurant and I decided to confront him. After all, that's why we came here, isn't it?'

'Sam, what's this all about?' Gina was confused.

Emma turned to her and smiled. 'Sam came to see me before he flew out here. He was worried that Marco had plans to make life even more difficult for you. We agreed that he had to be stopped. I persuaded Sam to let me come and talk to him – but neither of us guessed exactly what those plans were.'

'Sam, is this true?'

'Yes, Gina. Marco had said something to Emma about there being some scandal in your past. We thought that he was going to drag it out into the open.'

'Oh no.' None of them noticed the despair in Gina's voice.

'So why didn't you confront me?' It was the first time Marco had spoken since Emma arrived and he sounded shocked.

'You were too quick for me. At first I thought that you'd gone back into your hotel but then I caught sight of you leaving the town square. I followed you –' She stopped and gave a bitter laugh.

'What is it, Emma?' Sam asked.

'I almost gave up at that point – it suddenly occurred to me that he might be going to meet a woman –'

'Emma –'

'Don't sound so wounded, Marco. Do you think I'm a fool?'

He didn't answer and she continued, 'Thank goodness I didn't give up there and then. Something made me go on and I followed him even when he left the town behind him and began to climb up the mountain path.

'I soon guessed where he was heading. I imagine that he wanted to take you by surprise – you would have heard a car approaching – seen its lights from a distance.'

'How long have you been standing there? In the garden?'

'I wasn't far behind you, Marco. I've heard everything.'

Marco closed his eyes and sighed. He seemed to diminish suddenly. But then he said, 'I did it for you, Emma.'

'What exactly did you do for me? Have an affair with Nadine? Make her pregnant?'

It wasn't only Marco who flinched at Emma's

words and Gina stepped forwards and placed a hand on Sam's arm.

'No – you know what I mean. I want my daughter – and I thought you would want her to – would love her –'

'Of course I would have loved her – and of course I want her –'

'No!' Gina cried out.

'It's all right, Gina,' Emma said softly. 'Natalie is staying with you, there's no question of that. Marco gave up any right to be a parent a long time ago.'

'That's cruel!' Marco's voice was full of pain and Emma walked towards him and took his hands in her own.

'We're going home now, Marco. First of all back to your hotel and then, tomorrow, we're going back to Ireland to get my poor dogs out of the kennels. It's a while since you've been home – you owe me a few days at least.'

She was talking to him as if he were her child. Suddenly, Marco seemed to diminish. 'OK,' he said, 'if that's what you want.'

'How – how will you get back to town?' Gina asked.

'The way we came,' Emma said. 'It's a lovely night for a stroll.'

'Wait,' Juan called after them as they began to walk away along the terrace. 'I can drive you back – really, I insist.'

Marco raised a faint smile. 'Don't you trust me to see myself off the premises?'

Juan didn't answer. He stared at Marco coldly.

'Oh, don't worry, lead the way, I'll do whatever you say.'

'I'll see you off,' Sam sounded bleak and Gina watched as he went with them. He was talking quietly to Emma.

She was alone on the terrace and she couldn't believe that it was over. She knew that it was only Emma's intervention that had forced Marco to give up the fight for his daughter and she blessed Sam for bringing her here.

Even though Sam and Emma had not known the exact nature of Marco's threat they had been prepared to help her.

Then, she suddenly realized that it might not be over. Marco had accused her of not being a suitable guardian for Natalie. He had dredged up those ugly rumours from her past and, of course, Sam probably still believed that she was having an affair with Juan.

Whatever Sam had just said about not taking Natalie away from her, that could simply have been an argument to use against Marco. Now, more than ever, he might want to have guardianship of his niece himself.

Without realizing it, she had been backing away along the terrace. Suddenly she wanted to escape – to be alone – to try and make some sense of everything that had happened, before she could even think of what to do. She turned and sped down the steps into the garden.

As she ran along the winding paths, she heard only the sounds of the night. The breeze whispering through the leaves of the trees and the occasional rustle and snap of a twig as some small, nocturnal creature explored its territory.

A pale shape leapt across her path and she stopped in fright. She held her breath and stared down. Two bright eyes glinted up at her in the moonlight. 'Claude!' she breathed and kneeled down to stroke Natalie's new little kitten.

Claude began to purr but, suddenly she hissed and raised her back into an arch. The next moment she turned and vanished into the undergrowth.

'I'm sorry, I didn't mean to frighten anyone.'

Gina twisted round and raised her head. A tall figure was standing over her. Sam. He offered her his hand and pulled her up.

'Why did you run away?'

'I'm not sure.'

'I thought you'd be glad – glad that the threat was over.'

'But is it?'

'What do you mean?'

'You heard what Marco said – about my first job with the Harringtons – about why I had to leave. Are you going to try to take Natalie away from me?'

'I knew about that old story, Gina. I've known all along. David told me at the outset. Before he employed you, Robert Hargreaves had investigated your background and he assured David that Jeremy Harrington had forced his attentions on you and you were completely innocent. Robert said that you had been badly wronged.'

'You knew!' Gina shook her head almost in disbelief as she remembered the anguish that what she imagined to be her 'secret' had caused her. 'And Juan?'

'It seems that I have been as naïve as my sister must have been. It was never Juan and you, was it? It was Juan and David.'

'Don't condemn him, Sam. Juan made David happy, he returned his love, when David had long ago accepted that he was never going to find human happiness.'

Sam began to walk along one of the paths that led to the orchard. She didn't know if she should follow him. Then he turned and said, 'Walk with me?'

The apple trees were brushed with moonlight. The land sloped down towards the river and they could glimpse its dark waters shimmering here and there with reflected light as it wound its way along the valley. Beyond it, the mountains rose steeply, towards the stars.

They didn't stop until they reached the boundary wall. The ancient stones had retained the heat of the day; they leaned against them and looked down on to the rooftops of the sleeping village.

'I'm sorry that you had to find out this way,' Gina said.

'Find out about what? My sister and Marco? That her marriage to David was a sham?'

'No! Don't say that!'

'David should never have married her.'

'Why not? He had the best of intentions.'

'I can't help thinking that what Marco was suggesting might be true – that he needed a cover. "The successful artist is also a happily married man."'

'Sam, David told me that for many years that was all he ever wanted – to be happily married. He had lots of girlfriends when he was at college, didn't he?'

'Yes – he was very attractive.'

'But none of the relationships ever lasted – ever deepened into love, did they?'

'That's true. I used to tell him that he would know when the right girl came along.'

'Eventually, the right person did come along.'

'Juan.'

'Yes, Juan. I don't think David had really accepted his true nature until then. So don't think badly of him for marrying Nadine. He truly wanted to help her.'

'You're very understanding, Gina. David was very lucky.'

'David lucky? No – I was.'

Below them, the lights of the village began to wink out. Faint sounds of laughter echoed up the hillside as the inn in the cobbled square shut its doors for the night.

Sam turned to Gina and asked, 'Why do you think that he left me his house?'

'You'd been going there for years –'

'That's hardly a good enough reason.'

'Well, I've been thinking – perhaps – perhaps he wanted to make amends.'

'Amends? What for?'

'For parting you and me.'

'Yes,' Sam's smile was strained. 'That must have upset his plans – when he saw that I was in love with you. He must have already known that he was terminally ill. He must have already decided to marry you – for whatever reason.

'The irony is that when I realized he'd never given you my letter, I assumed it was sexual jealousy. I was wrong.'

'So David wasn't a saint,' Gina said, 'but he wasn't evil. He thought he was doing the best for those he loved. You must go on thinking of David as a good friend. And as for the house, I think he realized that leaving it to you might bring us together somehow. But, Sam –' Suddenly her voice was anxious.

'What is it?'

'Is it too late?'

'Is what too late?'

'For us to get together again – I mean – Sally . . . Sally Maxwell?'

'A friend, nothing more. A good friend.'

'Ah.'

'Gina, do you know what I think?' Sam had taken hold of her shoulders. She looked up into his face, but could make nothing of his expression.

'Tell me.'

'That we should stop thinking for a while.' Gently

he drew her into his arms. 'We're wasting the moon-light.'

His head dipped towards hers and she raised her lips expectantly. He brushed them with his own, softly, experimentally, and then he sighed.

'What is it?' she asked.

'I suppose we'll have to make some decisions . . .'

'And what are they?'

'We'll have to decide which house to live in when we're married – yours or mine. And then we'll have to decide whether Natalie should go to school in France or in England. And then, wait a moment –'

He pulled her even closer so that her body seemed to be touching his at every point. He kissed her again, this time his lips parted hers and his tongue began its sweet exploration. She felt herself begin to tremble.

When he stopped and raised his head, she looked up at him, questioningly. He smiled and said, 'And then we'd better decide –'

'Sam, stop!' She reached up and, taking his face in her hands, she drew it down towards her own once more.

'Gina,' he breathed, as they sank down on to the warm earth. 'I've never stopped loving you . . .'

THE EXCITING NEW NAME
IN WOMEN'S FICTION!

PLEASE HELP ME TO HELP YOU!

Dear *Scarlet* Reader,

As Editor of *Scarlet* Books I want to make sure that the
books I offer you every month are up to the high standards
Scarlet readers expect. And to do that I need to know a
little more about you and your reading likes and dislikes. So
please spare a few minutes to fill in the short questionnaire
on the following pages and send it to me.

Looking forward to hearing from you,

Sally Cooper

Editor-in-Chief, *Scarlet*

QUESTIONNAIRE

Please tick the appropriate boxes to indicate your answers

1 Where did you get this Scarlet title?
Bought in supermarket ☐
Bought at my local bookstore ☐ Bought at chain bookstore ☐
Bought at book exchange or used bookstore ☐
Borrowed from a friend ☐
Other (please indicate) _____

2 Did you enjoy reading it?
A lot ☐   A little ☐   Not at all ☐

3 What did you particularly like about this book?
Believable characters ☐   Easy to read ☐
Good value for money ☐   Enjoyable locations ☐
Interesting story ☐   Modern setting ☐
Other _____

4 What did you particularly dislike about this book?
_____

5 Would you buy another Scarlet book?
Yes ☐   No ☐

6 What other kinds of book do you enjoy reading?
Horror ☐   Puzzle books ☐   Historical fiction ☐
General fiction ☐   Crime/Detective ☐   Cookery ☐
Other (please indicate) _____

7 Which magazines do you enjoy reading?
1. _____
2. _____
3. _____

And now a little about you –
8 How old are you?
Under 25 ☐   25–34 ☐   35–44 ☐
45–54 ☐   55–64 ☐   over 65 ☐

cont.

9 What is your marital status?
Single ☐ Married/living with partner ☐
Widowed ☐ Separated/divorced ☐

10 What is your current occupation?
Employed full-time ☐ Employed part-time ☐
Student ☐ Housewife full-time ☐
Unemployed ☐ Retired ☐

11 Do you have children? If so, how many and how old are they?

_____

_____

12 What is your annual household income?

under $15,000	☐	or	£10,000	☐
$15–25,000	☐	or	£10–20,000	☐
$25–35,000	☐	or	£20–30,000	☐
$35–50,000	☐	or	£30–40,000	☐
over $50,000	☐	or	£40,000	☐

Miss/Mrs/Ms _____

Address _____

_____

_____

Thank you for completing this questionnaire. Now tear it out – put it in an envelope and send it, before 30 June 1998, to:

Sally Cooper, Editor-in-Chief

USA/Can. address
SCARLET c/o London Bridge
85 River Rock Drive
Suite 202
Buffalo
NY 14207
USA

UK address/No stamp required
SCARLET
FREEPOST LON 3335
LONDON W8 4BR
Please use block capitals for address

Scarlet titles coming next month:

MARRIAGE DANCE   Jillian James
Anni Ross is totally committed to her career in dance. She's positive that she's got no time to spare for falling in love! But attractive lawyer Steve Hunter has other plans for Anni's future . . .

SLOW DANCING   Elizabeth Smith
Hallie Prescott is plunged into the world of glitter and glamour when she accompanies her screenwriter husband to Hollywood. But it's not long before the dream goes sour. Can Grant Keeler help Hallie rebuild her life?

THAT CINDERELLA FEELING   Anne Styles
Out of work actress Casey Taylor will take any job she can find. Which is how she ends up delivering a kissagram to the offices of Alex Havilland, a businessman who has no time for frivolity and who is definitely *not* amused!

A DARKER SHADOW   Patricia Wilson
Amy Scott can handle any problem that the world of computers throws at her. But when it comes to coping with sudden and frightening events in her private life, she doesn't know where to turn. Until her arrogant and disapproving boss Luc Martell decides to intervene . . .